A Passionate Pupil

To his surprise, Aurelia approached the bed. Thomas nearly stopped breathing.

He lifted the thick pile of bedcoverings, silently inviting his wife to join him. Truthfully, he was so hot he needed a dose of cool flesh to slow him down, keep him from frightening the dear girl to death.

Heart pounding, but spirit willing, Relia snuggled down next to him, *A-ah!* Poor darling, he must indeed be freezing, for there was a part of him that seemed stiff as a board. Men were built very oddly, it seemed. Her lips curved in a soft, secret smile. It was high time she learned the why of male anatomy.

Mr. Lanning was all too willing to demonstrate. . . .

The Lady and the Cit

Blair Bancroft

A SIGNET BOOK

SIGNET
Published by New American Library, a division of
Penguin Group (USA) Inc., 375 Hudson Street,
New York, New York 10014, USA
Penguin Group (Canada), 10 Alcorn Avenue, Toronto,
Ontario M4V 3B2, Canada (a division of Pearson Penguin Canada Inc.)
Penguin Books Ltd., 80 Strand, London WC2R 0RL, England
Penguin Ireland, 24 St. Stephen's Green, Dublin 2,
Ireland (a division of Penguin Books Ltd.)
Penguin Group (Australia), 250 Camberwell Road, Camberwell, Victoria 3124,
Australia (a division of Pearson Australia Group Pty. Ltd.)
Penguin Books India Pvt. Ltd., 11 Community Centre, Panchsheel Park,
New Delhi - 110 017, India
Penguin Group (NZ), cnr Airborne and Rosedale Roads, Albany,
Auckland 1310, New Zealand (a division of Pearson New Zealand, Ltd.)
Penguin Books (South Africa) (Pty.) Ltd., 24 Sturdee Avenue,
Rosebank, Johannesburg 2196, South Africa

Penguin Books Ltd., Registered Offices:
80 Strand, London WC2R 0RL, England

First published by Signet, an imprint of New American Library,
a division of Penguin Group (USA) Inc.

First Printing, February 2005
10 9 8 7 6 5 4 3 2 1

PUBLISHER'S NOTE
This is a work of fiction. Names, characters, places, and incidents either are the
product of the author's imagination or are used fictitiously, and any resemblance to
actual persons, living or dead, business establishments, events, or locales is entirely
coincidental.

If you purchased this book without a cover you should be aware that this book is stolen
property. It was reported as "unsold and destroyed" to the publisher and neither the author
nor the publisher has received any payment for this "stripped book."

The scanning, uploading, and distribution of this book via the Internet or via any other
means without the permission of the publisher is illegal and punishable by law. Please
purchase only authorized electronic editions, and do not participate in or encourage
electronic piracy of copyrighted materials. Your support of the author's rights is
appreciated.

To the dedicated staff and volunteers of the
Sarasota County Library System,
who consistently acquire for me
the most extraordinary research books

Prologue

Miss Aurelia Trevor unhooked her knee, disengaged her stirrup, and slid down from her sidesaddle unaided, tossing the reins of her lathered horse to a startled groom. Grabbing the long tail of her sable velvet riding habit and tossing it over her arm, she stalked down the drive with a purposeful stride seldom seen in well brought up young ladies. She plunged down a set of outside steps to the basement of Pevensey Park; her riding boots beat an echoing tattoo on the flagstone hallway. After throwing open the door to the spacious estate room, she came to an abrupt halt, glaring at its sole occupant. Mr. William Tubbs—a sharpfaced man with nearly sixty years in his dish—was seated at the broad estate desk, silhouetted against a jumbled background of shelves holding an astonishing variety of leatherbound books, from estate records to serious treatises on agriculture. Mr. Tubbs took his time in rising to his feet. His eyes flicked over her. Assessing.

Ah, but he had never done that when her father was alive! "Mr. Tubbs," Miss Trevor demanded, "why is no work being done on the weir?"

William Tubbs smirked at her. Yes, confound it, that was the only word Miss Trevor could think of to describe the look on her estate manager's face.

"Lord Hubert says the work isn't necessary," Tubbs told her.

Miss Trevor's fine bosom heaved as she took a deep breath. Unfortunately, she caught Mr. Tubbs's sudden interest in her fitted jacket. Nearly sputtering with rage, she declared, "You know quite well Lord Ralph told you to see to that work as soon as the harvest was in. It was one of his very last orders. You cannot ignore it simply because Lord Hubert hasn't the slightest idea what it takes to run a property of this size."

Mr. Tubbs shrugged, making not the slightest effort to disguise his disinterest in her opinion. "No choice, miss. Lord Hubert holds the purse strings, as you very well know."

"That may be," Miss Trevor raged, "but Pevensey Park is mine, and we will have floods in the spring if that weir is not fixed. And the work must be done before winter sets in."

"Can't be helped, miss. You've no say in the matter. Lord Hubert is master here now."

"Lord Hubert is an—" Miss Trevor choked off an unseemly criticism of her uncle and guardian. "By the time I gain control of my own property, it will be in ruins," she declared from between gritted teeth.

"There's no help for it," William Tubbs repeated stubbornly. "I take my orders from Lord Hubert."

For a moment Miss Trevor was silent, a sly look gradually taking the place of fury. "I have some pin money put by, Mr. Tubbs. Order the work done, and I shall pay for it myself."

Mr. Tubbs, whose own mother considered him ferret-faced, shook his head. "Can't do it, miss. I'd get the sack for sure."

"I wonder, Mr. Tubbs," said Miss Aurelia Trevor of Pevensey Park, Kent, "whether it has occurred to you that in the fullness of time I shall have total control of my lands. It is possible—and I am certain you will agree—that you are merely postponing the day when you are sacked."

With this Parthian shot, Miss Trevor turned in a flurry of swishing dark velvet and stalked off down the hall, startling Cook and her helpers as she dashed through the kitchen, sporting a ferocious scowl, before ascending into the rarified atmosphere of the state rooms on the ground floor. She ran up the great front staircase, waved off her maid Tilly, and flung herself onto one of the window seats in her corner room. *Think.* She had to think. Five more years of her uncle's domination was inconceivable. It wasn't supposed to have been like this. Pevensey was hers. She would not let it be destroyed!

Chapter One

And now, a scant six weeks after her confrontation with Mr. Tubbs, Miss Trevor's dreams and hopes were down to a last slim thread dangling in the wind. Clasping a fine cashmere shawl around her shoulders to stave off the nip in the October air, she stood, all alone, on the flagstones of the south terrace and surveyed her acres.

For the fourth time in five generations the ownership of Pevensey Park had descended through the female line. Originally built by the Duke of Alburton as a wedding gift for a favorite younger son, the estate had escaped entail by passing, as a marriage portion, through a nearly unbroken succession of daughters. Whether this was a curse or a blessing depended entirely on one's point of view. Or gender. Until the last two months Miss Trevor had considered it a blessing. At the moment, however, she was truly frightened. She was on the verge of losing, and rapidly discovering desperation.

Aurelia leaned against the stone wall at the outer edge of the upper terrace, yearning for the days of loving security, when her mama and her papa were alive, and all was right with the world. When Pevensey Park was a wonder to be savored and enjoyed, and not a dreadful burden over which she had no control.

Pevensey. Beautiful Pevensey. A young landscape gardener, greatly under the influence of Lancelot "Capability" Brown, had convinced her grandfather to remodel his park in the wilderness style so much in vogue in the mid-eighteenth century. Therefore, below the terraces was a vast sweep of well-scythed grass, gradually descending to a deliberately invisible ha-ha, with fat white sheep dotting the far upslope of the Kentish hills. Irregularly shaped and carefully placed clumps of trees framed the grassy slope, with a blue-gray pond lying in the shade of the spinney on the left.

Also on the left, a wooden bridge led to a small rotunda, placed with exquisite care to the view, on the far side of a bubbling stream. Though Miss Trevor might have preferred a medieval ruin as a playhouse, the small rotunda, with its six columns and domed ceiling, had been her particular hideaway as a child. A surge of nostalgia, almost pain, swept over her, as she recalled the excitement of running over the lawn, crossing the arched wooden bridge, and entering a world of magic and imagination such as only a child can know.

She loved Pevensey Park. Every tree, shrub, and blade of grass. Every sheep on the hillside, every wheat field, hop vine, and dairy cow; every last flower, fruit, and vegetable grown in the market garden hidden behind the picturesque stands of trees. For Pevensey Park, having no great family fortune to support it, had been forced to make its own way in the world. And, fortunately, the Park had been blessed with a succession of levelheaded, commonsensical owners. It was a thriving concern. And its present owner, Miss Aurelia Trevor, was quite determined it would stay that way.

Slowly—almost fearing the impact on her current heightened emotions—she turned and looked at the house. Although not the product of the great Inigo Jones himself, Pevensey Park was classic Palladian, its cream-colored façade and perfect symmetry shimmering in the early-afternoon sun. The terraces on which she stood were also a remnant of the Palladian era, her grandmother having refused, in no uncertain terms, the landscape architect's attempt to sweep away all vestiges of the old formal gardens. For which Aurelia was most grateful. Even now, in early October, she could lean on the cement balustrade and look down on geometrically laid out beds of dahlias, mums, snapdragons, asters, and roses, backed by a few lingering hollyhocks and Rose of Sharon. Green was lovely, but what a bleak world it would be if there were no flowers.

"Miss? Miss Aurelia?" Biddeford, the Park's butler, was beside her, holding a silver tray on which rested a visiting card. "Lord Hanley is here."

Lord Hanley. Her last hope. Would he be the savior Pevensey Park needed? If only she had been able to have a Season, find the proper consort for her acres . . .

But first her beloved mama had succumbed to a slow wasting disease, and then, while they were still in mourning, her dear papa had passed on as well. From a broken heart, everyone said, and Aurelia was inclined to agree. Once, they had all been so happy. . . .

And now here she was, only six months after her papa's death, and already several weeks into a search for a husband, having been forced into giving up all hopes of independence by a calamitous combination of events on which she did not care to dwell. And yet she must. For without a stern enumeration of the anguish, disappointments, and frustrations of the last few months, how would she gather the courage to extend a proposal of marriage to a perfect stranger?

Miss Trevor sagged back against the balustrade, eyes closed, fighting for composure.

Papa, how could you?

Yet, truthfully, how could Lord Ralph have anticipated that his trusted friend and neighbor, Marcus Yelverton, would pass on—also well before his time—leaving her to the sole guardianship of Lord Hubert, her papa's greedy younger brother? The Trevor brothers, younger sons of the Marquess of Huntsham, had come into the world well hosed and shod, as the saying went. Nonetheless, the marriage of Lord Ralph, a second son, to the only child of the owners of Pevensey Park had been considered a coup of no little proportion. Lord Hubert Trevor, the third son, had had to settle for a lady with a much less impressive dowry, and had never quite forgiven either his eldest brother for being heir to a marquisate or Lord Ralph for acquiring Pevensey Park.

And yet that old saying—*Blood is thicker than water*—

proved true. Lord Hubert had been appointed coguardian
with Mr. Yelverton, and until Miss Aurelia Trevor reached
the advanced age of five and twenty, they must approve
even the slightest expenditure. And now, since Mr. Yelverton's unfortunate demise, her fate was in the hands of Lord
Hubert, who was proving to be impossible. Obstinate. Heedless, if not positively stupid. Or perhaps—the ugly thought
kept popping up—simply vindictive.

Worse yet, Lord Hubert had a son—known since infancy
as The Terrible Twyford. And, quite shockingly, Twyford
had begun making assumptions about his inevitable union
with his cousin even before Lord Ralph's casket was lowered into his grave. Horrified, Aurelia had nearly boxed his
ears. His mama had dragged him away, but Aurelia caught
that part of her scold where Lady Hubert informed her son
he was a silly boy for rushing his fences—as his papa had
told him, "slow and easy over the ground" would do it.

Slow and easy. *Twyford?* Neck or nothing was more his
style.

Nor was her precarious situation aided by William
Tubbs's continued obstinance, nor the intransigence of her
papa's solicitor. Not even Pevensey's close neighbor, Squire
Stanton, could be brought to believe that a female should
have any say in governing her own property. In fact, less
than a week after her disturbing scene with Mr. Tubbs, Miss
Trevor received a visitor. Harry Stanton, son of the squire
and a friend since childhood, came trotting up to Pevensey
Park's impressive front portico. He was dressed in his Sun-
day best, looking fine as a fivepence. Aurelia scarcely recognized him.

Nor did she recognize his fidgets. Harry had run tame at
Pevensey since he had been old enough to sit a horse. But on
this particular day he looked as if his cravat were strangling
him, his thick neck showing as red as raw beef beneath the
not-so-perfectly arranged folds of white linen. His dark blue
superfine jacket managed to look crumpled in spite of being
stretched tight across his broad shoulders, and his waistcoat
appeared in danger of popping a button or two as it strained

over a figure already showing a tendency for a too-great enjoyment of food and drink.

Yet because the thought of Harry as a suitor had never once occurred to her, Miss Trevor was considerably surprised when, after solemnly greeting Aurelia's companion, Miss Augustina Aldershot, he hitched his satin-upholstered chair across the Axminster carpet and leaned close to whisper to Aurelia, "Father sent me. He—*we*—well, 'tis plain to see what's happening here, Relia. We know you're in deep mourning, but we—*I*—want you to know you have friends. You can count on us." He glanced down at his large hands, which had fallen between his knees, bit his lip, picked an invisible speck of lint off his biscuit-colored jersey trousers. "What I mean is, Father thinks—" Blankly, he gazed over her shoulder, regrouping. His cravat bobbed up and down as he swallowed hard. "I mean, I'd be glad to marry you, Relia. Always friends, don't y'know. Good basis for a marriage, my mother sa— I mean, I think we would suit, and then you'd be rid of your uncle and your cousin."

Harry sat back in his chair, breathing a sigh of relief that he'd finally done as he was told. "Know it ain't proper—mourning and all that—but everyone knows that old sour puss, your uncle, is throwing Twyford at you, giving you no peace—"

"And no money."

"And no money." Expectantly, hopefully, her long-time friend regarded Miss Trevor from the deep brown eyes that revealed only a modicum of apprehension.

For a moment she was almost tempted. Harry was a vast improvement over her cousin Twyford. But what she felt for him was the love for a brother, not a husband. And, worse yet, she knew quite well he felt the same. Harry had no more wish to be married than she did, though their reasons for succumbing to the necessity for a leg shackle were the same. Control of Pevensey Park. Her acres would increase the squire's holdings ten times over.

Very carefully, Aurelia said, "It would seem that we could be of use to each other, Harry, but we are, I think, too good friends to settle for cupboard love. We would both be miserable. Do you not agree?"

He stared at her a long moment, manfully controlling his relief, Miss Trevor suspected, only by dire thoughts of what his papa was going to say. Then Harry stood, bowed, and strode out of the room.

Miss Trevor did not, however, discount him as a husband. As a last resort Harry Stanton would do. But could she bring herself to use her old friend in such a dastardly manner to keep herself out of the clutches of Twyford Trevor?

Oh, yes. She very much feared she could. For she would be saving Pevensey Park and its people, as well as herself.

That evening, after dinner, Aurelia attempted to put off the inevitable. Curling into a tapestry-upholstered wingchair set before a toasty fire, she buried her nose in a particularly lurid novel. Her efforts, however, were futile.

Miss Aldershot raised her head from her needlework and said in her customary forthright manner, "It is time to act, child. There is no escape from your uncle, from Mr. Tubbs, nor that twiddlepoop Twyford except marriage."

"Twyford is merely an annoyance." Aurelia did not raise her eyes from her book. "I will not have him. I've made that clear."

"You are far too intelligent, child, to be so naive," declared Miss Aldershot with considerable severity. "Twyford will not accept your rejection. Your papa, dear soul, is scarce five months departed, and already 'tis plain as the nose on your face the family means to haunt you until the deed is done." Miss Aurelia Trevor hunched her shoulders and bent her head closer to her book.

Miss Augustina Aldershot had come to Pevensey Park as governess when Aurelia was five, staying on, with glad heart, to support Miss Trevor through her mother's long illness and her father's decline. Though not much above forty, she was an angular female, who had long since acknowledged that lack of beauty, lack of fortune, and a sharp tongue had forever relegated her to spinsterhood. And since the sole moment of love in her life had ended in bitter disappointment, her opinion of men tended to be dour. Known to her few intimates as Gussie, she was fiercely loyal to her long-time charge and felt it her duty to protect Relia Trevor in any way she could.

At the moment, Miss Aldershot decided a change of tactics was in order. "It is most unfortunate," she ruminated quietly, "that the cream of the younger sons—all much in need of a wife with a fine estate—are off to war. Most thoughtless of that horrid Bonaparte to wish to conquer the world at just this moment. If only . . . ah, yes, what a fine prospect young Alan Fortescue would have been. Now there's a man after my own heart." Casting a speculative glance at the stubborn Relia, Gussie Aldershot heaved an elaborate sigh.

Miss Trevor scowled at her book, a vision of Lieutenant Alan Fortescue in his scarlet regimentals completely obliterating Mrs. Radcliffe's rather dreary hero. Gussie was right. Alan, younger son of the Earl of Gravenham, had looked quite splendid even *before* donning his imposing shako and scarlet coat with gold lace. With the earl's country house not ten miles from Pevensey Park, she had encountered Alan at irregular intervals for as long as she could remember. And, though memories of childhood frequently faded, Relia was quite certain she was only four when she had tumbled into love with the tousle-headed twelve-year-old who had accompanied his parents to a picnic at Pevensey Park. But that was sixteen years ago, and the earl's younger son was far, far away, somewhere in Portugal or Spain.

"Lieutenant Fortescue followed General Wellesley off to war without a backward glance," Aurelia told her companion. "And if he *had* looked back, it certainly would not have been at me. We have partnered each other at assemblies, nothing more. And at the rate the war is going, I will have reached my twenty-fifth birthday before he ever comes home."

"Yes, dear, but I do believe mention of his name has captured your attention," Miss Aldershot declared with bland innocence.

"Gussie!"

"In the natural course of things," Miss Aldershot continued inexorably on, "you would be granted a decent period of mourning. But this is not the case. The wolves are gathering—mark my words, your cousin Twyford will find a way to have you, no matter what nastiness it takes." Gussie allowed this statement to hang in the air between them, like some poisonous cloud.

Face forlorn, Miss Trevor laid her book onto the small round table beside her chair. "You know I do not wish to marry at all unless I can find someone who will let me manage Pevensey as I choose. Papa raised me for it, Gussie. Trained me. Unlike other girls who must leave home when they marry, Pevensey is mine, all mine. I will not hand it over to some man who plans to do with it as he pleases."

"Nonetheless, young Harry has shown us the way. You must marry the moment you reach your majority. We are already into September, so the second of November is not that far off, my dear. We must embark upon a search *immediately*."

"Immediately? You cannot think that Twyford would . . . would—"

"Ravish you? Indeed, I do. Since the beginning of time men have done such things to gain land. It is simply accomplished more discreetly in this day and age."

Silence reigned. The fire crackled in the fireplace, sparks drifting down from the raised grate. "We must face the truth, Relia," Gussie said at last. "No matter you are still in your blacks, we must go husband-hunting. Except for Stanton and Fortescue, this area has always been sparse of suitable young men. Nor can you go to the local assemblies or up to London for the fall season without encountering grave censure—"

"Nor would I care to!" Aurelia interjected. "For I *am* in mourning, Gussie. I miss Papa and Mama quite dreadfully."

"As do I, child," Miss Aldershot murmured. "But we cannot let our grief overwhelm us. We must act. I believe . . . yes, I will write to two or three friends, asking their assistance."

"I do not want them to think I am begging!" Aurelia protested.

"No, no, child. I will merely indicate there is a reason why you must marry so soon after your papa's death. Heiresses in distress are too common for anyone to doubt the truth of it."

As the ladies stared at each other, eyes wide with anxiety compounded by resignation to the inevitable, Biddeford entered, bringing the evening tea tray. By the time Aurelia had poured out, she was becoming slightly more reconciled to the awful necessity of marriage. A young woman of no little intelligence, she had not failed to recognize the import of Harry Stanton's visit. Even her closest friends and neighbors considered her fair game.

"I will write to my godmother," Aurelia conceded. "Lady Morville is well situated in town, a pillar of the *ton.* Surely she will know of someone."

"An admirable plan," Miss Aldershot approved. "If we can but stave off the twiddlepoop's advances until we find a savior." Even as Gussie said the words, horrid possibilities filled her mind. "You must not ride out alone anymore, child. And tell Biddeford to check the locks on every door each night without fail."

"Truly, Gussie, I cannot believe Twyford would go to such an extreme."

"Twyford is worse than a beast, Aurelia. He is a sly beast. He will do as he pleases, leaving his parents none the wiser. And if they *should* suspect, after the fact it will not matter. You will have no choice."

After the fact. In spite of the warmth of the fireplace, Aurelia shuddered.

Chapter Two

*T*he next morning found the ladies frowning over their letters, quills in hand, appropriate words refusing to separate themselves from the jumble in their minds. Was there any subtle, pride-assuaging way to state that an heiress in mourning was in immediate need of a husband? And, even if it were possible for the young lady to swallow her pride, how did one go about stating her preferences? For, of course, not just anyone would do.

"My dear," Gussie declared as she looked up to discover Aurelia nibbling the feathered end of her quill, "I fear we have not thought this problem through. What are your requirements for a husband?"

Requirements. Aurelia jabbed her quill back into its stand, clasped her hands tightly in her lap, and glared at the offending piece of blank parchment lying on her marquetry escritoire. She supposed that sometime in the not-so-distant past—when she had sat, creating air castles on the white marble bench in the rotunda—she had indulged in girlish dreams of love and happily ever after. But her knight errant, her pirate captain, her prince, had somehow remained faceless. Nothing more than a glow in her heart, a naive promise that someday she, like the heroines in novels, would find the one great love of her life. They would live together, raise children together . . . and never, ever, leave Pevensey Park as long as they both should live.

In a voice so cold and uncompromising Aurelia surprised

even herself, she pronounced, "He must be willing to let me live at Pevensey Park."

Miss Aldershot, taking a fresh sheet of paper, dutifully recorded: *Must have no estate of his own.*

"He must have enough money that I know he is not marrying me solely for my wealth."

"Aurelia dear, almost all marriages in the *ton* are made for reasons of acquisition. Land, dowries, prestige—it is the way of the world. You cannot expect—"

"Write it down."

Must have respectable fortune was added to the list. "Do you not care about his age, dear? His looks?" Gussie inquired.

"Naturally, I would prefer a man not more than ten years older than myself," Relia responded with what sounded suspiciously like bitter resignation, "and one pleasing to the eye. But I am not a fool, Gussie. I will not sacrifice Pevensey Park for a pretty face. My first two requirements are the important ones."

Miss Aldershot did not add age or physical characteristics to the list. "Anything else?" she asked.

Aurelia toyed with her quill, rearranged the inkstand, heaved a sigh that was closer to a groan. Her chin went up. "I want a husband who will support my authority, not usurp it. One who has other interests and will allow me to control Pevensey, as I was brought up to do."

"Oh, my dear," Gussie breathed, "I do not believe I can put that in a letter. My friends would think you quite mad. And not a man in England would agree to such a condition."

Aurelia hung her head. "I know. But record it, if you will. Until this moment, I had not fully recognized how much it matters to me. If you write it down, no matter what compromises I must make, I will at least have a record of how I felt before this horrid business of husband-hunting began."

"Relia . . . almost every female in the land must leave the home of her birth, cling to her husband—"

"*Whither thou goest,*" Miss Trevor quoted with considerable scorn.

"Indeed."

The room darkened as the sun was obscured by a cloud. Presently, Aurelia picked up her quill. With her thoughts coalesced at last, she began her letter to Lady Morville.

Miss Augustina Aldershot, ignoring her misgivings, followed her employer's lead. Having once, if briefly, known love, she had hoped that Relia, like her parents, would find a true and lasting love. Evidently, it was not to be. In the careful penmanship she had imparted to Aurelia when she was her governess, Gussie wrote the promised letters to her friends, informing them that Miss Aurelia Trevor was in search of a husband, landless but not impoverished.

Gussie's letters bore first fruit. Just over a fortnight later a post chaise drew up to the front portico of Pevensey Park, disgorging a tall man of uncertain age. As Aurelia heard Biddeford striding across the tiles toward the front door, she scampered away from the window, where she had been peeking at their guest, and plumped herself down upon a gold- and cream-striped satin settee, whose scrolled fruitwood arms gleamed with beeswax polish.

In a few moments Mr. Oswald Pitney was bowing before her. He was so tall and thin, so solemn, she almost expected him to creak as he straightened up, rather like the bending of a giant pine or perhaps one of the marble statues in the park. But he was not unpleasant in appearance, Relia noted with relief, for, in spite of her grand words, she *would* have to look at him for the rest of her life. He was just a bit . . . well, craggy—rather like a mountainside she had once seen when the family had visited Wales.

After her guest was perched, somewhat awkwardly, on the edge of a chair that matched the settee, Miss Trevor said, "I understand you are an academic, Mr. Pitney?" She had been hopeful for exactly this reason, as her papa, though a conscientious landowner, had spent the better part of each day in his library, surrounded by his beloved books.

Mr. Pitney stretched his long neck, as if his cravat were interfering with his thought processes, then declared, "Indeed, Miss Trevor, I have been quite content in my quiet residence in Oxford. Happy with access to the many treasures there. But when I heard Pevensey . . . that is, when I was informed there was a lady in distress—one to whom I might give assistance—I felt it my duty to meet with you."

"I see." Aurelia seized upon the faint hope in these words. "Then you find your studies, your quiet life, fulfilling? Worthy of absorbing all your time?"

"I do indeed," Mr. Pitney responded with the first sign of animation she had seen from him.

Excellent. Kent was some distance from Oxford. Mr. Pitney might spend considerable time away from Pevensey Park.

"My father is a baron," her guest offered with cool pride, "able to provide me with a comfortable independence. I was intended for the church, but found my calling is to books and not the cloth. Although I have never been in the petticoat line, I am not so unworldly as to eschew an advantageous marriage when coupled with the impelling call to provide guidance to a female left rudderless in this harsh world."

Rudderless indeed! Miss Trevor determined on the instant to eschew Mr. Oswald Pitney. If at all possible. In a few short minutes she thanked the solemn Mr. Pitney for journeying all the way from Oxford into Kent. She was considering several suitors, she told him, and would inform him if he would be required to uproot himself from the hallowed halls of academia. Though obviously shocked by a gentle maiden demonstrating calm control of such a delicate situation, Mr. Pitney made a stiff farewell and took himself off.

As the front door shut behind him, the Pevensey ladies looked at each other and rolled their eyes.

"He is, nonetheless, a possibility," Aurelia sighed. "I doubt he would be much bother."

"My dear child," Miss Aldershot sputtered, "I doubt you'd ever get a child out of him!"

"Gussie!"

"Aurelia, there are certain things we have never discussed. I will say only that when a rake is over thirty and unmarried, no one questions his virility. But *that man* was thirty-five, if he was a day, and not a sign of an interest in anything but books."

"He was panting over my acres—you know quite well he was."

"Undoubtedly—what else could you expect? But," Gussie added ominously, "if there is one thing I know you want besides Pevensey itself, it is an heir, someone who will love and care for the Park as you do. And I tell you, *that man* won't do."

The ladies waited, but, alas, Miss Aldershot's three letters produced only Mr. Oswald Pitney. Their last hope was Lady Morville, who finally communicated her triumph in a letter recommending a Darrell Carswell, Viscount Hanley. She would send him down to Pevensey Park directly.

And now—a scant three weeks before she might wed without her guardian's consent, and with little time left for vital repairs before winter set in, Lord Hanley was here. Aurelia's knees threatened to fail her as she walked through a succession of finely decorated rooms on her way to the drawing room. Twyford. Harry. Mr. Pitney. And now Lord Hanley. Surely, it was time for fortune to smile on her.

Relia paused at a pier glass in the small Red Ante-Chamber just outside the drawing room. What would Lord Hanley see? She smoothed the fall of her silver-gray silk gown, its hem banded in narrow strips of black lace. The honey brown curls tumbling artfully over her ears had not been disarranged by any mischievous gust on the terraces. The rest of her hair was piled high on her head and fastened with mother-of-pearl combs. The face staring back at her was round, young, and surprisingly sweet, giving little hint of the stubborn and aristocratic nature beneath. Except for her eyes, which were an intense gray-blue. Swiftly, Relia lowered them, as she noted their sharp, penetrating stare was not completely disguised by her long, thick fringe of lashes. Gentlemen did not care for intelligent women. Controlling women, they despised.

Nor was she in her best looks. Mourning, even gray, did not become her. And the strain of her husband-hunt was showing. Her eyes seemed more deep-set than usual, and there were smudges—more truthfully, visible half circles—

beneath them. Yet, surely, a woman, even six months into mourning, might not be expected to look as dewy fresh as a schoolroom miss.

Lord Hanley was waiting.

Aurelia took a deep breath, ordered her lips into a smile, and entered the drawing room.

Oh, my! Darrell Carswell, Viscount Hanley was positively beautiful. Dressed in perfect town attire of finely fitted blue tailcoat, striped vest, fawn trousers, and mirror-polished Hessians, Lord Hanley showed his gleaming white teeth in a charming smile and took her hand, feathering a kiss just above her knuckles. *The devil!* Kissing a lady's hand was a greeting from her parent's generation. But was there a lady of any age whose heart did not flutter, at least a trifle, over such an intimate gesture?

His pockets are sadly to let, Lady Morville had written, *but his prospects from a favorite aunt are excellent, so I do not consider him in true need of an heiress. Although,* she had added judiciously, *the boy would be a fool to ignore such a splendid opportunity as Pevensey Park.*

"The boy" was, Aurelia judged, not more than five or six and twenty. But he exuded what was known as town bronze from every square inch. In fact, in spite of his charming façade and apparent good nature, she felt herself diminishing from Lady of the Manor to country mouse. *Control.* She must seize control.

"You enjoy life in London, Lord Hanley?"

His blue eyes lit with what Miss Aldershot would later describe as a fanatical gleam. "I guarantee you will love London, Miss Trevor. It is the only place to be, don't y'know? All that's important happens in town."

Relia's heart plummeted, but perhaps things wouldn't be so bad. . . if Lord Hanley preferred to stay in town and was willing to leave her in the country—a common arrangement, she knew. "You do not care for the country then?" she asked.

"The country?" Viscount Hanley made a brave effort. "An occasional weekend is acceptable," he allowed. "A bit of shooting, a hunt now and again."

"Am I to understand you prefer to live in London year-round?"

"Is there anything else?" he asked with an arch look ameliorated by an insouciant smile. "Just think, Miss Trevor," he continued, positively quivering with eagerness, "if we are wed, we can furnish a townhouse with nothing but the best, give the finest parties, become leaders of the *ton*—"

"I—I fear I have no interest in London, Lord Hanley," said Aurelia, clinging desperately to a mask of calm, even as she felt her last hope being wrenched asunder.

"Dear girl," he cried, "you cannot expect me to live in the country? Why . . . good God, it *smells*!"

Pevensey Park. Which smelled of fresh-scythed grass and flowers. Of waving stands of wheat and ripening fruit. Of hops and oast houses. Of sheep and cows and pigs. New-turned earth. Spring rains and summer lightning. Of fish in the stream and the sweat of dedicated labor. Of life—birth, death, renewal.

Here she was and here she would stay. Somehow she would find a way.

"You're mad!"

Since Thomas Lanning's least whisper could be more intimidating than a bull's roar, his solicitor and longtime friend, Charles Saunders, retreated into the depths of the burgundy leather wingchair that faced the broad expanse of his employer's desk and contemplated another approach. Truthfully, Thomas, who was once again bent over the paperwork on his desk, looked as immovable and as impervious to change as the Rock of Gibraltar. A handsome man was Thomas Lanning, Mr. Saunders had to concede—until you looked into the depths of those piercing gray eyes and began to wonder if he had any of the weaknesses of mortal men. Yet in the matrimonial market he was considered a fine catch. If his bride did not mind a man with the resilient strength of a Toledo blade . . . and the sharp cut as well. Not that Thomas Lanning was arrogant or aloof—he was much too clever to offend his colleagues in the City or his high-flying acquaintants in the *ton*. But for all the bonhomie he could display on occasion, no one ever quite knew what Thomas was thinking. But this time . . . this time Charles had to make him listen.

But first . . . a diversion.

Mr. Saunders sat forward in his chair and made an elaborate inspection of the walls of Thomas's spacious office, a well-appointed suite of rooms in a building close by the Royal Exchange. "You've acquired another Turner, I see."

"A good investment," Mr. Lanning returned shortly as he swirled his signature with a bold hand at the bottom of a long piece of parchment.

"Can't say as I understand what you see in his work. It's like someone draped a houri's veil over a perfectly good landscape. Or like a mist came down, obscuring all the good parts." Charles shook his head. "Take my word for it, Thomas, in twenty years' time they won't be worth a ha'penny on the pound."

"If you have nothing more to say, Charles, you may leave."

"Don't be a nodcock, Thomas. This is important!"

Slowly, Thomas Lanning rose to his full six feet, one inch. He placed his large hands flat on top of his desk and leaned down to glare at his friend. "I am a man of the City," he declared, biting out each word as if they were bullets. "I do not *want* a country house. I do not *need* a country house. And, most particularly, I do not need an heiress who is such an antidote she cannot find a husband."

"Sir Gilbert swears to me she is not an antidote," Charles protested. "Her mother was ill for some time before she passed on, and then her father—"

"No! Stop nattering, Charles. I won't have her."

"Her grandfather was a marquess. Old Huntsham. Fine family." Mr. Saunders was growing desperate.

"If I wanted a wife, there is no lack of candidates. I scarcely need you to play whoremonger."

Charles Saunders shot up out of his chair. Though not as tall as his friend and employer, he still managed to direct a lightning bolt of anger straight into Thomas's gray eyes. "Miss Trevor is a lady of spotless character, with some of the finest bloodlines in England. Her estate is considered a gem—well cared-for, productive. You have no call to insult her . . . or my judgment."

Thomas subsided into his chair, waving Charles back into his as well. Idly, he tapped a finger on the papers he had just signed, while he reined in his temper. "I have heard all your arguments, Charles, but—for the last time—I have no interest in marriage."

"You didn't let me get as far as *why* Miss Trevor is in immediate need of a husband." Mr. Lanning drew a harsh breath, which subsided into a resigned wave of his hand. "She had two guardians, you see," Mr. Saunders began, "but one—Marcus Yelverton—passed on quite unexpectedly. Dropped dead at an Assembly, straight in the middle of a country dance. So now Miss Trevor and all that goes with her are under the control of her uncle, Lord Hubert Trevor, who is not about to let such a treasure slip through his fingers. He's pressing her to marry his son Twyford—"

But Thomas wasn't listening. "Yelverton? Marcus Yelverton, the MP? Lives somewhere between Maidstone and Tunbridge Wells?"

"That's the one."

Thomas steepled his hands; his lips twitched into a faint smile. "Your genius is usually infallible, Charles, but in this instance I had begun to think you fit for Bedlam." Mr. Lanning's smile broadened into a feral grin. "But you have redeemed yourself. You may tell Miss Trevor's solicitor that I will be delighted to meet with her at her convenience."

Of course. Silently, Charles swore at himself. What an idiot he had been to think that a wealthy heiress with excellent bloodlines and a fine estate would be of interest to Thomas Lanning. His friend's ambitions ran much higher than those of ordinary men. Thomas already had wealth. It was power he craved.

Chapter Three

V iscount Hanley's failure to live up to expectations was a bitter blow to the ladies of Pevensey Park. But the very next morning Miss Trevor, ever resilient, ordered up her carriage and journeyed into Tunbridge Wells. There she consulted Mr. Josiah Eastbridge, a rival solicitor to the man who had served her father for so many years and who now, apparently, served only her Uncle Hubert. Mr. Eastbridge, a gentle soul, could scarce believe he was to be entrusted with any modicum of the Trevor family business—however secretive Miss Aurelia might be about her true purpose. He was, therefore, only too happy to recommend a solicitor in London. His old schoolmate, Sir Gilbert Bromley, a man of rare perspicacity, sometimes known—he informed her proudly—as the Solicitors' Solicitor.

Miss Trevor, pleased with both Mr. Eastbridge and her own daring, gave her maid and Gussie Aldershot only minimal time to pack before the three women set off for London. After securing a fine suite of rooms at Grillon's—for which Relia gave thanks that her papa's will had included a generous pin money allowance—a letter of introduction was despatched to the much-vaunted Sir Gilbert Bromley. The solicitor responded with flattering promptness.

The ladies made the considerable journey across London from Albemarle Street to Lincoln's Inn Fields in near silence. Aurelia did not hesitate to peer out the window, fascinated by the sights, sounds, and smells of a town she had seen only on rare occasions before her mother's illness. She looked on it as a spectacle—something to be viewed, even savored for a few moments of time—then left behind. With relief. For everything was so squeezed together—how could people live this way? Miss Trevor welcomed the park-like green of Lincoln's Inn Fields with pleasure. London's solicitors and barristers had displayed surprisingly good taste in choosing this spot as their own.

For a man who had been described to her as "distinguished," Sir Gilbert Bromley was, on first glance, a disappointment. A man of perhaps fifty, his body was as rotund as Squire Stanton's, his face as round as a cartwheel, as was the shining bald spot on top of his head. But his eyes, Relia saw, were a clear blue, the kind that could see to far horizons or penetrate the depths of a murky pond. *Thank you, Mr. Eastbridge.*

After the ladies were seated, Sir Gilbert smiled benignly and said, "And now, ladies, what may I do for you?"

As Miss Trevor talked, the solicitor's smile faded. A wealthy, landless husband—strong enough to deal with a greedy uncle, an importunate suitor, and a cowardly steward, yet disinterested enough in country affairs to let the reins of Pevensey Park remain in his wife's hands? "Good Gad, woman!" Sir Gilbert burst out. "Have your wits gone begging? I'm no matchmaker. And even if I were, your demands are outrageous."

But Relia fluttered her long lashes and looked so woebegone, the brilliant London solicitor never stood a chance. Such a beauty . . . granddaughter of a marquess. Such a fine property . . . and magnificent income. And then Miss Trevor named a fee that might have tempted the Prince Regent himself. Sir Gilbert Bromley shook Miss Trevor's hand, bid Miss Aldershot good day, and promised to give the matter his most serious consideration.

And now the fateful moment was at hand. Miss Trevor was armored in the best half-mourning gown a London modiste had hastily remodeled to fit her petite client, whose golden guineas took precedence over the reluctant payments offered by the countess for whom the dress had been intended. Of lavender lustring, with hem and matching spencer piped in black, it was far more flattering than Miss Trevor's previous mourning gowns. Her warm brown hair, though unfashionable by London standards, was piled high on her head. Pearl drops with a lavender cast depended from her ears. Leather slippers, dyed to match her gown, adorned her small feet. She was, in short, as ready as a young woman could be to interview a possible candidate for the position of husband.

Sir Gilbert, wishing to give Miss Trevor the advantage, requested that she arrive at his office early, so she might be on hand to greet the proposed suitor. Much as if she were interviewing a prospective butler, sniffed Miss Aldershot. But both ladies were forced to conclude that Sir Gilbert's suggestion had merit. Now, however, Relia was sorry. For she had been twenty minutes early, and the miserable Cit was late. Late to a meeting so vital to his future! Miss Aurelia Trevor could not, in fact, imagine what had made her accept Sir Gilbert's suggestion. Marry a Cit? A man her friends and neighbors would scorn. A vulgarian who actually had to earn his keep. A man of no land, no family, a mediocre education . . .

Good Lord, what if he truly smelled of the shop? For how Lord Hanley could say the country smelled when London was positively *rank* with odors, Aurelia completely failed to understand. What if Thomas Lanning were one of those self-made men who had pulled himself up out of the coal mines, the textile factories, the merchant fleet, or a *butcher shop*? What if he wore a moleskin waistcoat or—horrors!—what if his accent were simply *impossible*?

The office door opened. One of Sir Gilbert's clerks announced, "Mr. Thomas Lanning."

Relia was terrified. What had she done? She had to call on every ounce of family fortitude before she could force her eyes to look.

Dear God, here was a *man*. A man who made Viscount Hanley look like the shallow boy he was. A man who caused her toes to curl, her stomach to feel as if she had swallowed a swarm of butterflies. A man who awakened parts of her she had not known existed.

Thomas Lanning stood, slightly slouched, as if refusing to display himself to full advantage for the ladies' delectation. Yet it was clear he was tall, impeccably dressed, without any of the excesses found in young men of the *ton*. His dark brown hair was uncompromisingly short, allowing only a slight wave to dangle toward his ears. Gray eyes, veiled at the moment, looked indifferently down from a face so much stronger than Lord Hanley's that it nearly took Relia's breath away. Handsome, yes, but only if one cared for a man of granite.

Yet Thomas Lanning was the stuff of dreams. Everything a girl might desire.

Or nothing. Relia could not imagine this man giving up control of anything.

Somehow the introductions were over, Mr. Lanning was seated in a chair across the table from Miss Trevor. Sir Gilbert, looking vastly pleased, and perhaps a trifle sly, bowed himself out. Miss Aldershot promptly effaced herself to a chair in the farthest corner of the imposing conference room, leaving Miss Trevor and Mr. Lanning to gaze at each other in open, and slightly hostile, assessment.

Young, so young, Thomas thought. Too young to be entering into a hardheaded marriage of convenience. And lovely. Surprisingly so. Petite. She would scarcely reach his shoulder. And arrogant as a duchess, by God. The chit was examining him with narrowed eyes and considerable skepticism, as if she had fully expected someone who had just crawled up out of the gutter. Did she think he had made his fortune selling pasties from a barrow?

Thomas, nobody's fool, had made a condition for his attendance at this most unusual confrontation. Miss Trevor would be told only what she needed to know. Mr. Lanning was a Cit of acceptable fortune with no country estate. His business interests were in London, where he could be expected to spend a goodly portion of his time. At this preliminary, and highly shaky, stage of their negotiations, this was quite enough information for Miss Aurelia Trevor.

The silence was becoming oppressive. Mr. Lanning leaned back in his chair, stretched out his long legs beneath the conference table and drawled, "I understand you are in need of a dragonslayer, Miss Trevor."

Drat the man! She should have spoken first, of course. It was she, Aurelia Trevor, who had a position, however unorthodox, to offer. She was the employer; he, the supplicant.

"If I had control of my finances," Aurelia informed Mr. Lanning in glacial tones, "I would not need a dragonslayer." Mr. Lanning examined her with such leisurely impertinence, Aurelia felt her skin begin to heat. Desperately, she hoped she was not blushing.

"You are what—seventeen?" he inquired.

"Twenty!"

"Ah!"

To Aurelia, Thomas Lanning's raised eyebrow was as good as a red flag to a bull. "I reach my majority in a week's time," she declared from between clenched teeth, "but little good it will do me without the funds to run the estate. If I were a boy—"

"If you were a boy, you would still have a guardian, and marriage would not be the least bit of help."

True. But she would never acknowledge it.

Aurelia forced herself to examine Mr. Lanning with the same leisurely intensity he had turned on her. But she was a newcomer to the game. Her fingers and toes seemed to freeze into ice, while her insides swirled into scorching flames. Her mind threatened to panic. She had trusted Sir Gilbert to find a man who met all her qualifications. (Well . . . possibly she had had a few qualms.) But *this* . . . this confident Cit with his almost insolent manner . . . this too-perfect imitation of a London gentleman, with an accent as pure, if perhaps more precise, than Aurelia's own . . . No, no, no! This was not at all what she had imagined.

He was the epitome of every woman's dreams.

He was terrifying.

And he was laughing at her. From the lofty height of male superiority and what must be close to ten more years on earth, this Cit—beneath his bland, maddeningly quizzical façade—was amused. Relia's temper and the Trevor family pride surged through her, sweeping away both maid-

enly fears and female flutterings. She was Miss Aurelia
Trevor of Pevensey Park, Kent, and she had a task to complete. A husband to find. Who was Mr. Thomas Lanning to
find her amusing? His only advantage was that while she
might find this experience unique, Mr. Lanning must be
quite accustomed to offering his services for hire!

Miss Trevor squared her shoulders, folded her hands on
the shining surface of the conference table. "Pevensey Park
comprises some five thousand acres," she informed him. "In
addition to a fine park, we grow wheat and hops. Our sheep
are the finest merinos. Our dairy farm, in addition to fulfilling our own needs, supplies milk to much of Tunbridge
Wells. Most of the produce from our market gardens—
vegetables, fruit, and flowers—goes all the way to London."
Miss Trevor looked Mr. Lanning straight in the eye. "Since
Pevensey Park is a *business*—though most landowners eschew such a title—I am willing to consider a man of business as my—ah—dragonslayer."

With satisfaction Aurelia noted that, as she talked, a
quiver of emotion had shaken Mr. Lanning's bland expression. He had not known Pevensey Park was one of the most
profitable estates in England, she was sure of it. And no
man was so wealthy, he was not attracted by the thought of
augmenting his assets.

Dear God in heaven! With something akin to horror, Aurelia recognized what she had done. In her mind, she had already chosen him. This one would do.

Thomas Lanning. When just looking at him caused her
heart to pound, her stomach to churn—

The women of Pevensey Park were made of sterner stuff!

"You will, of course, wish to visit the Park," Aurelia announced, "to make sure I have not painted too rosy a portrait. That is"—she broke off, mortified by her possible
misinterpretation of his silence—"that is, if you have any interest in proceeding with a possible—ah—contract."

Brave girl! Almost, Thomas applauded. There were men
of forty and fifty who quaked in their boots at thought of negotiations with Thomas Lanning. But did she truly have any
idea what she was doing? Any thoughts beyond her precious

Pevensey Park? Had she considered what marriage would mean? Did she think him a tame tabby to lie down and purr for the sake of an occasional pet?

Had she thought as far as children? And how they were made?

He doubted it.

From the corner of the room Thomas heard a slight sound. The companion—he'd forgotten all about her. Had that been a sob or a prayer? For surely she, too, recognized this was the crucial moment. Would he go to Pevensey Park, or would he get up, say, "Thank you for considering me, Miss Trevor," and walk out of her life forever?

Hell and damnation but she was an attractive female! So much more than he had expected. Courageous. Intelligent.

Vulnerable. So very much in need of a knight errant.

And Pevensey Park was in the same part of Kent as the home of Mr. Marcus Yelverton, deceased.

"I have a number of commitments here in town which I must meet," Thomas said carefully, "but I will rearrange my schedule for the following week. You may expect me the day after Guy Fawkes . . . if that is convenient?"

For a moment a mist passed before Miss Trevor's eyes. *What had she done?* She heard a choking sound from Gussie. Mr. Lanning was still sitting there, looking politely indifferent, as if they had not just taken a giant step toward the most momentous decision of their lives.

"It is quite convenient," Aurelia told him over the near-strangling lump in her throat. "We look forward to your visit."

Mr. Thomas Lanning unfolded himself from his chair, stood up, bowed—most precisely—to both ladies, and strode out of the room.

Miss Aurelia Trevor dropped her head onto the conference table and shook.

Chapter Four

*M*iss Trevor gave London not so much as a glance as their coach made its way out of town, the four horses gradually picking up speed until they were bowling along the road toward Kent at a pace that brought a gleam to the coachman's eye and a whistle to his lips.

Aurelia knew what her father would have said. That she'd made a rare mull of it. Blackened the family name. No—far worse—she was obliterating the family name. Exchanging it for that of a Cit. A Cit who acted as if he were doing her a favor even to consider her offer!

And Squire Stanton would go purple with rage. Harry, as well. That she should stoop so low—choosing a Cit—when she could have had a fine country gentleman known to her since the cradle.

Perhaps Lord Hanley was, after all, the wisest compromise. If she gave him enough to support himself in London in lavish style, he would seldom trouble her . . . beyond the requisite heir and a spare.

Heir. She had always thought children quite wonderful. As an only child, Aurelia had dreamed of filling Pevensey Park with the sounds of running feet and joyous laughter. Children skipping and tumbling across the expanse of park toward the wondrous world inside the Palladian rotunda, as eagerly as she once had done. But now . . . the thought of children threatened to stop her heart. Though necessarily vague, her concept of how children were made was perhaps a trifle too influenced by being a country girl for all of her twenty years. Her only knowledge of marital matters was confined to the violent mating of barnyard animals and the censorious horror evinced by her housekeeper when one of the maids strayed into the family way. Aurelia could, just barely, imagine herself doing her wifely duty with Harry or Lord Hanley. But with Thomas Lanning . . . ? Her courage would fail her. . . . She'd expire at his feet. Drop dead, all of a heap.

Leaving the miserable Cit in sole charge of Pevensey Park.

Never!

"Relia . . . Aurelia!" said Gussie Aldershot. "Another mile of that glum face and I swear I shall scream. How can you have second thoughts? The good Lord has smiled on you. And the Park as well."

"But he's so—so—"

"Indeed he is! And you may thank Providence for it."

"But he'll never allow—"

"Allow you to rule? Of course he won't. Nor would young Harry, for all he's little more than a nodcock. Nor can I believe *my* Aurelia Trevor, whom I have known since you were a tot of five, would be fool enough to take a witless boy like Lord Hanley when you could have a man like Thomas Lanning."

"I will allow him the visit," Miss Trevor conceded, rather grandly. "It would be rude to turn him away. And then we shall see."

Miss Aldershot regarded her charge with grave concern. "Relia, I do not fool myself into thinking Mr. Lanning will make an easy husband. It will be, I think, much like loosing a jungle tiger on the unsuspecting Kentish countryside. But that is not such a bad thing. You know the old saying about 'fresh blood.'" Miss Aldershot leaned back against the velvet squabs, a tiny smile curling her thin lips. "And I believe we can be quite certain Mr. Lanning's blood is very fresh indeed." The only response Gussie received from Miss Trevor was a swift intake of breath followed by seething silence.

The ladies were so anxious to be home that they passed through Maidstone without stopping to take a bite to eat or stretch their legs. Home. Miss Trevor thought she well might burst into tears at the sight of Pevensey Park. Was she mad to have risked so much? In spite of Gussie's words, should she settle for the tried and true? For Harry, who was a solid English countryman. Or Viscount Hanley, whom she could wind round her little finger . . . or buy off with judicious applications of coin of the realm?

And run far and fast from Thomas Lanning? Who, when he came to Pevensey Park, would be like a fish out of water. A man of the City, lost in the rolling green hills of Kent, shunned by the landed gentry. While she, Miss Aurelia Trevor of Pevensey Park, would be pitied for having fallen so low. Married to a Cit. A man who worked for his living.

As did nearly all the inhabitants of the county of Kent.

Strange. She had not thought of that before. In a sense, her father had also worked for his living, closely supervising his steward, riding his thousands of acres, always keeping a careful eye on the needs of his land and his tenants. Until her mother's death had sent him into a downward spiral from which he had never recovered.

Was it so simple then? If a man owned land, he was a gentleman. But if his living was not derived from the land, then he was a Cit? After her meeting with Thomas Lanning, Sir Gilbert had confided that Mr. Lanning's wealth had been made from "investments." So what was so heinous about that? Her papa had investments. Not just in consoles, but in more risky ventures as well. So why . . . ?

Best not to question the way of the world, Aurelia sighed. Nor why she was sitting here making excuses for Thomas Lanning . . . attempting to justify their possible union, even though the thought quite frightened her out of her wits.

"At last!" Gussie declared, peering out the window. "I see the tops of the oast houses. We are nearly home."

Relia felt a rush of tears to her eyes. But by the time they were trotting smartly down the long drive lined with lime trees, augmented with the occasional colorful splash of a copper beech or the exotic silhouette of a Cedar of Lebanon, she had wiped her cheeks, gazing with joy at the splendid panorama of Pevensey Park. Here, she was cocooned in beauty. Surrounded by those who loved her. *Safe*.

Illusion, all illusion—as Miss Trevor discovered as soon as Biddeford welcomed her into the house, his butler's bland mask unable to hide his distress. As Aurelia and Gussie stepped into the intricately tiled front entry, their footsteps slowed, came to a halt.

"What is happening here?" Miss Trevor demanded, as two footmen heaved a large wooden crate up onto one of several stacks of boxes already piled in the entry hall.

"Lord Hubert, miss," Biddeford choked out. "He's clearing the bookroom. Says he can't abide clutter. Sending them all to the attics, he is. But it's too much for our poor lads. He's storing them here 'til he can hire extra help."

"Lord Hubert is *here*?"

"Yes, miss. Arrived just after you left for London. And in a rare taking he was to find you gone. Sent for Lady Hubert. And Mr. Twyford." The elderly butler, looking even more woebegone, announced, "They have moved in, miss. Taken over the east wing. There was nothing—"

"Of course not, Biddeford," Aurelia interjected, appalled by the butler's obvious distress. "He is my guardian. There is nothing you could do. But as for my father's books . . ." Miss Trevor, eyes kindling to fury, gazed at the wooden crates, stacked between two elegant white columns. "Biddeford, where shall I find my uncle?"

"I believe you will find him in the estate room, miss. He said he wished to examine the account books."

"James, Peter," Miss Trevor said to the two footmen, who were hovering next to the stack of boxes, clearly waiting for their mistress's reaction, "you will cease what you are doing and take our portmanteaus upstairs. Then you may report to Biddeford for further instructions."

The footmen could not quite restrain their grins as they crossed the entry hall and gathered up the ladies' luggage, waiting respectfully for Miss Aldershot to precede them up the stairs. Gussie's gaze, more than a trifle grim, followed Aurelia's slight figure as she exited the entry hall on a quest destined to be as futile as her encounter with Mr. Tubbs.

Miss Augustina Aldershot, with her shoulders slumped and a tear in her eye, trudged up the stairs to her room.

"My lord," said Miss Trevor as she entered the estate room. Her tone was arctic.

Lord Hubert Trevor, a silkily handsome man of considerable height, with a fine head of gray hair topping his still pleasing countenance, had put aside the estate books—if he had ever opened them, Relia thought—and was leaning back in his comfortable chair, looking thoroughly pleased with himself, while the fingers of his left hand toyed with a snifter of brandy. As always when she saw her uncle, Miss Trevor experienced a nasty qualm, for his resemblance to her beloved papa was marked. A resemblance which was, alas, only skin-deep. Lord Hubert rose slowly to his feet, one hand surreptitiously clutching the desk. The brandy bottle, Relia noted, was nearly empty. "If I had been aware you planned to visit me, uncle, I would have been here to greet you." Miss Trevor did not curtsey, nor so much as nod in greeting.

"And where have you been, miss?" Lord Hubert demanded, even as he listed alarmingly toward the desk.

"As I am certain Biddeford informed you, Gussie and I went to London. I have decided to go into half-mourning and needed to order new gowns." Aurelia felt only a slight quiver of conscience as she had, indeed, spent a goodly portion of her time in town improving her wardrobe.

"Your aunt and I were most alarmed, Aurelia. When will you understand you are no longer free to do as you please?"

"Since I did not expect your visit," Miss Trevor returned in clipped tones, "it never occurred to me my journey might alarm you."

"Sit, sit," Lord Hubert mumbled, swaying to and fro as he waved his niece to a chair in front of the estate desk.

It was hopeless, Aurelia thought as she clasped her hands tightly in her lap and stared at her uncle. She would be fortunate to get any sense out of him at all. Much of her anger dissipated on a sigh of despair. "Uncle, you know Pevensey Park is mine, to order as I please. Papa made that quite clear in his will. My majority is nearly upon us. You may be trustee of my money for another five years, but this is *my* estate. My inheritance. You have no right to order the packing up of my papa's books."

"Can't abide a mess," Lord Hubert returned, on what sounded suspiciously like a whine. "Nor can Lady Hubert. Books everywhere, don't you know? Books on tables and chairs, on the floor—some of 'em stacked as high as a man can reach. Can't live with that, child. Clutter, my lady wife calls it, and rightly so. Too much to carry to the attics, so I am having it packed off to the stables. Practically empty, they are. Plenty of room for books."

"The stables?" Relia echoed faintly. "They'll be ruined!"

"Take an army to get 'em to the attics," Lord Hubert grumbled. "Can't expect me to auth—author—agree to such an expense. Wouldn't be right."

Though stunned by her uncle's high-handed behavior, Miss Trevor realized she was missing something. Something possibly even more vital than the fate of her father's books.

"Uncle?" she said as the silence grew heavy. "I fail to see why Papa's books should concern you. You do not live here."

Lord Hubert, looking sly and perhaps a trifle uneasy, took a deep gulp of his brandy. "Did not Biddeford tell you?" he inquired. "I was so concerned when I found you gone that I sent for Lady Hubert and Twyford. We have decided we have been remiss in our care of you. Obviously, a young woman of your tender years and noble station cannot live alone. We have, therefore, decided to make Pevensey our home until you are safely married."

"*Your home?*" Relia murmured, wishing, as she heard her feeble echo, that she had managed to imbue her voice with some semblance of outraged indignation instead of simple shock.

For a moment her uncle's blue eyes—tinged with gray, as were her own—appeared to sharpen, his mind grasping at sobriety. "It has occurred to me, Aurelia, that Ralph's books would make excellent tinder for the Guy Fawkes bonfire."

Miss Trevor sat, perched on the edge of her chair, eyes closed, while the safe haven of Pevensey Park crumpled around her. There must be a proper response to all this, but her mind was filled with a whirlwind that refused to disgorge a single coherent thought.

Escape. She had to escape.

"And, Relia," her uncle added as she rose to her feet, "you had best hurry your dressing for dinner. Lady Hubert prefers to dine at six o'clock. That is when you will be expected at table."

Miss Trevor glided out of the estate room on a miasma of pain, but by the time she reached her bedchamber, her sharp senses were recovering. She could, she *would* deal with this situation. Harry Stanton, Lord Hanley, even Oswald Pitney, would be better than *this*.

Even a Cit was better than this. For Pevensey Park, for the sake of children yet unborn, she would do *anything*.

Except what her Uncle Hubert and her Cousin Twyford wanted.

That night Aurelia toyed with her food while Lord Hubert sat in her father's place at the head of the elegant cherrywood table and Lady Hubert presided at the foot. In the place that had remained empty since her mama's death. Twyford, fortunately, was absent. Dangling after some tavern wench, Aurelia supposed, wishing that each additional pint might project him further into the oblivion of forgetting he was now living at Pevensey Park. Miss Aldershot was close-lipped, choosing to ignore the fact that Lady Hubert treated her as if she did not exist. It was not a pleasant meal, but worse was yet to come.

Lady Hubert, once plain Miss Eustacia Middlethorpe, had been so enamored with acquiring a title, along with the youngest son of a marquess, that no one except her mama had dared address her by her Christian name since the moment of her marriage. Lord and Lady Hubert carried this practice to the extreme by using their titles when referring to each other. Twyford had once been heard to speculate, when in his cups, that he wondered if his parents continued this affectation into the throes of passion. A wayward thought, immediately vanquished, as, truthfully, Twyford could not imagine passion and his parents in the same room, let alone the same bed. Not even when an equally foxed friend poked him in the ribs and reminded him that his very existence was confirmation of at least some brief moment of connubial bliss.

Although Lady Hubert's conversation at table had consisted primarily of laments on her son's continued absence, the moment the ladies had settled themselves in the drawing room, leaving Lord Hubert to yet more brandy, she went on the attack. "Your conduct, Aurelia, is disgraceful," she declared, sitting primly upright on the striped satin settee, looking down her prominent nose, which was set in a thin face marked by lines inflicted through years of disapprobation over the many—and inevitably malicious—annoyances that had marred her passage through life. "How could you run off to town in such a fashion, leaving us to wonder if you were dead or alive? Set on by highwaymen, kidnapped for ransom—"

"Ma'am," Relia interjected, "I believe the road between here and London is one of the best kept and most traveled in the kingdom. And we took two outriders. Truly, there was no danger."

"You have no right, child—none at all—to go haring off without informing Lord Hubert. You are headstrong, Aurelia. Your father indulged you to excess. It is high time you fully understand your uncle is your guardian. It is he who says when you may come and go. He who holds the reins of Pevensey Park."

Anathema as it was, her aunt was all too correct. Aurelia knew it. She had pushed her independence past what was pleasing when she had gone off to London without at least informing her uncle. Although, with legal age so close at hand, surely the question should be moot. She had only to bide her time and play the dutiful niece, while guarding her tongue and waiting for the plans she had set in motion to develop. But pride is a terrible thing, as was the Trevor temper. "If you think to force me to marry Twyford, you are very

much mistaken," Relia fumed. "I shan't do it. Never! I'll
marry a man off the streets, a blacksmith, a—a *stablehand,*
the second footman, before I'll allow Twyford to touch me."

"Aurelia!" Gussie gasped.

Lady Hubert dropped what little pretense of polite conversation that still lingered. "You will marry Twyford and
like it. Pevensey Park stays in the Trevor family."

Yes, it would, Relia vowed. But only through Miss Aurelia Trevor. Sole heiress.

Quite suddenly, Mr. Thomas Lanning's granite strength
seemed to take on the glow of polished armor. She would
write to Sir Gilbert this very night—sneak the letter to
James or Peter for posting in the village. She would take
back control of her life. She *would.*

Thomas Lanning was dependable. Although he had made
his fortune on 'Change with more than a little creativity and
daring, his reliability was known the length and breadth of
the City. Indeed, renown for his acumen and the excellence
of his financial advice had long since overflowed into the
esoteric realms of Mayfair. So much so that Mr. Lanning
had been termed "Prince of the Exchange" by no less a per-
sonage than His Royal Highness, the Prince Regent.

But to Miss Aurelia Trevor he was a frog—an ugly one at
that. Thomas was certain of it. The arrogant chit was using
him, as she would her coachman, to steer her clear of rough
roads. Charles might natter on about the girl's difficulties till
he was blue in the face. What did he, Thomas Lanning of the
City of London, care if some heiress in Kent was being
forced to wed her cousin—even if he *was* known as The Terrible Twyford? The so-called gentlemen of the *ton* did it all
the time. *Keep the money in the family*—wasn't that the hidden motto behind most Coats of Arms?

When he had performed his service of rescuing the Fair
Maiden, Aurelia Trevor would offer her polite thanks and
shoo him back to London. So, in spite of his promise, he
would not journey to Pevensey Park. There must be a hundred—a thousand—young men willing to chase off a few

minor dragons in order to ally themselves to a lucrative country estate. . . .

He would send his regrets.

Regrets. The regrets would be his. A fine country estate—the power base he needed, whistled down the wind because he—confound it!—because he hesitated to use a vulnerable young woman as she was using him.

Analyzing conflicting information was Thomas Lanning's trade. He was an expert—even adept at conducting arguments with himself. He should, in all conscience, turn his back on the chit. Yet . . . was his personal ambition worth a leg shackle? How hard could marriage be? From Miss Trevor's cool indifference, he did not believe she would be a demanding wife. Indeed, quite the opposite. The sooner she saw the back of him, the better.

Thomas glanced down at the papers on his desk and, just for a moment, discovered they made no sense at all. Hell and damnation, the fiendish chit had scrambled his wits! He slammed open the top right drawer of his desk, seized a fresh piece of parchment, jabbed his quill into the ink, and dashed off a note to Miss Trevor. Mr. Thomas Lanning deeply regrets his inability to keep his commitment to visit Pevensey Park. He is unavoidably detained by—Thomas raised his head, frowned—by an urgent journey to Scotland. There, that ought to be far enough away. No need for the aristocratic witch to know he didn't plan to leave his desk in London.

"Thomas, Thomas!" Charles Saunders dashed by Mr. Lanning's long-suffering clerk. "I've just had a note from Sir Gilbert—"

"Go away, Charles. I have a meeting with Nathan Rothschild in an hour."

"There's trouble at Pevensey—"

"I don't want to hear about it. I've washed my hands of Miss Trevor and her precious Park."

"But, Thomas, you can't!" said Mr. Saunders, appalled. "You *promised.*"

"I have made my reputation on being able to distinguish sound investments from foolish ones. I will not go to Kent."

"*Foolish*? Are you mad? Pevensey is one of the best-run estates in England, its income unrivaled by properties twice its size."

"It comes with a life sentence I do not choose to undertake. Good day, Charles. I have work to do."

"But Sir Gilbert has had a letter from Miss Trevor this morning. Lord and Lady Hubert have moved into Pevensey Park, along with The Terrible Twyford."

Thomas Lanning dropped his head into his hands, his fingers combing his dark brown locks. He swore, long and colorfully.

"Shall I order up your white charger?" Charles inquired blandly. "Your sword and lance?"

"Don't forget the chainmail," Thomas sighed.

Chapter Five

T o Miss Trevor's infinite relief, Twyford Trevor did not return to Pevensey Park for two days. But the night before, in the wee hours of the morning, she had heard him stumbling up the stairs. For the first time in her life she had locked the door to her bedchamber.

So this morning she was bent on escape. Wearing a mourning gown the color of an imminent thunderstorm, and with spirits to match, she strode briskly across the sloping green park in front of the great Palladian house. The sun highlighted her honey brown hair, confined solely by a black velvet ribbon tied at the nape of her neck. In spite of her stiffened shoulders and brisk pace, she looked absurdly young. A drab waif lost in a vast expanse of green.

Time had just run out on her husband-hunting. Her problem was now so tangled she was caught in a vortex of conflicting emotions. In order to think, she had to escape the house. Escape the oppressive atmosphere that radiated from her aunt and uncle. Escape the imminent appearance of her cousin, who was likely to pop out of the woodwork at any moment.

Relia paused on the top of the high point of the arched wooden bridge. Gazing upstream toward the cascade, she managed a weak smile. At the time the park had been reconstructed by the eager devotee of Capability Brown, the natural slope of the stream had been enhanced by dredging, and a cascade had been constructed of layer upon layer of flat stones. The stream now fell in a tinkling waterfall over three natural-appearing terraces, which were framed in ferns and other graceful water plants, with a willow tree at the top of the cascade, adding its picturesque droop to the man-made scenic beauty. Relia closed her eyes, letting the sooth-ing rush of the water slide into and over her bruised soul.

Her cousin Twyford wasn't truly evil. *Overindulged, self-ish, willful* were the words that came to mind. Even as a child, he would do whatever was necessary to get his own way, regardless of the rules his elders had attempted to im-part—whether the rules of God from the vicar, the rules of polite society from his governess, or the rules of mathemat-ics from his tutor. Twyford, in short, could not be trusted. Relia sincerely doubted her cousin would go as far as rape, but a midnight visit—if only to demonstrate how easy it would be . . .

If only to demonstrate her total vulnerability.

Relia tore her mind from the brink of the abyss, moving abruptly across the bridge to the open rotunda, with its cir-cle of six columns topped by a classic domed roof. But the fancies of her childhood were only distant memories. Secu-rity. Why had she never appreciated it while she had it? Gaz-ing down at the deep pool of water at the foot of the cascade, Relia pictured her papa sitting in his library, surrounded by his books, her mama writing letters at the marquetry es-critoire in the morning room overlooking the terraces.

A crow broke through her wishful thinking, jabbering an-grily at a squirrel. An ugly sound, amply suited to the day. The bird's garb was darker and shinier than her own, Relia noted idly, his voice louder and more strident. Fortunate bird, to deliver his epithets and be able to fly away, leaving his annoyances far behind. Relia heaved a sigh, for she feared her problems had gone far beyond the realm of an-noyances. And she was earthbound. Powerless.

Unless . . .

No. He would not come. Thomas Lanning would cry off, she knew it. The man had had far more pride than she had expected. He had actually been reluctant . . . *reluctant* to consider her offer. Her predicament had *amused* him! Only an invitation to view the Park had whetted the man's appetite. The shocking nerve of the upstart merchant! No, she could not count on Mr. Lanning. She must, therefore, choose among Harry, Lord Hanley, and Mr. Pitney.

Nausea swept over her. Relia's stomach cramped. She bent forward, arms locked over her midsection, rocking in pain.

"Poor cuz, have I come at a bad time?"

The worst possible. The only good thing about the arrival of Mr. Twyford Trevor at the rotunda was that the shock of seeing him stiffened Aurelia's spine, transforming her acute attack of nerves into cold defiance. For if Lord Hubert resembled his brother Ralph, Twyford was nearly his uncle's image. Indeed, he might have stepped straight out of the portrait of the young Lord Ralph, which was prominently displayed at the head of the great front staircase. This, of course, could only add to Miss Trevor's general disgust at the thought of marriage to her cousin, making an alliance with The Terrible Twyford seem close to incest.

There were few, however, who would deny that Mr. Twyford Trevor was a well-favored man, even though lines of dissipation were beginning to mar his classically handsome face. His figure was still slim, his clothing the work of Weston, his boots by Hoby, and his hats by Locke. Sandy hair, styled in the latest Brutus cut, topped eyes of the Trevor blue-gray. His mouth was, perhaps, a shade too thin, the lips of a man more given to petulance than to smiles. Grandson to a marquess and heir to a comfortable estate, if not a title, Mr. Trevor was generally considered a most desirable *parti*.

He made his cousin Relia's skin crawl.

"Good morning, cousin," Miss Trevor replied calmly enough, having managed to close a shell around her pain.

Hands behind his back, Twyford towered over her, looking thoughtful. "I believe we need to come to an accommodation, Relia. I have no more liking for the parents' ordering my days than you do. Set a wedding date, and we shall be rid of them."

"You forget—I am still in mourning," Relia murmured, eyes downcast, so her cousin could not see the turbulent emotions that hovered there, threatening to burst forth.

"Six months of mama ordering your household? I think not. You forget, Relia. I have known you all your life."

Clever of him, this attempt to put them on the same side, with Lord and Lady Hubert as the enemy. Was it possible her uncle and aunt were truly concerned about propriety and held only some vague hope propinquity would bring about the desired match between Twyford and herself? Or was their appropriation of her household all part of some diabolical plot to seize Pevensey Park?

How long did she have? Was her imminent birthday forcing their hands? Did they fear her legal right to say no? And did Gussie have the right of it when she declared Twyford was truly to be feared? And, if so, how long would he wait before he cornered her somewhere—perhaps here and now—and dragged her off into the woods, a deserted bedchamber, an empty cottage?

"I will consider the matter," Relia temporized. "You are quite right, cousin. The situation is untenable. A solution must be found." She managed a faint but appealing smile, reaching out a hand, as if in supplication. "I know you understand what a surprise this has been—coming home to find you all in residence. I am certain you will grant a poor female time to gather her wits and decide what must be done." She fluttered her long, thick lashes and allowed her voice to trail away to a whisper.

Twyford, who was far from gullible, gave her a sharp look. "Try your die-away airs on someone else, Relia. Three days only, and then we must set a date. You know quite well my father is a dreadful skint. There'll be no money from Pevensey until the reins are in my hands. No, no, dear heart, spare me your protests. I'm well aware you've no taste for female fripperies, but just think, m'dear—if Lord Hubert has his way, cottage roofs may fall around your tenants' ears, dams give way, the stables go to rack and ruin, the gardens grow up to weeds and the park remain unscythed." Twyford leaned down until his solid bulk blotted out his cousin's view. "You would not care for it, Relia, I promise you." Abruptly, Mr. Trevor straightened. "Three days, cuz. Do not forget."

As Twyford turned on his heel and strode back across the park, air whooshed back into Relia's lungs. Somehow—oddly—she trusted his word. She had three days of grace before he settled the matter by more nefarious schemes.

Three days. Whether Lord and Lady Hubert were part of a plot or merely greedy bystanders, she could not count on them for help. Her need for a dragonslayer was immediate. Which was why she had dashed off her urgent note to Sir Gilbert. But Mr. Lanning was busy with his own affairs. He did not really want her. He would not come.

And that left Harry Stanton. She would ride to the Stantons' at once! But when Aurelia reached the stables, the head groom, abjectly apologetic, informed her that Lord Hubert had given orders she was not to ride or drive out until further notice, a punishment for her headstrong jaunt to London.

Once again, James, the footman, was called upon to smuggle out a note. But that night after supper, the tick of the ornate brass and mahogany clock on the mantel in the drawing room seemed to grow louder with each passing minute, counting down to her moment of doom. She hated being female, Relia decided. She hated Pevensey Park. In medieval times she might, at least, have gone off and joined a nunnery. Men were the very devil. That she should be dependent on one to rescue her was intolerable.

No matter whom she married, she would hate him forever. Because by an accident of birth, the world considered him superior. Not only in strength, but in wisdom, education, training—

Impossible! Miss Aurelia Trevor threw the embroidery hoop Lady Hubert had thrust into her hands after dinner halfway across the drawing room, where it came close to knocking over an Imari vase of which she was quite fond.

Nonsense! When Harry called on her in the morning, she would throw herself into his arms and beg him to save her. She would grovel. She wanted Pevensey Park, and she wanted children. Since not only the laws of England but the laws of nature decreed that a man was necessary, then a man she would have. And to the devil with the Hubert Trevors and all their machinations.

But Miss Trevor, caught up in the desperation of her plans, had forgotten she no longer had the ordering of her household. When Mr. Harry Stanton rode up the driveway, promptly at ten the following morning, and handed his hat, his gloves, and his riding crop to Biddeford before waving the butler away with the hearty assertion there was no need to announce him, Aurelia's anticipation of a private interview with her old friend was immediately quashed.

"You may show our guest to the drawing room, Biddeford," Lady Hubert declared as she paused, with regal stance, on the gallery above the entry hall, her nose almost visibly aquiver as she sensed a challenge to her fondest wishes. "You may then inform Miss Trevor we have a visitor."

Mr. Stanton, agog at this high-handed usurpation of rights at Pevensey Park, followed blindly on Biddeford's heels, where he was relieved to find Relia and Miss Aldershot eagerly awaiting his call. But before he could do more than utter polite greetings to the ladies, Lady Hubert swept into the room. Harry, who had just taken a seat close to Aurelia, shot back to his feet.

"Good morning, Mr. Stanton," Lady Hubert declared. "To what do we owe the honor of so *early* a call?"

Harry, who had been up since seven, gulped, shot a desperate look toward Relia, swallowed hard, and stammered, "Was out and about, ma'am—my lady. Thought I—I'd drop by. Known Relia—Miss Trevor—since she was in the cradle, don't y'know."

Lady Hubert, after an audible sniff, waved Mr. Stanton back into his chair. After the necessary pleasantries about his parents' health were accomplished, an awkward silence descended. Miss Aldershot, sitting as straight as the uncompromising lines of her Chinese Chippendale chair, exchanged a significant look with Miss Trevor. A look Aurelia ignored, as she and Gussie had found themselves in strong disagreement that morning, with Miss Aldershot insisting that Mr. Lanning would not let them down, and Miss Trevor insisting he would. And, besides, they did not have time to wait on Mr. Lanning's pleasure. Far better Harry Stanton than cousin Twyford.

"Harry," Relia burst out, "you will recall the matter we discussed the last time you were here?"

For a moment Mr. Stanton looked puzzled, then his gaze sharpened, focusing on Miss Trevor's anxious face. "Is it possible you have changed your mind?" he inquired, Lady Hubert's inimical presence forgotten.

"Indeed, I—"

"Ah, here you are!" declared Twyford Trevor, striding into the room with the supreme confidence of the grandson of a marquess defending his turf from the upstart son of a squire. "Young Stanton, is it? Haven't seen you in years, m'boy. How are things in the countryside? As bucolic as ever, I trust."

Once again, Harry bobbed to his feet. "Trevor," he said with a cool nod.

"Oh, do sit down, man. Mustn't stand on ceremony with old friends, what? Must make m'father's apologies, I fear. Too early for him. A two-bottle man, don't y'know," Twyford added, tapping the side of his nose.

Harry, still stiffly erect, said, "No doubt it takes a while to become accustomed to country hours."

"Now what may we do for you?" Mr. Trevor inquired, settling onto the striped gold-and-cream settee next to his mother, where he leaned back and stretched out his feet, very much the picture of the master of the house.

"I merely stopped by to pay my respects to Re— Miss Trevor and Miss Aldershot. Now that I know your family is visiting, Trevor, I will make the squire aware of your presence."

"We are not visiting," Lady Hubert pronounced with considerable emphasis. "We are here to provide the proper background for Aurelia as she returns to society, now that she is out of her blacks."

"You are going to *live* here!" Harry exclaimed in a tone his dear mama would have deplored.

"Indeed." Twyford crossed his long legs at the ankles and smiled at Mr. Stanton.

"Mr. Thomas Lanning," Biddeford intoned.

Thomas was never quite sure why he had insisted on leaving London late the previous afternoon, thus sentencing himself to a night at a hostelry that in no way met his standards. But, somehow, there had been such a note of urgency in Sir Gilbert's communication . . . almost as if the cousin the solicitor referred to as The Terrible Twyford would actually stoop to coercion. Or worse. So he had set out immediately, even though more than a little chagrined by his urge to charge to the lady's rescue. It was only as his coach drove through the vast Pevensey acres, past the pointed cones of the oast houses, past fields of fall vegetables and orchards full of fruit, and finally turned into the long drive toward the great house itself, that Mr. Lanning wondered if he was off on the most egregious wild goose chase of his life. The owner of all this could not possibly need his help, and even if she did, he did not belong here. This was not his milieu, by God. No, indeed!

And then he saw the house. And groaned. It was too much. If he married her, the arrogant young chit was welcome to it. No wonder Pevensey Park had as many productive arms as an octopus. It must take them all to support the blasted house and grounds!

Fortunately, the butler seemed to recognize a man of substance when he saw him, even as his slight frown indicated he could not quite place Mr. Thomas Lanning on the customary ladder of precedence assigned to callers. But he had heeded Thomas's wave to silence as they stood in the doorway, catching the last part of the conversation in the drawing room.

Two suitors already on the scene, Thomas noted. Perhaps Miss Trevor needed him after all. Certainly, if the look on her face when she saw him was any indication . . . Thomas cast a hasty glance over his perfectly fitted jacket, waistcoat, pantaloons, and boots. Was it possible Miss Trevor had caught a glimpse of shining armor beneath his conservative London attire?

"Mr. Lanning," Miss Trevor breathed, as she dropped into a curtsey worthy of His Majesty himself.

"And who might you be?" roared a voice from a doorway at the opposite end of the imposing drawing room.

"Good morning, uncle," Relia trilled, her fears and desperation unaccountably flown on the breath of fresh air that accompanied her latest visitor's arrival. "Mr. Lanning is an expert from the City. He is here to offer advice on the business of running Pevensey Park."

"Advice? I asked for no advice," snapped Lord Hubert as he stalked across the deep pile of the Axminster carpet. "Nor need it," he added on a decided grumble.

"It was Miss Trevor who consulted me," Thomas responded in his most conciliating tone, the one he used while finalizing negotiations that always seemed to end to his vast benefit.

"My niece had no right to do so." Lord Hubert made violent shooing motions with his hands. "So go back where you came from. We've no need of you here."

Mr. Lanning, evidently a trifle slow-witted, did not seem to take offense. "But I am vastly interested in the workings of Pevensey Park, my lord, and Miss Trevor promised to show me the many enterprises under her command—"

"Under my command!"

Mr. Lanning bowed. "Of course, my lord." Not in the least discomposed, he turned to Aurelia. "I have come a long way, Miss Trevor. I would be delighted if you would be kind enough to drive out with me so that I may see the estate your uncle is so conscientiously guarding for your benefit."

"You heard my father. You may leave!" Twyford declared, rising to his full height, which was still an inch short of Mr. Lanning's own.

Thomas looked at Miss Trevor and most sincerely hoped he was correctly interpreting what he saw there. They were supposed to have had time. . . .

Time to think . . . time to adjust . . . time to consider all the ramifications . . .

But there was no time, no time at all. For if he left, these people would never let him near her again. And the fate of

Aurelia Trevor at the hands of The Terrible Twyford was not to be contemplated.

Thomas looked Miss Trevor straight in the eyes, shrugged, and smiled. "I fear we have no choice, my dear," he said. "We must be truthful." With a remarkably well-executed look of chagrin, he turned to the avid spectators of his little drama. "We had hoped to keep our secret a trifle longer, but I can see there's no help for it, we must tell all. Aurelia—Miss Trevor—and I are betrothed. In fact, I have the special license in my pocket." Mr. Lanning patted the left side of his fine corbeau-colored tailcoat. "We plan on being married immediately."

Chapter Six

"*M* arried, is it?" bellowed Lord Hubert. "And pray tell how you will do that without my consent?"

"She's to marry me!" Twyford blustered.

Mr. Lanning seemed almost apologetic as he peered at the two men before turning remarkably limpid eyes on Miss Trevor. "You did say you would reach your majority in the next few days, did you not, my dear?"

"Two days." Aurelia and Gussie spoke nearly in unison.

"Well, there you have it," said Mr. Lanning, with every appearance of a man completely unaware of the sensation he was causing. "That gives us quite enough time to speak to the vicar, does it not, Aurelia, my love?"

"Who is Thomas Lanning, pray tell?" Lady Hubert demanded, finally finding her voice after the intruder's startling announcement. "What manner of man are you? Who are your parents? . . . Where is your home? How dare you aspire to the hand of an heiress? Indeed, how could you have met her? Not a word have I ever heard about a family named Lanning. Except Twineham's, of course, and if you had the slightest connection to the dear duke, I assure you I should have heard of you."

Mr. Lanning bowed politely. "My father would have been sorry to hear that, ma'am. He was, I believe, rather well-known in the City before his unfortunate demise on a journey to Dublin."

"The *City*!" Lady Hubert clutched her heart. Her husband

and son gave almost identical snorts of derision. Harry Stanton muttered something beneath his breath.

"You're a *Cit*!" Twyford exclaimed. "Good God, man, you could not come within a mile of wedding a lady." He rounded on his cousin. "And you, my girl, should be ashamed of yourself for contemplating such a match, even for a moment."

Miss Trevor, as demure as the most shy young maiden at her first ball, clasped her hands in front of her and declared, "But do you not recall that I accompanied Mama to Tunbridge Wells for the waters in the early days of her illness? It was there I met Thomas, so, you see, we have been acquainted for some time now and are quite certain of our feelings in this matter. Naturally, Papa had his doubts, but as my majority approached and I realized I would be free to marry where I would, I went to London to see . . ." Miss Trevor had the grace to blush before giving her alleged beloved a tremulous smile. "To see if he were still of the same mind. He was, and now he is here, and we are to be married."

Fortunately, Mr. Lanning had actually visited Tunbridge Wells, so he had no difficulty continuing the deception. *Clever minx.* They must discuss the matter as soon as possible in order to get their details straight. But, for the moment, Thomas felt grim satisfaction at noting how poorly the news of a long-standing attachment was sitting with Lord Hubert and his family. Father and son had, in fact, turned an unhealthy shade of purple, while Lady Hubert looked as if her face had been showered with rice powder. But the ability to tolerate one's adversaries was part and parcel of being a successful man of business. Making mortal enemies of his betrothed's closest relatives was not sensible. And, although a man of great energy and determination, Thomas Lanning always tried to be sensible.

His marriage to Miss Aurelia Trevor was definitely sensible. Yet . . . with each new investment, contract, or acquisition, he faced the challenge with enthusiasm, certain of his ability to deal with any problems that might occur. But marriage to Miss Trevor . . . to Pevensey Park, to farms and

fields, cows and sheep, to a scornful family of arrogant aris-
tocrats was, perhaps, not the wisest thing he had ever done.

Thomas suddenly realized he was standing silent, letting
epithets fly around him unheard. Miss Trevor was beginning
to look decidedly anxious.

"So it is quite settled, you see," Thomas declared with
what a goodly portion of his audience considered obnoxious
good cheer, "and I believe it is time to begin as we mean to
go on. Aurelia, my dear, it is a fine day for a drive. You may
show me Pevensey Park while we put the finishing touches
on the plans for our wedding." With a glint of steel in his
eye, Mr. Lanning held out his arm. "Shall we?"

Miss Trevor, delighted to escape, slipped her hand
through the crook of his elbow while Biddeford, who had
had his ear to a crack in the door, called for Miss Aurelia's
shawl and bonnet before opening the door wide for the betrothed couple to exit the drawing room. Mr. Lanning, however, came to a halt just before passing under the lintel.
Turning Miss Trevor and himself about with easy grace, he
said to the dumbfounded occupants of the drawing room,
"We shall, of course, wish you to attend our wedding. But
after that . . . naturally we would prefer privacy. I am sure
you understand. I doubt we shall take a long wedding journey"—Mr. Lanning smiled down at his betrothed and patted
her hand—"perhaps a few days at Tunbridge Wells. Lord
Hubert, my lady, Mr. Trevor . . . I trust it will not inconven-
ience you to remove yourselves from Pevensey Park while
we are gone. Lord Hubert, when we return from our drive, I
will give you the name of my solicitor so we may begin the
business of settling Miss Trevor's trust."

After offering a regal nod to his noble but gaping audience, Mr. Lanning gently turned his betrothed back toward
the door. They strolled leisurely across the tiled entry hall,
pausing only long enough to accept Aurelia's shawl and
bonnet from Biddeford, who looked suspiciously moist
about the eyes.

Miss Trevor came to an abrupt halt on the landing, some
twelve stairsteps above the gracefully curved drive where
Mr. Lanning's post chaise awaited him, the postilions snap-

ping to attention as they caught sight of their employer. Thomas, ever polite, paused, raising one dark, inquiring brow.

"I cannot ride with you in *that*!" Miss Trevor proclaimed, eyeing the yellow post chaise and four lively horses with something closely akin to horror.

Thomas Lanning, who had far more experience with the workings of the male mind than the female, could only stare in amazement.

"It is a *closed* carriage," Aurelia explained. "Ladies do not ride with gentlemen in closed carriages. Alone," she added when he continued to stand there, looking for all the world as if she had suddenly sprouted a second head.

"We are betrothed," Thomas declared. Sweeping his arm around her waist, he started for the stairs.

Miss Trevor dug in her heels. "Nonetheless—"

Thomas halted, thrust her from him. "Shall I send you back then?" he demanded. "They're in there, waiting, you know—your precious family connections. Squabbling among themselves, each blaming the other for whistling your fortune down the wind. They will, no doubt, welcome you back with open arms."

Aurelia, unaccustomed to being manhandled by anyone, most particularly a Cit who did not own his own carriage, drew herself up to her full five feet three inches, while searching frantically for a proper rebuttal. How *dare* he?

"This was your idea, was it not?" Mr. Lanning persisted, his tone growing more aggrieved with each word. "You sought a dragonslayer, and now that you have him, you object because his charger is yellow instead of white?"

Aurelia drew in a sharp breath. "I object because his charg—because that vehicle is not *proper*!"

Thomas raised his hat. "Good day, Miss Trevor. Although I regret the waste of my valuable time, I find myself greatly relieved that my services are no longer needed." Mr. Lanning clapped his tall beaver back onto his head, and loped down the stone steps of Pevensey Park with all the alacrity of a Frenchman escaping the guillotine.

Aurelia stared after him. A postilion was opening the

bright yellow door, the steps were lowered. Mr. Lanning was climbing in. . . .

Miss Trevor picked up her skirts and flew down the stairs. She couldn't—*wouldn't*—lower herself to calling after him, but . . .

The door of the post chaise slammed shut. One postilion was already mounted, the other about to join him. The horses, sensing the imminent departure, snorted and stamped the ground.

No-o-o! Aurelia reached the carriage, pounded on the door. Then, mortified, she jumped back, head hanging, tears of humiliation rushing to her eyes.

The post chaise did not move. The door opened. A shining pair of boots appeared, biscuit pantaloons, a corbeau jacket . . . a hand reached out, tilting up her chin. "Was I harsh?" Thomas said. "I come from several generations of bankers, you know. Or perhaps you did not. We tend to be more at home with numbers, ledgers, and other males than with the gentler sex. Tears, Miss Trevor? I fear I am not at all what you had in mind."

Miss Trevor was forced to steady her lower lip before she could reply. "And 'tis plain *you* do not like me. We are a sad pair, are we not?"

"Truthfully," Thomas said, suddenly dropping his hand as he realized he was still cupping Miss Trevor's chin and her spirited yet vulnerable countenance tended to unsettle his customarily steady nerves, "I believe we may be of use to each other. If I did not, I would not have come. Yet I fear accommodation between us is unlikely to be smooth. This is your home, your land. This fantastical husband-hunt was entirely your idea. Therefore, it is you who must choose, so let us be quite clear." Thomas crossed his arms, turning as stern and serious as she had yet seen him. "If you marry me, I promise I will slay your dragons, then return to my own life, allowing you complete—within reason—" he qualified, "freedom to run Pevensey Park as you choose. But when we are together, you will give me the respect due a husband, including riding in any vehicle I should provide—"

"But we are not yet married—"

"Blast it, woman! Will you get into the chaise or not?"

A closed carriage. A small closed carriage with only two seats. He actually expected her to show herself to her tenants in such an intimate posture? It was as good as a declaration . . .

Fool! Was that not exactly what she wanted? A man of strength and intelligence was poised to enter the lives of everyone at Pevensey Park. His advent would affect most of those in the village of Lower Peven as well. There was no longer a need for secrecy. To escape the rule of her Trevor relatives, she would marry Thomas Lanning even if he were the devil himself.

Head erect, her back ramrod straight, Miss Aurelia Trevor allowed Mr. Lanning to hand her into the post chaise. He climbed in after her, giving the postboys the office to start. As the chaise began to move, Aurelia sank back into the far corner of the leather squabs, wondering, quite rightly, into what impossible imbroglio she had just thrown herself. In London, Mr. Thomas Lanning had been the man with whom she was negotiating a lifetime contract. Aloof, competent—but unable, or unwilling, to hide his condescending amusement. Yet he was a man who met all her requirements and was, astonishingly, pleasing to both eye and ear. When he visited Pevensey Park, she had thought to have a leisurely opportunity to advance their acquaintance, discuss the pros and cons of their proposed alliance.

But now, with no further explorations of their respective characters, their family backgrounds, or current problems, they were well and truly betrothed. Miss Aurelia Trevor of Pevensey Park, bound to a chameleon who changed his coat to match his audience. A man who slipped from dragon-slayer to conciliatory idiot to . . . *obsequious* Cit, then, from one step to the next, turned back to knight errant, cutting a broad swath through her openmouthed relatives. But for her, he had not a single gentle word that was not part and parcel of his theatrical performance. Not even the simple good manners of understanding that she, an unmarried female of good family, could not ride alone with him in a closed carriage.

Relia peeped at her betrothed, who was staring straight ahead, quite as if she were not there. Even his profile was distinguished—if, of course, such a word could be used to describe a Cit. Fortunately, he seemed to understand his place among the landed hierarchy of Kent—quite at the bottom of the barrel—even though he was, alas, all too stubbornly male regarding relations with his wife. This could be a problem, but, as Gussie kept reminding her, she had made her bed and must now lie in it.

A most unfortunate thought! Relia felt a hot blush rushing straight up from her toes to her face. Indeed, her whole body was blushing. Hastily, she turned her head away, hoping to hide behind the all-too-small brim of her bonnet.

"Which way?" Mr. Lanning inquired, seemingly indifferent to his betrothed's disturbed emotions. "We are at the end of the drive. Which way do you wish to go?"

Miss Trevor responded, soon finding herself caught up in extolling the virtues of the many enterprises at Pevensey Park, where, as she expected, necks craned, hands waved, and speculative looks were quickly followed by the light of recognition. Miss had done it, by God, and found herself a man. And a right fine one, if looks were not deceiving.

As Miss Trevor and Mr. Lanning spoke with the wide-eyed milkmaids at the dairy farm and the workers manning the drying racks at the oast houses, or accepted a basket of ripe red apples from a farmer and his wife—all of whom beamed ear to ear upon being the recipients of Mr. Lanning's sudden return to bonhomie—Relia wondered once again at her betrothed's ability to put on different faces for different people. Outside the chaise, he was all that was affable. Her tenants seemed to take to him immediately. Inside, the chaise might as well have been suffused with the icy winds of January.

Yet was she not participating in the same game? Smiling and gracious when playing lady of the manor, sulking in a corner when she was not?

They were on their way back now, and Relia knew she must assert herself. Mr. Lanning had made an almost too-fine impression on her people. Somehow they had

looked . . . well, as relieved as she was. If not more so. Miss
Trevor was not altogether pleased. Her tenants, after all, did
not have to live with the man!

Did they realize what a sacrifice she was making? Relia
glared out the window, for once not appreciating either the
beauty or the profitability of her acres. "Mr. Lanning," she
declared, emerging from her corner to slide an inch or so
closer to her betrothed. "There is a matter we must discuss."

"Yes?" Though his facial features did not change, Relia
was quite certain his tone turned instantly wary.

"I had thought to bring this matter up during your visit,
so it should not come as a surprise. But now . . ." Miss
Trevor clasped her hands, transforming into a vulnerable,
beseeching maiden. "My father quite doted on Pevensey
Park, and I would like to keep his name alive. Therefore I
wish you to assume his name. I believe you will find Trevor-
Lanning has a fine ring to it."

As she caught the look on his face—now very far from
blank—Relia slid back into her corner. She had been pre-
pared for an initial objection, but it appeared Mr. Lanning
was about to burst out in a roar that would blow her straight
out of the chaise. Yet as she watched in horrified fascination,
he leaned back, knuckled his forehead, and began to laugh.
His shoulders shook. His other hand gripped his knee. Finally, he produced a handkerchief and wiped his streaming
eyes.

"Miss Trevor," he said at last, "before agreeing to our initial meeting, I had my solicitor look into the history of
Pevensey Park. The name of the owner has changed with all
but one generation for well over a hundred years. Your re-
quest is outrageous, but all of a piece for a young woman
with enough pride and presumption to employ a solicitor to
find her a husband. Oddly enough"—Mr. Lanning sat up
and looked directly at her—"oddly enough, I admire your
courage. Will I change my name? No. Will I allow my poor
children to be saddled with such an awkward mouthful as
Trevor-Lanning? No, I will not. As for our marriage . . . ?"
Thomas Lanning shook his head. "If we do not kill each
other in the first month or so, I believe we may deal well to-

gether. Certainly, you are no niminy-piminy creature without an ounce of backbone. You may annoy me at times, but you do not disgust me." Unfortunately, Mr. Lanning chose that moment to end his monologue.

Miss Trevor opened her mouth, closed it. She did not disgust him. How utterly delightful. The temperature in the chaise, warmed by Mr. Lanning's laughter, plunged back to bleak winter. Relia eyed the basket of bright red apples on the floor at her feet and conjured dire thoughts of a Cit who could be so charming to the lower classes and treat his betrothed as if she were dirt beneath his feet.

She needed him. Pevensey Park needed him. But as soon as Lord Hubert and his family were chased away and Squire Stanton realized her acres would never be added to his . . . and William Tubbs understood he was to follow her orders, then Mr. Lanning could go back to his precious City. She would be rid of him and mistress of the Park once again. For this—as she had concluded long since—marriage was a sacrifice she could make. After all, it was not as if Mr. Thomas Lanning were going to be under foot for more than a minimal amount of time.

"Ah, yes, I nearly forgot," said Mr. Lanning, as if just remembering a vail for the postboys, "I have something for you." Reaching inside his jacket, he produced a small white plush box. "It seems Rundell and Bridges had your size in their records, so it should fit." To Miss Trevor's complete chagrin, he flipped open the box to reveal a brilliant sapphire surrounded by a ring of diamonds. "I believe a ring is the expected confirmation of a betrothal." He removed the ring from the box, holding it between his thumb and forefinger, waiting . . . challenging . . .

Anxiety clutched Relia's throat, sending sharp spears of pain through her chest. They were actually making this perfectly horrid, cold-blooded match. She was lowering herself to marry a Cit. A Cit who was far too bold and domineering.

Yet he had remembered to buy her a ring. Thomas Lanning was, in fact, sitting there offering her the most beautiful ring she had ever seen.

Relia thought she might be ill.

Slowly, fearfully, Miss Trevor extended her left hand. Mr. Lanning was right—the ring was a perfect fit.

If only their marriage could be such an exemplary match.

Shivers ran up Relia's spine. There could be no doubt. She had just made a disastrous mistake.

Chapter Seven

Seldom has a wedding been marked by so many inimical countenances. Seated in the Trevor pew—with its high back, ornately carved door, and kneelers done up in petit-point by Aurelia's dynamic great-grandmother—were Lady Hubert and her son, looking for all the world as if they were attending the funeral of their nearest and dearest. Behind them were Squire Stanton, his good wife Margaret, and their stairstep children—Harry, the hope of the family, and three of his four younger sisters and brothers. The squire and his wife might have been riding a tumbril to the guillotine for all the enjoyment they seemed to be deriving from the wedding of Miss Aurelia Trevor and Mr. Thomas Lanning. Young Harry's mood seemed to swing wildly from belligerent indignation to brow-wiping relief. Miss Chloe Stanton, age eighteen, was not seated in the Stanton pew as she was to be the bride's sole attendant. The three youngest Stantons, however, were so intrigued by the hostile undercurrents filling the modest church that they peeked, eyes dancing, across the aisle of the old stone church to see if the groom—a Cit, imagine that!—had any friends at all.

Apparently, he did not. That side of the church was empty, while various townspeople, including the mayor of Lower Peven, upper servants from Pevensey Park, and a number of Miss Trevor's tenants squeezed in behind the Stantons. Everyone looked solemn. Glad they might be to see Miss Trevor married, but a man of the City was not at all what they had imagined for Miss Aurelia. *Time would tell*

was the general consensus, while an occasional dire muttering could be heard here and there.

Since white was an accepted mourning color under special circumstances, Miss Trevor was wearing a gown of
stark white velvet. It did not become her any more than deep
black. Instead of a radiant bride, the congregation saw a
young woman looking nearly as pale as her gown, a washed-
out wraith who, some said, looked as if she would run for it
if she only had the strength. And Lord Hubert? Well, there
wasn't a soul who didn't know what he thought of these pro-
ceedings. Cut out, he was, and not liking it one little bit. Instead of the organ playing in the loft, a body could almost
hear the drums beating a deadly tattoo to a hanging. Old
Gloomy Guts, that's what he was. 'Twas a wonder Miss had
gotten him to escort her down the aisle.

Briefly, the Stantons allowed their frozen expressions to
thaw as their Chloe walked by, looking demurely lovely in
peach silk with amber mums woven into her blonde hair. A
fine sight, all agreed. But the congregation soon shifted its
fascinated attention to Miss Aurelia Trevor and her uncle, as
they paced solemnly toward the altar. Who knew?—m'lord
might drop into an apoplexy at any moment.

And then every eye was riveted on the man stepping forward to greet his bride, with what must be yet another Cit at
his side. Well, a man had to have at least one friend, did he
not? That the friend was almost as tall as the groom, with an
open countenance marked by a shock of blond hair and
seemingly sincere blue eyes, did Mr. Lanning no discredit.
Those in the congregation who had seen Mr. Lanning before
nodded, a few poking their neighbors in the ribs. See—not
so bad . . . for a Cit, that is. Of course, if'n she'd had more
time, Miss Aurelia c'd o' done better. Bad thing, her pa and
old Yelverton sticking their spoons in the wall at near the
same time. Heads nodded sagely.

Weren't weddings supposed to be joyous? Relia clutched
her bouquet of white and gold mums until the stems dug into
the palms of her hands. Somehow she stopped where she
was supposed to stop. Someone tall loomed up beside her.

An intimidating stranger. Never mind that brief meeting in London, their drive around Pevensey Park, or the past two days in which Thomas Lanning and his solicitor Charles Saunders had spent most of their time closeted with Lord Hubert and Lord Ralph's solicitor, pouring over documents in meetings that were occasionally punctuated by Lord Hubert's bull-like roars of protest.

Proper settlements or no, she was about to be married to someone she barely knew.

You started it! her conscience chided.

Dear God, she had.

"Dearly beloved . . ." said the vicar, who, taking his cue from the somber faces around him, did not offer the benign smile with which he usually began the wedding service.

The whole thing passed in a blur. Relia heard herself say the words, heard strong repetitions from Thomas Lanning, but could not distinguish, or ever recall, any individual words. Except . . .

"You may kiss the bride."

Kiss the bride? But the moment was over before she could protest. Mr. Lanning bent his lips to a brush of her cheek, and then they were turning, facing the congregation, moving so fast down the aisle Relia had to rush to keep up. If this was how the miserable man planned to control her life . . .

He did. They rode back to Pevensey Park in an open landau, with Mr. Lanning constantly urging her to smile and wave, for all the world as if he were the owner and she the bride newly arrived in Lower Peven. And then she remembered he was exactly that. For all he had doubled her generous quarterly allowance and granted equally munificent dower rights, Thomas Lanning now owned Pevensey Park. Blast the man! She was totally dependent upon his keeping to the spirit, as well as the legalities, of the trust and marriage settlements.

The wedding breakfast—attended only by the wedding party and their relatives, plus the mayor and his wife—was sumptuous but over rather quickly, with only Mr. Saunders and the mayor offering toasts. In all too short a time the new

Mrs. Thomas Lanning found herself being divested of the ghostly white velvet and inserted into a silver-gray traveling ensemble with spencer and bonnet trimmed in vertical rows of pin-tucking. And then they were in the well-appointed Trevor coach, and Mr. Saunders was assuring her husband that he would "take care of everything." If that meant dislodging Lord Hubert and his family, perhaps this nightmare wedding had been worth it, Aurelia grumbled to herself as she sat bolt upright on the edge of the blue velvet squabs, refusing to be comfortable. Refusing to relax her guard in Thomas Lanning's presence.

With a sigh of relief that their charade of a wedding was over, Thomas leaned into the coach's luxurious upholstery—and discovered he was gazing at the back of his wife's bonnet. Good God, if the chit planned to sit like that, he should ready himself for a lapful of female at the first deep rut in the road. Undoubtedly, she was expressing her displeasure about something. Again. Though what he had done this time . . .

Not what he had done, Thomas amended. It was more likely what he had *not* done that rankled. Taming Lord and Lady Hubert and The Terrible Twyford without leaving his betrothed bereft of relatives at the altar had taken all of his diplomatic skills; while, during the same past two days, his head for business had concentrated on protecting Miss Trevor's interests, his own interests, and the future of Pevensey Park, again without completely alienating the Hubert Trevors. Settlements had been made—from his own monies—of which his bride knew nothing. And would not have believed even if he had told her.

Which he had not, as they had exchanged no private words since their tour of Pevensey Park the day of his arrival. So it was scarcely a wonder she was sitting there with her back ramrod straight, being shaken by every little bump in the road. Truthfully . . . yes, he had ignored her. Avoided her. Had had no idea what to say to her.

Had he feared he would blurt out the truth? Feared his

sense of fair play would overcome his hard-headed ambition?

Or . . . silently, Thomas mouthed an expletive. Was it possible those stiff little shoulders had nothing to do with his neglect of her? Was it possible his courageous, determined Miss Trevor was *afraid*?

Of him?

"Aurelia?" She stretched her body, sitting even taller and straighter. It took considerable effort to keep from putting his hands about her waist and pulling her back until they were sitting side by side. "Aurelia, I apologize. I should have warned you that dragonslaying is a time-consuming occupation. I fear the Fair Maiden frequently finds herself waiting, all alone and uninformed. And then with the wedding hard on the heels of triumph . . ." Thomas let his voice trail away. Miss Trevor—Mrs. Lanning, he corrected, not at all certain he cared for the sound of it, even if it was far better than Mrs. *Trevor*-Lanning—paid him no heed. She might as well have been riding in the gig behind them with her maid and the luggage. Was that not why he had banished the maid from the coach—so he might have this time alone with his bride?

"Aurelia," he tried again, "there are matters we should have discussed, and I am well and truly sorry I did not find time to do so before the wedding." His wife's chin descended, just a trifle, encouraging Thomas to continue. "Aurelia . . . you need have no fear of me. I have given the matter some thought, and I believe we should leave our marriage one in name only until we are better acquainted—perhaps until the end of your year of mourning?" His voice rose into a question at the end, but the only sound within the coach was the steady crunch and whirr of the wheels, the thud of the horses' hooves.

"You are, of course, a busy man," his wife declared at last, in a voice as tight as her shoulder blades. "Naturally, you will wish to return to London immediately. It was . . . kind of you to suggest a few days at the Wells in order to put the cap on our charade."

"I was not thinking of appearances," Thomas retorted.

She turned toward him, opening her eyes wide. "Truly?" his wife mocked. "I had thought to employ a dragonslayer. Instead, I find myself wed to a man who talks his enemies into submission. A man who stoops to bribing the dragons to go away. I suppose you will retire Mr. Tubbs to a cozy cottage—"

"I have already done so." Hell and damnation, of course Lord Ralph's attorney had told her! He could handle all the dragons, find the right face and deft hand to confront every problem, but his agile mind and vast experience seemed to desert him when it came to his wife. "Aurelia," Thomas ventured on a more humble note, "I believe I have not offered my felicitations on reaching your majority. It is scarcely fair, I fear, that you are forever condemned to celebrating your birthday and your wedding anniversary on the same day."

"You are assuming I will wish to celebrate my wedding anniversary," his bride responded coldly.

Devil it! He'd done everything she asked of him. Was he now being cast off? Dismissed like some hired outrider when the danger was past?

Relia was not at all certain why she was so incensed. The miserable Cit was right, of course. She had been utterly terrified of the night to come. She knew many brides were bedded by near strangers, but she could not—simply could not—picture herself doing whatever husbands and wives did with a man like Thomas Lanning. A London nobody. Who was large . . . commanding . . . impossibly sure of himself.

What a faradiddle! The truth was . . . the truth was, although she *had* been terrified, now she was insulted. He did not want her. He had gained Pevensey Park and was now free to reveal how little interest he had in what went with it. *Horrible man!*

Relia's hand flew to the hangstrap as the coach hit a nasty bump. Strong arms dragged her back, placing her against the squabs in a firm, no-nonsense display of strength. "Now stay there," her husband growled, "or you're like to break your silly neck."

A silence, seething with carefully repressed emotions

from both bride and groom, reigned during the remainder of
the distance to Tunbridge Wells.

The Swan was a gracious inn, providing the most imposing façade among the classic colonnaded buildings fronting
the terraces and shops known as The Pantiles. Only a short
walk along the top terrace was Tunbridge Wells's version of
the famous Pump Room in Bath. Three levels of broad flagstone terraces, built into a hillside, were visible from the
front entrance of The Swan. Each level had its own picturesque assortment of fountains, shops, pubs, and dwelling
places for those who had come to take the waters. At intervals, shallow steps led from one terrace down to the next, a
distance of four or five feet with no protective railing. The
flagstones simply came to an abrupt end with a sheer drop
to the terrace below.

The overall effect, however, was charming—smaller and
more intimate than Bath. And more colorful, as fall flowers
spilled from baskets hanging between the long row of white
columns on the upper terrace. If only the Wells were not
filled with so many sad memories. . . .

"You are pleased with our rooms?" Mr. Lanning inquired, as they stood in front of The Swan, inspecting the
panorama of The Pantiles.

"They are most acceptable," Relia told him, careful not to
reveal the enormity of her relief when she saw that he had
meant what he said. Or seemed to. They had a spacious
suite, with a sitting room and two bedrooms, though there
was no dressing room to accommodate her maid. Tilly, poor
soul, must share a room in the servants' quarters. Of course,
it *was* supposed to be her wedding night—

"Would you care to visit the Pump Room?"

"No!" Sharply, Relia drew back from the arm her husband was offering.

"I beg your pardon," Mr. Lanning muttered. "I had not
thought. You were here with your mother, of course. At The
Swan?" Relia nodded. "Then I am truly sorry. I have been
gauche. We should not have come—"

Surprised, Relia could only stare up at the genuine regret

she saw reflected in her husband's gray eyes. He meant it. If he had thought about the actual memories this town held for her, he would have taken her elsewhere.

"Do you wish to leave?" he asked. "We can go to Brighton, although I fear the fashionable set has returned to London by now."

Calling on the prideful bearing of generations of noble ancestors, Relia put her hand through her husband's arm. "Not at all, Mr. Lanning. Tunbridge Wells is a lovely town, and I know you are anxious to return to London. I will not keep you. We will make a show of enjoying our brief wedding journey, and then you may be gone."

They had moved past three shop windows before the customarily silver-tongued Mr. Lanning found his voice. "I would be pleased if you could call me Thomas," he said.

Relia peered into the shop window, as if half-boots and silk slippers were of all-consuming interest. "I daresay I should," she conceded, still intent on the shoes. "For the sake of appearances." But she did not repeat his name.

They walked on. Making a turn where the Pump Room jutted out to block most of the terrace, they strolled back along the outside edge of the flagstone terrace, a vantage point from which they could better view the lovely line of colonnaded buildings, the flowers and fountains, and the colorful parade of people come to enjoy the delights of Tunbridge Wells. Among them was a group of boys in nankeen breeches and short coats, obviously scions of the gentry, or they never would have been allowed to tear along at such a pace in the midst of the strolling adults. Relia smiled at their exuberant high spirits. Her flagging spirits were brightened to see a group so full of cheerful, even boisterous, energy. This was, after all, her wedding day. And surely someone should be filled with joy.

The colonnade came to an end. "Would you care to explore the next terrace?" Mr. Lanning inquired politely. "Or would you prefer to examine the shops we missed on this level?"

"I believe . . . I believe I should like to go down," Relia

told him. For all her husband's promises, it seemed better to put off returning to their rooms for as long as possible.

They started back along the terrace, heading for the nearest steps, with Thomas walking on the outside, gallantly shielding her from any possibility of a fall. But just as they reached the stairs, the horde of galloping boys, now on the lower terrace, charged toward the steps from below. Why she thought they would give way for her, Relia never could quite understand, but as she reached the top step, the boys dashed up, one of them jostling her hard enough that she lost her light grip on Thomas's arm. She staggered, missed her footing completely. The stone steps, the sharp edge of the upper terrace, the rock hardness of the lower terrace five feet below flashed across her vision in a blur of horror. Breath rushed out of her lungs. The world swirled. She fell.

And then there was a jerk on her arm. Around her waist. And she was standing on firm flagstone, her nose pressed hard to her husband's chest. Heart pumping hard, her breath coming in gasps, her head so dizzy she would have fallen if Thomas had not held her up.

Chapter Eight

"*V*icious scamps!"
       "Imps of Satan!"
   "Tan their hides, I would!"
   Comments from the crowd whirled round her, never quite penetrating the cocoon of safety Relia had found within the arms of the stranger she had married that morning. Just as she became aware that they were the cynosure of an ever-growing crowd, Thomas began to move, people parting before him like chaff on the wind. A blur of terrace, the hotel lobby . . . she was swept up the stairs with her toes skimming the steps . . . and then she was lowered into a well-padded chair in their sitting room and a small snifter of brandy was being pressed to her lips.
   Relia swallowed, coughed, shivered . . . and recognized how much the incident had unsettled her when she caught herself regretting the loss of her husband's touch. A cozy shawl was wrapped about her shoulders. Thomas Lanning was making it very difficult for her to dislike him, even if he wanted her only for her acres.
   She had bought him, had she not? Very well. How fortunate he seemed intent on giving good service.
   Relia took another sip of brandy, then raised her eyes. *Dear God!* She had seen him with many faces, but nothing like this. If she had not known his glower was not directed at her, she would have been terrified. She rather hoped the boys had safely hidden themselves away, for their youthful

heedlessness did not deserve to have this particular Thomas Lanning descend on them.

"I must apologize," he declared stiffly. "You should have your maid to attend you. Shall I send for her?"

"No . . . truly, I am fine. I am . . . ashamed to have made such a piece of work of it."

"It was a close-run thing."

"Yes . . . and I have not properly thanked you for saving me. I am most grateful." *Heavens!* She sounded as if she were speaking to a chance-met acquaintance.

"That is what men are for, are they not?" Mr. Lanning countered just as coolly. "Protecting the weaker sex is one of our duties."

"But I don't wish to be weaker!" A telltale tear surprised her, slipping out of one eye and rolling down her cheek.

Her husband lowered himself until he was hunkered on his heels, his sharp gray eyes on a level with his bride's. His grim look had turned to one of concern, with a hint of puzzlement. "You are a brave woman, Aurelia. In scarcely more than a year you have suffered a series of blows that would have sent most females into strong hysterics. But you fought through your problems and achieved your own solution. Now, however, what I cannot understand is that you seem sorry for it."

"I am not sorry! I merely—" Relia sniffed, searched for a handkerchief. Thomas handed over his. "'Tis bridal nerves," she pronounced at last, squaring her stubborn Trevor chin. "I will recover. And are my nerves not allowed to be a trifle o'erset by nearly breaking my neck?" she added on a slightly more plaintive note.

With a shake of his head, Thomas unfolded himself to his full height. An odd sort of female, his bride. Most women he knew would be prostrate on their beds, clutching their vinaigrettes, perhaps even sending for the doctor. He should not be surprised, of course. From that very first meeting he should have known he was getting an Amazon wrapped in a pint-sized package. Men made marriages of convenience all the time—it was both expected and accepted. But for a female to choose a husband in such a manner, without the aid of any male member of her family, was almost unheard of. And he, who prided himself on being a hardheaded man of business, attentive to his own gains, had found her so appealing—in spite of her arrogance—that she had touched some hidden streak of gallantry, nearly causing him to refrain from joining his empire to hers.

Dragonslayer. Knight Errant. The temptation had been too great.

And just now . . . if he had not moved so fast out on the terrace, she might be dead. And Pevensey Park and all its enterprises would have been added to his other acquisitions. All of which would have turned to dust. For the arrogant little minx attracted his interest as no woman ever had before.

Thomas strode across the room, yanking the bell pull so hard it nearly came off the wall. He had a few words with Tilly before the two women retired to his wife's bedchamber so she could change into the garments he had dictated.

Relia made straight for the chest on which rested a delicately painted porcelain pitcher and bowl, lavender soap, and a stack of embroidered linen towels provided by The Swan. The water, deliciously cool, brought sudden relief to her oddly heated body. As she dried her face, Relia sank onto her bed, wondering that such an incident, however close to disaster it might have been, should have overset her nerves so badly. She was not cowardly, never inclined toward fits of the vapors. So why . . . ?

She did not care for the answer that popped into her mind, although, in all fairness, she could not reject the notion out of hand. The flush of heat that had wracked her body was not so much due to her near fall as to her shocking proximity to Mr. Lanning. Her husband.

Thomas. Who did not choose to exercise his husbandly rights.

For which she should be heartily thankful.

"Come now, miss. You'll feel ever so much better when you're out of your stays."

Intent as Relia had been on washing away the strange sensations that had somehow taken over the emotions of the sensible, pragmatical young woman she had thought herself to be, she had failed to notice the clothing Tilly was laying out for her. Her steel blue eyes opened wide. "I cannot wear *that*. 'Tis scarcely past tea time."

"M'lord ordered it, miss—ah, ma'am."

"He is not a 'm'lord!'"

"Yes, ma'am." Tilly bobbed a curtsey, adding irrepressibly, if somewhat softly, "But he sure acts like one, don't he?"

Indeed he did. Relia was uncertain if she wanted to smile or continue the good cry she had almost begun in the sitting room. For close to the thousandth time she wondered what she had done to herself. Who *was* Thomas Lanning? She now bore his name yet she knew almost nothing about him.

And why was that, pray tell? Quite simply, because she had not demanded that Sir Gilbert tell her. Because it had not seemed to matter. Because she had been so arrogant she had thought to hire Mr. Lanning's services, like a steward or a butler, based solely on the recommendation of others and on a brief personal interview. He met her list of qualifications; she was desperate—what else mattered?

Forcefully, Relia reminded herself that many women had made far worse bargains. No. Most women had this kind of bargain made for them. They could always have the satisfaction of railing against father, brother, or guardian, while she had no one to blame but herself.

With some deliberation Relia laid the damp towel over the top of the pitcher, then stared at the garments Tilly had placed over the coverlet at the end of the bed. The beautifully embroidered, though nearly transparent, linen bedgown and midnight-blue velvet dressing gown were among the many items of elaborate nightwear Gussie had insisted she purchase while they were in London. Since Relia had not wished to think about this aspect of her marriage, she had simply allowed Miss Aldershot to do as she pleased. And, naturally, Tilly had packed her newest and best for this short journey to Tunbridge Wells.

Beneath her breath Relia muttered a word overheard in the stables. "Miss!" Tilly declared, much shocked.

But she wasn't a miss—she was a wife, Relia thought glumly. Though like to be a virgin . . . for *months*. Maybe years, maybe forever.

Wasn't that what she had wanted? An itinerant dragon-slayer, who would do his job and ride on, leaving her exactly where she had said she wanted to be?

Relia's eyes took on a calculating gleam. Very well, she would do as her new husband ordered. After all, the fine linen bedgown would be completely hidden beneath the heavy velvet dressing gown . . . and it *would* be infinitely more comfortable. Surely one of the more unexpected advantages of being married.

And perhaps, just perhaps, she might once again jog Mr. Lanning's amused tolerance of her. For there could be little doubt that her near accident had torn through his indifference. If only for a short time, he had *cared* what happened to her.

Stoo-pid. Thomas Lanning would have felt the same for any female under his escort.

The former Aurelia Trevor, every inch the daughter of Pevensey Park, turned and presented the row of tiny buttons down her back to her maid. "Very well," she pronounced with regal indifference, "we will do as commanded. *For now.*" Relia lifted her chin another notch, while Tilly failed to stifle a giggle.

Thomas sat slumped in a wingchair set before a crackling fire, idly twirling a brandy glass and wondering about what was beginning to seem like an ominous silence from his wife's room. Was she going to hide in there all night? With the demmed maid as chaperon?

What a fool he was. Had he actually thought he could carry this off like any other business contract? Just sign his name and acquire yet another vast holding? If he had, he'd been disabused of the notion when he saw his new wife about to be taken from him. Of course, no one and no thing, once acquired, was ever allowed to escape Thomas Lanning's control, yet . . . this had been different. As difficult as she could be, the new Mrs. Lanning had some rather remarkable qualities. Besides being an all-too-tempting morsel—

A soft snick of the door . . . and there she was, turning scarlet the moment she saw him looking at her. *Virgins!*

Lord, what else could he expect? Her only contact with men was likely her father, the dastardly Trevors, and that son of the squire, who was likely so backward he hadn't even tried to steal a kiss. And her mother may well have died before having time to impart the necessary female information. Not that she would need it tonight, of course. But Thomas began to realize that his body had failed to get the necessary message from the more rational part of him. *Devil it!* Bridegrooms should be granted immunity from fashionable tightly knit trousers. He could only hope his wife was too innocent to notice. Thomas Lanning, rock hard man of business, brought low by the sight of a female—*his* female—enveloped from neck to toe in a cocoon of dark velvet. Thomas Lanning—Prince of the Exchange, the man who prided himself on never being at a loss for words—rose to his feet, cleared his throat, and held out his hand. "Do join me, Aurelia." Somehow he could not call her Mrs. Lanning, in spite of the vicar's words, the music, the avid congregation, and his signature on so many official documents. The reality of it would not settle in his mind. "You will find the fire . . . warming," he added, with little of his usual glibness of tongue.

Relia fixed her gaze on his hand. He was adept at holding out a hand, was he not? Both literally and figuratively. But—*dear Lord!*—what was he wearing? Or not wearing.

"I trust you have no objection to dining *en déshabillé?*" her husband ventured, as he waved her toward a tall upholstered chair next to his.

Relia had strong objections. No gentleman would think of dining with a female with his jacket off and his waistcoat quite shockingly unbuttoned, revealing so much of his fine lawn shirt that she could see the shadow of something dark beneath. *Merciful heavens!* She had occasionally seen shirtless workers in the field and knew many men had hair on their chests, but surely not *here* in her very own room!

Their room. This very morning she had married this man.

But, of course, Thomas Lanning was not a gentleman, so how could she expect gentlemanly manners? Relia rather suspected he had . . . had *stripped* quite deliberately—

"Come, come, my dear, no need to look so wary. How could I tell you to dress comfortably and not do the same myself? I would have looked quite foolish in coat and cravat when you were . . ." Thomas sketched a graceful wave toward her garments, his voice trailing away, to be replaced by what Relia could only characterize as a salacious grin. She remained immobile, her lower lip jutting into something that might, in a lesser female, be called a pugnacious pout.

"Aurelia," her husband said, still holding out his hand, "may I remind you we are married? We are about to enjoy our wedding supper. Think of it as *en famille* rather than *en déshabillé*."

For a few moments Thomas Lanning seemed to have justified her tightly held fears. He had turned into what she had expected when she married a Cit—the man with vulgar manners and a mediocre education. And now, spouting French as easily as English, he was simply Thomas Lanning. The man who had saved her life in more ways than one.

But her feet refused to move toward his outstretched hand.

With easy grace, he strode toward her, as inexorable as the change from day to night. He clasped her hand, then paused, his gaze shifting to someone behind her. "Tilly, is it?" Thomas said. "You may have the remainder of the evening off." The maid bobbed a respectful curtsey and left, carefully closing the door behind her. "She cannot stay to attend you later," Thomas added quietly. "Indeed, she does not expect it, and we must maintain the façade. You would not, I think, wish everyone to know that I have not demanded my husbandly rights. Such news would reflect badly on both of us. There might even be legal repercussions from Lord Hubert, alledging that we are not truly married, and although I do not enjoy the reputation of being a man in the petticoat line, I would not care to have anyone question my manhood."

Relia, who had gotten rather a good look at his manhood in the past few moments, did not doubt the sincerity of his statement. She did, however, have grave reservations about the sincerity of his promise to maintain a *mariage blanc*. Five months until the end of her year of mourning. Did he have a mistress in London? Very likely. Yet his reasoning was not unsound. They needed the time he had so graciously offered. But somewhere deep inside, Relia was sorry for it. A bride was entitled to a true wedding night, was she not?

A foolish female fantasy. An air-castle constructed from too many Minerva novels and too little attention to the tragic romances of the classics. She, Aurelia Trevor Lanning, was a means to an end. Thomas Lanning had acquired what he wanted. Now he had little use for her. He would go back to his London life and his London women, while enjoying all the luxuries the income from Pevensey Park could offer.

How appallingly fortunate to be born male!

By the time the bridal couple had enjoyed the fine supper provided by The Swan and downed a good many glasses of wine to go with it, they had worn the rough edges off some of the awkwardness of their situation. How could any man object to so lovely a bride, even if she did occasionally display the tongue of an adder? And the bride ceased to have heart palpitations every time her husband moved so much as a finger. By Relia's second glass of wine she was even able to swallow a bite of beef without feeling that it was going to choke her. By the moment she found herself nibbling daintily on a meringue while watching Mr. Lanning—Thomas— finish a compote of peaches and the rest of the meringues, Relia had nearly forgotten her pique with him.

At least it could be said she had postponed it for another day.

It might have been a good moment for Mr. Lanning to forget his solemn promise. Unfortunately, he had made his considerable fortune and sterling reputation by always keeping his word. He was not about to shatter a lifetime of principles, however calculated and conniving they sometimes might be, in regard to the woman he was destined to live with for the remainder of his life. She had to trust him, did she not?

And how long would trust last after she discovered the *real* reasons why he had married her?

Mr. and Mrs. Lanning lingered in front of the fire, the small round table set between them now cleared of all but the requisite bottle of port. Thomas poured a glass for his bride. She shook her head, then changed her mind. Tonight it seemed she could not deny her husband—Thomas, her rescuer—anything.

They talked desultorily of places she had visited in London and Bath, of Aurelia's father and mother, while somehow avoiding all talk of Pevensey Park and the Trevor relatives. It never occurred to Relia to ask about Thomas's family. By the time they realized the hour had grown late, the newly married couple was in considerable more charity with each other. But when Thomas Lanning walked his bride to her bedchamber, he left her at the door, with no more of a kiss than the one he had bestowed on her at the altar.

Then he turned and stalked toward his own bedchamber, pausing only long enough to take up the bottle of port. An observer might have said Mr. Lanning was close to running. His bride, however, did not notice, for she had slammed her door and was leaning back against it, eyes closed, bosom heaving. She had done it! The legalities of her marriage were a triumph.

Why then, was the actuality such a bitter disappointment?

Chapter Nine

*T*hroughout the next two days Mr. and Mrs. Lanning, keeping well away from the precipitous edges of the flagstone terraces, explored every shop on the hillside known as The Pantiles. They sat on conveniently placed benches and enjoyed the fountains, while watching the slow parade of those who had come to take the waters, to shop, to see and be seen. They dined, meticulously attired, in The Swan's elegant dining room. They spoke in bland tones of nothing, as if they were chance met at a teeming London rout party.

Yet at no time did they come close to the all-too-brief rapport they had reached for a few hours in front of the fire on their wedding night. For each had retreated from the brink of what neither wished to acknowledge, enclosing themselves in a shell of pride and willful misunderstanding. Mr. Lanning reminding himself, sometimes forcefully, that his bride was merely enduring his Cit presence, wishing him back to London as fast as he was able. Mrs. Lanning was equally certain that her husband wanted nothing from her that he had not already acquired, and that he could scarcely wait to be released from the obligation of his wedding journey so he could disappear down the London road behind a team of fast horses, unlikely to return for some time to come.

On the third morning after their wedding, the newlywed couple, carefully repressing mutual sighs of relief, boarded their coach and set off for Pevensey Park. The journey was accomplished in near silence, as they had already exhausted every innocuous topic of conversation from books to the weather. If Thomas recalled that he had arranged for his wife's maid to travel and sleep as far from her mistress as possible so that he might become better acquainted with his bride, he gave no sign he now recognized the futility of this plan. That they were, in fact, almost as close to being strangers as they had been on the day they met.

Miss Augustina Aldershot, not standing on ceremony, was waiting on the landing with open arms as Relia descended from the coach. Thomas Lanning, his perfectly bland façade firmly in place, watched as the ladies embraced. One would think he and his wife had just returned from a year's journey to the far side of the world.

"Thomas, welcome home!" And there was Charles beaming at him, shaking his hand, spouting nonsense, as if Pevensey were truly his home. "I must whisk you away, I fear," his friend said. "You've only been gone from London a sennight, and already the walls of the Exchange are crumbling. Come now, into the library. Your bride will forgive us, I know. Undoubtedly, she wishes to change out of her travel clothes."

Charles, Thomas noted, was quite right, for his bride had already disappeared into the house, without so much as a backward glance at either her husband or her acting steward. So be it. He handed his gloves and hat to Biddeford and followed Charles Saunders to the bookroom.

"Relia. Relia!" Gussie huffed as she followed the new Mrs. Lanning's rush up the grand staircase. "There's something . . . My dear, you're going the wrong direction!"

But Relia paid her companion no heed, dragging off her bonnet, spencer, and shawl and throwing them carelessly onto the counterpane of her wonderfully familiar bed. "Oh, it is so good to be home, Gussie. I am always happiest when surrounded by my very own things." Relia turned slowly around, arms outstretched, absorbing the comforting atmosphere of the bedchamber that had been hers since she was old enough to leave the nursery. She frowned. "Gussie . . . why are the dressers bare?" With purposeful step, she walked to the chest of drawers against the wall, pulled open the top drawer. It was empty. She dashed to the tall wardrobe filling one corner of the room, flung open the door. "Gussie," Relia inquired on a more ominous note, "what have you done with my things?" For everything was gone—from gowns, bonnets, and shoes to chemises, reticules, and handkerchiefs.

"But, my dear," Gussie protested, "surely you must realize you cannot stay in this room. We have all worked very hard while you were gone to move your things into the master suite. Relia," Miss Aldershot added, as the new Mrs. Lanning looked at her in horror, "you are married now. You and Mr. Lanning must share the suite that belongs to the owners of the house. Relia? Dear child, somehow I have failed you. I cannot believe you did not understand—"

"You have moved my things into my *mother's* room?" Relia whispered.

"Oh, my dear," Gussie breathed.

"And—and my—and the *Cit* into my papa's chamber?"

"Relia," Miss Aldershot said on a note close to the sternness of her days as a governess, "it is the way of the world. He is now owner of Pevensey Park. It would have been a dreadful insult to do anything else. And you are his wife. Therefore you must share the suite. Not to do so would cause a scandal and likely have your uncle and your cousin down about your ears quicker than cat can lick an ear.

"Most young ladies," Gussie continued more softly, "do not face this dilemma. They leave home when they marry, and only the husband must face sleeping in his father's bed. Men do not, I believe," she added judiciously, "suffer from an excess of sensibility."

"Excess?" Relia cried. "You call it 'excess' because I do not care to live in the room where I watched my mama slowly wither into a husk of her former self? Because I do not care to sleep in the bed in which she died?"

"But it is such a grand bed," Gussie wailed, "with draperies that match the wallpaper."

"I will not sleep in it!"

The two women, who had moved from a relationship of

teacher and pupil to that of companion and friend, stared at each other, both betraying a mix of anger, frustration, and sorrow. They were at an impasse.

Biddeford, fixed just inside the doorway to the library, cleared his throat. "Begging your pardon, Mr. Lanning, I fear there is a bit of a contretemps above stairs."

"Not now, Biddeford," Thomas snapped. "Can you not see we are busy? I leave domestic matters entirely in your hands."

"Begging your pardon, Mr. Lanning, but the matter concerns Miss Trev—Mrs. Lanning—and is of some urgency."

Thomas and Charles, frowning, raised their heads from the papers spread out before them. "Very well," Mr. Lanning said, rising to his feet. "You may tell me about it as we go up." He waved the butler toward the stairs, with Charles Saunders following close behind.

Thomas found his bride sitting stiffly on the edge of a chaise longue near the window, while Miss Aldershot sat, even more upright, on a chair across the room. He wished he might have found Biddeford's tale a web of nonsense, but he had to concede that his wife's stubbornness was not totally misplaced. He could, unfortunately, see her point. "We will redecorate the entire suite," he told her in a voice that left no room for argument. "Charles tells me I must go up to London immediately, so I will choose the colors for my bedchamber while I am there. Then I will send the upholsterer to you, Aurelia, so you may choose what you wish. You may, if you wish, order a new bed or have your old one moved to your new room. The choice is yours. During the renovation you will, of necessity, sleep in your old room. I shall tell Biddeford to have your things returned to this room immediately." Thomas gave a regal nod, then stood quietly, watching his wife with some interest.

Relia's exultation was short-lived. She had won . . . so why did she feel so very peculiar about her victory? Possibly because, no matter the odd English legalities about males owning their wive's property, Pevensey was hers, and she must not ever let him forget it.

"*You* will choose the colors for your bedchamber?" Relia challenged.

"Do *gentlemen* not choose the colors for their bedchambers?" Thomas responded, presenting the epitome of innocent ignorance.

"Not in *my* house!"

"Ah . . . but I thought it was mine. I wonder how it is I could have made such a mistake." Suddenly, Thomas laughed, while, out in the hallway, Mr. Saunders and Biddeford heaved sighs of relief. "I beg pardon, Aurelia, but if you could but see the look on your face. No matter. From what Charles tells me, I must be off to London immediately. You will be untroubled with my presence for some time to come. Biddeford!"

"My lord— Beg pardon . . . Mr. Lanning?"

"See to the removal of Mrs. Lanning's things back to this room. Miss Aldershot, Charles, a few moments alone with my wife, if you please. And close the door on your way out."

In a remarkably short time Mr. Thomas Lanning and his wife found themselves alone. He stood, with his hands behind his back, gazing down at her bent head. Her victory and his imminent departure had not produced the blazing triumph he had thought to see on her face. "Aurelia . . . I am sorry for this. I did not expect our marriage to be so full of . . . drama. It seemed a fortunate arrangement for both of us. I believe it may still be that, but . . . there have been a few more bumps along the way than I had anticipated. I will be returning to London within the hour, and with all that awaits me there, it may be some weeks before I can return.

"Aurelia . . . look at me." When she did, Thomas could not fathom what he saw in the depths of those blue-gray eyes. Not animosity, however. At least he dared believe she did not actively dislike him. "It is possible I may not return until the renovations are complete. When they are—as soon as they are—I shall expect you to move in. It is essential we keep up appearances. Do you understand me? There can be no control over Pevensey or any of its inhabitants if they think you and I are at odds. Do I make myself clear?"

"Yes."

"Yes, what?"

"Yes . . . Thomas."

"And, Aurelia, while I am gone, pray remember that you sought me out. You, in essence, offered for me. Now that you have me, do not turn missish and succumb to a fit of the vapors. I may be off to London, but I am here in Pevensey Park to stay. You will not be rid of me as easily as you are undoubtedly anticipating at the moment." Thomas cocked his head to one side, studying his bride of three days, whose look was now easily identifiable as defiant. "Something to remember me by," he declared with considerable cheek and dragged his wife up from the chaise, his grip as firm as the one he had used to rescue her so handily in Tunbridge Wells.

The embrace he offered her was even tighter, longer . . . and far more punishing. His lips met hers before she could even think to pull away. Shock and tumult struck them both. And then he was stepping back, charging for the door even faster than he had run from her on their wedding night. Relia's knees gave way. She sat down hard upon the chaise longue.

She had not married a Cit. She had married a barbarian!

Dinner that night was a near silent affair, with Miss Aldershot offering a series of conversational ventures, to which the new Mrs. Lanning replied in monosyllables. It was very quiet. Never before had Relia noticed how silent the vast expanse of the house was at night. Somehow, with Thomas Lanning's departure, life seemed to have been drawn from the structure, a revelation she found most displeasing. In truth, her husband had run off with such haste that he would likely be forced to spend the night at an inn instead of in the warmth and comfort of Pevensey Park.

It was, of course, quite possible he did not find warmth and comfort at Pevensey Park.

Relia chewed a mouthful of apple tart that, to her disordered senses, might as well have been wrapped in bark instead of Cook's flaky pastry. She had made such a desperate effort to find a husband, and now that she had him, what was she to do with him?

Very little, whispered the insidious voice of truth inside her head. It was more a question of what *he* would do with *her.*

"Relia, my dear," said Gussie brightly, making yet another attempt to penetrate Mrs. Lanning's inattention, "that nice Mr. Saunders is going to search out a new steward for us. Such a dear boy. He managed Mr. Tubbs so well I do believe the old humdudgeon is actually looking forward to doing nothing but living on his pension."

Miss Aldershot suddenly had Aurelia's complete attention. "Mr. Saunders is going to do *what*?" she inquired.

Slowly, Gussie put down her fork, staring at Relia in some consternation. "Find a new steward?" she offered.

"Mr. Charles Saunders, a *solicitor,* is going to find an estate manager for Pevensey Park? In *London*?"

"Relia," Gussie sighed, "Mr. Saunders is Mr. Lanning's personal friend as well as his solicitor. A young man of good family, I promise you, who is not at all ignorant about the requirements for a steward. Indeed, I found him most pleasant and competent."

"Pevensey Park is mine. I will find my own steward!"

"No, Aurelia, it is not. And you will not," declared Miss Aldershot in her governess voice. "Even though you do not seem to wish to lie in the bed which you have made, you have no choice. You threw out your net, and you caught a larger and more willful fish than you intended. You must learn to live with it."

"I . . . I can't," Relia murmured, suddenly sounding more like the five-year-old Miss Aldershot had first known than a married lady of one and twenty.

"You must. Recall, if you will, that your alternate choice was The Terrible Twyford—"

"I was going to accept Harry!"

"Piffle! You would have eaten the poor boy alive in a week. Or died of boredom. That," Gussie added with certainty, "will never happen with Mr. Lanning."

"*Et tu,* Gussie?"

"My dear, I have lived in this house for sixteen years. I have seen you grow from a child into a beautiful young lady. And now it is my dearest hope to see you grow into a wife and mother, with a new generation for me to mold into proper ladies and gentlemen."

Red stained Relia's face; the stubborn set of her Trevor chin began to wobble. Snatching what dignity she could, she attacked her longtime friend and companion. "He has won you over by agreeing you should stay on here."

"Oh, my dear," Miss Aldershot cried, "do you wish me to leave?"

Relia shoved back her chair and raced to her companion's side, throwing her arms around her, chair and all. "No, no, no, Gussie. You are all I have left in the world!"

Miss Aldershot squeezed her hand. "Thank you, my dear. But I believe you have acquired far more than you are willing to acknowledge. Only time will tell, of course, but you must try very hard to be fair. Your Cit is a good man, I think. And proud as Lucifer himself. He will not take what you do not offer."

Ah—if Gussie only knew.

Relia pressed a kiss to Miss Aldershot's cheek. Straightening, she clasped her hands in front of her and squared her shoulders, as if preparing for a recitation in the schoolroom. "You are, as ever, wiser than I," she stated with unaccustomed humility. "I promise I will make an effort to accommodate myself to this situation, which everyone quite rightly reminds me I have created for myself." Just for an instant, Relia's lips quivered before she got them firmly under control. "But I must tell you it will not be easy."

"I believe marriage is never easy, my dear," Gussie pronounced with all the wisdom of someone who has never known the felicity of that state.

"If you will excuse me," Relia said, "I will see if my things have been returned to my room." For a moment her head hung low as she trailed her fingers across the rich cherrywood of the dining table. "If my room is ready, I may stay upstairs. I—I have a good deal of thinking to do."

"Good night then, my dear," said Miss Aldershot, looking grave. "I promise you, all will look better in the morning."

Platitudes, Relia grumbled as she mounted the stairs. Platitudes would not be a speck of use against Thomas Lan-

ning. What she desperately needed was a detailed understanding of the relationship between a husband and wife. In
mind as well as body.

She supposed Gussie would say that was as good as asking for the moon. Yet Thomas Lanning was ten years her
senior, an experienced man of the world, while she was a
country girl who had never even had a Season. In birth, she
towered above her hired Cit husband. In experience, he was
the mountain, she the molehill. A lowering thought. Sadly
lowering.

Her room was quiet, magically transformed back to the
cozy refuge she had known all her life. A fire crackled in the
white marble fireplace, the heavy turquoise brocade
draperies were drawn across the windows. A wall sconce of
three candles twinkled above her dainty dressing table. With
purposeful steps Relia crossed to one of the rear windows of
the corner room, pulled aside the draperies, and looked out.
A harvest moon—still showing a pale orange—was rising,
bathing the terraces and sloping lawn in ghostly light. In the
distance—*ah!*—a red light flickered and grew, mounting
swiftly into a beacon that could be seen for miles. She had
completely forgotten it was Guy Fawkes Day. Allowing the
drapery to close behind her, Relia sat on the window seat
and watched the flames soar into the night sky on the rocky
hillside above her sleeping sheep. Surely, there had to be
some enormous irony in her tenants celebrating while she—

While she what? Felt sorry for herself? Felt her heart
would break because her Cit husband did not want her? Because the Cit husband she had used to save herself and
Pevensey Park did not bow down and kiss her feet?

Suddenly, all Relia's cares descended on her at once. Her
carefully masked features dissolved into anguish. Fighting
her way back through the draperies, she threw herself face-
down on her bed and wept. Great heartrending sobs no one
heard, as Miss Aldershot knew when to leave her charge
alone and Tilly, never suspecting her mistress might go to
her room hours earlier than usual, was seated at the broad
deal table in the kitchen, happily finishing her dinner and
flirting with the second footman.

Chapter Ten

*M*r. Charles Saunders stepped into his employer's office without knocking, folded his arms across his chest, and leaned against the jamb as if he hadn't a care in the world. "I've been sent to remind you that you are engaged for dinner this evening at the Greshams'."

"I sent my regrets," Thomas declared with no more than a fleeting glance at his longtime friend. "And pray tell me, Charles, at what historic moment did you exchange places with my secretary?"

"Since you frightened young Rollins so badly he's afraid to come near you. And," Mr. Saunders added with all the insouciance at his command, "I cancelled your rejection. You are expected at the Greshams' this evening."

Thomas's head jerked up. "The devil you did!"

"You need to get out and about, Thomas. You have the entire staff, not to mention some highly important colleagues, quaking in their boots. I swear you have not uttered a civil word to anyone since you came back. Including me," Mr. Saunders added under his breath.

"As you very well know, the Greshams are close to the Ebersleys—"

"And you are *hiding*?" Charles chortled, straightening off the door jamb. "The great Thomas Lanning hiding? From a *woman*?"

Thomas scowled. "A man does not willingly offer himself up for a scold. And, if you must have the wood with no bark on it, I have had enough female company to last me for some time to come."

Charles, suddenly sober, crossed the room and slumped into one of the chairs in front of his friend's broad mahogany desk. "Have I done you a grave disservice, Thomas? Should I have told Sir Gilbert to peddle his wares elsewhere? God knows you're just about the most dour new husband I have seen—and, believe me, I've known a good number of the newly shackled. Well? Do you wish me in Hades? And your bride along with me? Thomas," Charles prodded when his friend remained silent, "are you so unhappy that your view of all women is soured? I had thought an evening with Eleanor Ebersley was certain to sweeten your temper."

"You are right about one thing," Thomas said at last. "I am hiding. I had hoped to avoid Mrs. Ebersley. When vexed, she has a tongue that cuts sharper than the scorn in my dear bride's eyes. Oh, I admit an occasional rendezvous with the delicious Eleanor can be . . . ah—gratifying, Charles, but lately she's begun to look at old Ebersley as if she's counting the days 'till he sticks his spoon in the wall." To which comment Mr. Saunders had the good grace to keep his tongue between his teeth.

Thomas shuffled the papers on his desk. "And, Charles? I do not regret your conversation with Sir Gilbert. Just because my bride is a bit more intractable than I had presumed does not mean that the arrangement is not very much to my benefit. All will proceed as we have planned."

Mr. Saunders, suddenly animated, leaned forward in his chair, eyes aglow. "I say, Thomas, you're a great gun! You're really going to do it then?"

"I am."

"Does Mrs. Lanning know?"

Thomas looked over his friend's head, seemingly intent on a nautical scene by Turner. "Has that man-milliner and his fabrics left for Pevensey Park?"

"The upholsterer? Yesterday," Charles replied, suppressing a smile. "Ah—Thomas?"

"I suppose your family will expect you for Christmas?" Mr. Lanning inquired with seeming irrelevancy.

"Indeed they will."

"Then it would seem I will have to beard the young lioness in her den without your support. How fatiguing," Thomas drawled.

"You're not going to tell her until *Christmas*?" Charles burst out, much shocked.

"Perhaps not until the new year," Thomas murmured blandly. "Good day, Charles. And may I remind you that you are not the voice of my conscience. I actually have one of my own."

Charles Saunders was still shaking his blond head when he closed the door behind him. Softly, and with great care.

"Mrs. Stanton and Miss Stanton have called, ma'am," Biddeford declared. "Will you receive them here or in the drawing room?"

The Pevensey ladies were enjoying a sunny but chill morning in the cozy intimacy of the small morning parlor that overlooked the terraced gardens. Decorated in shades of rose and cream, it was a room both attractive and inviting. "Show them in here, Biddeford," Relia said. "The drawing room is undoubtedly quite arctic."

"My dear!" declared the squire's wife in hearty accents, rushing across the room to draw Aurelia into a firm embrace. "We have not visited until now as we thought to allow you the privacy due newlyweds, but what do I hear but that Mr. Lanning has gone off and left you. Abandoned you for his life in the city, they say. Can it be true, child? I have known you from the cradle and can scarce believe it. Has the man no sense at all?"

For all that the Squire Stanton remained firm in his conviction that his son had suffered a heartfelt disappointment when rejected by Miss Trevor, his good wife Margaret was under no such illusion. A stout woman with a generous nature, she could only thank the good Lord her son had been spared a leg shackle to Aurelia Trevor. It would take a man stronger than her precious Harry to manage her, indeed it would. But Mrs. Stanton was exceedingly fond of the girl and could not like to see her deserted three days after her wedding. It was unnatural, that's what it was.

Since the new Mrs. Lanning seemed momentarily speechless, Gussie directed the visitors to their seats and ordered Biddeford to bring refreshments. "We are delighted to see you," Miss Aldershot said to the Stanton ladies. "I fear it has been rather quiet here the past sennight."

Relia now had herself well in hand. "When we returned from Tunbridge Wells, Mr. Saunders had had word that Mr. Lanning was needed in London immediately. He is, as we all know, engaged in business there. He is not free to dash about or take his leisure as are—ah—most gentlemen." How very strange, but her tongue had refused to exclude her husband from the august realm of being a gentleman.

"But married only three days, my dear!" Margaret Stanton tutted. "When does he expect to return?"

Miss Chloe Stanton, blushing for her mama, swiftly interjected a question of her own. "I found Mr. Charles Saunders a most attractive man. Did you not think so, Relia?"

"Yes, indeed," Relia smiled, grateful for the interruption, as she had not the slightest idea when Mr. Lanning might return. "A true gentleman, I believe. I am told he is the younger son of a fine country family in Somerset."

But the squire's wife was not so easily put off. "And *I* am told he sacked Mr. Tubbs before he left. After all his years of service. Shocking, quite shocking."

"Mr. Tubbs," said Relia with some asperity, "forgot that I, not Lord Hubert, was the owner of Pevensey Park. I assure you, I was glad enough to have Mr. Lanning and Mr. Saunders to deal with him."

To cover her mama's most unladylike snort of disapproval, Miss Stanton asserted, "I never liked that man. Much too uppity. There were times he gave me a look that made me think he was trying to see straight through—beg pardon, Mama, but truly, Mr. Tubbs was not a nice man."

"And pray who is in charge of Pevensey Park?" Mrs. Stanton demanded.

"I am," Aurelia declared. "Mr. Saunders is currently searching for a new steward. Since I am sure we are all agreed he is as competent as he is charming, I am confident he will find an admirable candidate for the position." She could not possibly have said that! Yet it was true. Whatever one might say of Thomas Lanning or his friend Mr. Saunders, they were each remarkably capable men. For a moment Relia allowed herself to think of Oswald Pitney and Viscount Hanley. Where would Pevensey Park be if she had married either of them?

She shuddered. It did not bear thinking on.

Fortunately, Biddeford returned with a tray of tea and scones, and the conversation fell into a general exchange of country gossip. An illness here, a new baby there, a possible romance, the continuing (and quite delicious) feud between the wife of the dean of the village church and his vicar's wife. Indeed, the visit of Margaret Stanton and her daughter went far beyond the customary half hour, brought to an end only by Biddeford's reappearance.

"A Mr. Arnold has arrived, ma'am. The upholsterer Mr. Lanning said he would send down from London," he added with significant emphasis. Clearly, Biddeford felt the need to let their visitors know that Thomas Lanning had not totally abandoned his wife.

"You may tell him I will be with him shortly," Relia said, hoping she had managed to maintain a dignified façade even as her heart raced. He had not forgotten! Thomas had sent someone to effect the redecoration of the bedchambers, just as he had promised. He was coming back. When, she didn't know . . . but it would appear he expected to return. How very lowering to admit, even to herself, that she had, indeed, felt abandoned. Thomas Lanning had left her for the lure of London. Abandoned her to the pity of her neighbors. Thomas Lanning was an unfeeling lout. Despicable.

Thomas Lanning was the rock on which Pevensey Park would be fixed for the next thirty, forty, perhaps even fifty years. She had once believed she could endure almost anything for an assurance of that security. Surely, whatever Machiavellian plans her husband was making, she would be a match for him.

A sensible and admirably pragmatic concept. Yet, as it turned out, Aurelia was sadly mistaken.

Life soon settled back into the even tenor of earlier days at Pevensey Park. Aurelia ordered long-delayed repairs and improvements, for which the bills were so promptly paid by Mr. Josiah Eastbridge, who had been astonished to find himself in charge of a very large sum of Trevor funds, that Mr. Thomas Lanning's credit could not help but improve among the naturally suspicious tenants and villagers. Not what the nobles called good *ton,* paying bills so fast, but Cits understood about business, they did. Understood a man had to eat, feed his family. Looked like Miss Aurelia had done well for herself. For all of them.

Although Relia still suffered from the loss of the life she had had when her parents were alive, she reveled in her new power. Thomas Lanning had not lied. He had given her what she wanted. She had even managed to recapture the aura of serenity that had been so much the hallmark of life at Pevensey Park. With broad strokes of his pen on a stack of papers he had lifted the pall of threat over Pevensey Park, her terrible urgency to find a mate, and had returned her world to the beauty, the peace and tranquility she had once known.

Once Mr. Saunders found a steward, she would even be able to abandon the desk in the estate room, where she currently spent so much of her time. She would be able to indulge in books, as her dear papa had done. She might even take up embroidery again or possibly petit point. In a few months she would be out of mourning and able to attend parties. Yes, indeed, everything was exactly as she wished.

Be careful what you wish for. The old warning hissed at her out of the gloom of the December day.

It was *not* too quiet. She did *not* miss him! He might stay away forever.

The renovation of the two bedchambers and shared sitting room was nearly complete. Thomas would wish to see it. He would come to the country for the holidays. Of course he would.

"Ma'am?" Biddeford, looking a trifle shaken, appeared in the doorway of the estate room, which was lit only by windows high on the wall, thus requiring a good many candles, even in early afternoon. "Two young persons have arrived. I have put them in the Red Antechamber, ma'am. The female—a *young* female—says her name is Lanning."

"Lanning?" From behind the shelter of the broad estate desk, Relia stared up at her butler. "You are certain it was Lanning?" *Dear God, did Thomas already have a wife?*

Or perhaps a child?

He never said. . . .

Placing her palms flat on the desk, Relia forced her weak knees to straighten. She could, she would, meet this challenge, as she had met the last. How *could* she have been foolish enough to think that marriage would solve all her problems?

"And the person with her?" she inquired of Biddeford.

"Nate Fairchild's eldest, ma'am. Brought the young miss here in his farm cart. And may I say neither one looked too pleased about it?"

Relia took a deep breath, assumed her most arrogant Trevor countenance. "Very well, Biddeford, let us see what has been dropped upon our doorstep. And please send for Miss Aldershot."

"And there she be," Jake Fairchild declared, "a-sittin' in the common room, cryin' her eyes out—"

"I was not!"

"Yes, you wuz!"

"That is enough!" Relia roared over the two young people who seemed too intent on quarreling to offer any coherent explanation of what they were doing at Pevensey Park. "You will sit down. Both of you," she added as Jake Fairchild looked at the gold- and cream-striped satin chair and then at his well-worn brown cord breeches in something akin to horror. "And then you, Mr. Fairchild, will tell me your version, while you—Miss . . . Lanning, is it?"—the girl nodded vigorously—"remain completely silent. Is that understood?"

"But I—"

"Silence!" Relia looked up, relieved to discover Gussie standing in the doorway, surveying the scene with what could only be termed avid curiosity. When all four had settled into chairs—Miss Lanning with a flounce and Mr. Fairchild rather gingerly—Relia regarded the young man, whom she had known for many years, with what appeared to be nothing more than calm expectancy. She nodded encouragingly.

"It's like this, y'see," said Jake. "I was taking hay t' the Pig's Whistle this side of Maidstone and decided to 'ave a pint before I come home. And I see all t' men in the tap a-peerin' into the common room. And there she was on the settle, a-lookin' like she lost her last friend." Jake ducked his head, tugged a forelock of his straight brown hair. "I know I shouldn't 'ave spoke to her, miss—I mean, ma'am. Her bein' a lady and all—"

That remained to be seen! But Relia managed to keep her uncharitable thought to herself.

"I'd run out of money, you see," Miss Lanning interjected.

"*You,*" Relia snapped, "will have your turn. For now, pray do not speak!" The girl, who could not be a day over seventeen, slumped back in her chair, lower lip protruding in a decided pout. *Heavens,* Relia thought, *is that how I looked when I defied my parents?* "Pray proceed, Mr. Fairchild."

"Well, 'tis as she said. Seems like she'd set out for Pevensey Park without having enough of the ready. She'd had to sleep on the settle. Bill Tully, the landlord, woulda throwed her out, but Pevensey Park be magic words. His missus told him he might be sorry, for certain sure. So I told her—Miz Lanning—I'd bring her on. Had to get Mrs. Tully to say she'd known me since I was a nipper, but the young miss didn't have much choice, now did she? So that's what I did, and here she is, safe and sound. If not the most ungrateful wench I've seen in all my born days," Jake Fairchild added on a more plaintive note.

"That was very good of you, Jake," Relia told him. "We are all most grateful. I think," she added with a swift glance at Miss Aldershot before turning her attention to Miss Lanning—who was altogether too pretty, as well as lacking in manners. Dark hair, enormous green eyes. Even sleep-deprived and somewhat bedraggled, she was a stunning beauty. "And now," Aurelia declared, "let us hear who you are and what you have to say for yourself."

"I am Olivia," the girl said, nose in the air, as if that were all the explanation Aurelia Lanning should require.

"And who, pray tell, is Olivia?"

"Olivia Lanning, of course. I told that old butler, but he probably never said a word. He's so high in the instep you'd think he was master here instead of my brother."

"Brother?" Relia echoed faintly.

"Thomas. You *are* Mrs. Thomas Lanning, are you not? The heiress my brother married?"

"I am," Relia managed, though the words came out on a whisper. "I am so sorry. I'm afraid . . . Thomas never mentioned a word about you." As the girl's face fell—only for a moment before pride reasserted itself—Relia realized how grievously she had erred. "Where have you been living, Miss Lanning?" she inquired quickly. "And how is it that you found yourself stranded on the road? I am certain your brother would be appalled to learn of it."

Miss Lanning turned quite pale; her green eyes widened in horror. "Oh, you must never ever tell him. He would be furious. I have been living with my Aunt Browning, you see, my mother's sister, but I cannot like her, and I have been quite miserable. When Thomas wrote to say that he was married . . . well, you see, I just had to come. You will take me in, will you not? Thomas is my guardian, and I simply cannot bear to stay with my aunt another moment now that Thomas has a wife and a real house and—"

Relia held up a hand to stem the spate of words. Silence fell. She noted that both Gussie and Jake Fairchild were watching this family drama with avid fascination. "Am I to understand," the new Mrs. Lanning asked with care, "that you wish to live here at Pevensey Park?"

Miss Lanning clasped her hands in front of the top buttons of her rumpled green velvet pelisse. "Oh yes, oh please!

I'll be good, I promise. I beg of you, do not send me back to Aunt Browning."

And, of course, Aurelia could not. Yet how could Thomas not have told her he had a sister? The dangers the child had been subject to, traveling all alone from . . . from wherever she had lived.

Jake Fairchild was thanked for his timely rescue and taken off to the kitchen for a bite to eat and a replacement for his interrupted pint at the Pig's Whistle. And Gussie, patently overjoyed at the opportunity to exercise her governessing skills once again, was whisking Miss Lanning out the door when the newest member of the household paused, announcing, "I don't really like Olivia. I would much prefer to be called Eleanor."

"But what would your brother say?" Miss Aldershot asked.

"I daresay he won't mind," Miss Lanning replied airily. "Eleanor Ebersley is his mistress, and she's ever so grand. It is my fondest wish to be just like her."

Chapter Eleven

"*C* harles!" Thomas Lanning, clutching his wife's letter in his hand, bawled once again, "Charles!"

Since Mr. Lanning's many enterprises required Charles Saunders's undivided attention, the young solicitor had the sometimes dubious honor of a spacious office next to his employer's own. It was, therefore, not necessary for Thomas Lanning's furious bellow to carry all the way to Lincoln's Inn Fields.

"Oh, there you are!" Thomas growled as Charles appeared. He thrust the letter into his friend's hand.

"Good God!" Mr. Saunders breathed as he scanned the missive from Pevensey Park. "I knew Livvy was a minx, but this . . ." Charles pinned his friend with an accusing gaze. "Is it true you never told Mrs. Lanning you had a sister?"

"We departed rather precipitately, as you recall."

"You had three whole days in Tunbridge—" Charles broke off, his classically pale English complexion turning puce. "Beg pardon. Most stupid of me."

"If you are implying I was distracted by connubial bliss, you are fair and far out, I assure you," Thomas responded grimly.

"Whyever not?" Purple succeeded puce as Mr. Saunders choked, coughed, pounded his forehead with his fist. "Beg pardon. I fear I left my brains at home with my breakfast."

"No, no," Thomas demurred, "'tis I who am all about in my head. I had not anticipated . . . so many—ah—complications in this marriage. I was notified yesterday that

Nicholas has been sent down," he added with seeming irrelevance.

"The devil you say!"

"Charles," Thomas sighed, "are you quite, quite sure you cannot lend me support when I go down to Pevensey?"

"Quite," Mr. Saunders stated firmly. "M'mother would have me boiled in oil and served to the poor on Boxing Day like leftover Christmas goose."

"Then God help me," said Thomas Lanning.

Pride was a terrible thing, Relia conceded as she frowned, unseeing, over her ledgers. Her husband could stay in London forever; she truly did not care. But that he should be tending to business with one hand and enjoying the favors of someone named Eleanor with the other was outside of enough. Terrible man! Did he not recall that he was married?

It would seem he did not. For there had not been one word about a new steward, nor so much as a line in response to her letter about his sister. Though he must have received it, for a trunkful of Miss Lanning's belongings had arrived at Pevensey only that morning.

"Aunt Browning is delighted to be rid of me," Olivia had announced provocatively, but Relia thought she caught a rather woebegone plaint beneath Miss Lanning's bravado. Not that she could not sympathize with Olivia's Aunt Browning, for, in spite of her promises, the chit tended to be as willful as her brother. Prodded by a horrified Gussie, the girl had apologized for her remark about Mr. Lanning's mistress, but the words she had blurted out hung there, refusing to away.

Snap! Blankly, Relia stared at the now broken quill she had been holding in her hand.

Her husband was a rake.

Yet . . . could a Cit be a rake? Somehow Relia had always thought that a term reserved for gentlemen. Nor did the Thomas Lanning she had seen so far seem to be in the petticoat line—as Harry would say. Dear Harry. She should have taken him while she could and settled for the simple life of a country mouse.

Which she was, of course, compared to the grand, so-phisticated Eleanor Ebersley.

Scowling fiercely, Relia dug through the desk drawers, searching for another quill. When would the new steward ar-rive? Surely, there had been ample time. . . .

No doubt her dear husband was allowing her to become heartily sick of ordering supplies, supervising repairs, keep-ing meticulous account books, and dealing with all the daily cares of a vast estate. While he lived royally in London, chasing courtesans on *her* income!

A second quill snapped in half.

"Ma'am," said Biddeford, who had just entered the room, "Mr. Arnold has informed me that the refurbishment is com-plete. If you would be so kind as to inspect his work? I be-lieve he wishes to set out for London this very day."

Grateful for the interruption, Relia made the long climb from the basement to the bedchambers far above. Her praise for Mr. Arnold's handiwork was all that he could desire. The two bedchambers, their respective dressing rooms, and the sitting room set down between were truly so transformed that she could no longer picture her parents living here. Yet a second calculating look at her own bedchamber turned Mrs. Lanning's approving smiles to a frown. "I believe . . . yes, I believe I have erred," she mused. "The silk draperies and bedhangings are too light for winter. I fear I would take a chill."

"The satin is very thick, madam," Mr. Arnold protested.

"Nonetheless, I have decided I prefer velvet. These will do very well for summer, but for winter I must have velvet."

"Ma'am? I fear I have no samples of the proper color with me." Mr. Arnold's strangled tone revealed quite clearly he saw his return to London for the holiday disappearing on m'lady's whim.

"You are aware of my tastes by now, Mr. Arnold," Relia said, taking pity on the poor man. "On your return to Lon-don I trust you to select the correct fabric and send it to me. Along with your instructions for the seamstress. I am certain that after managing these"—Relia waved her hand at the silk-satin draperies and bedhangings—"she will have the new fabric done up in a trice."

"Thank you, ma'am," Mr. Arnold breathed, with a bow so deep Relia feared he would topple over. "I shall tend to the matter as soon as I am in town. But . . ."

"Yes?"

"May I say, ma'am, that velvet of that particular shade of peach may not be easy to find."

"I did not think it would, Mr. Arnold." Mrs. Thomas Lanning's lips turned up in a tiny little quirk. "I did not think it would."

"And who is this delightful young lady?" oozed the latest, and most unwelcome, visitor to Pevensey Park.

Aurelia gritted her teeth as Mr. Twyford Trevor whipped up his quizzing glass and examined Miss Olivia Lanning from the halo of dark curls framing her piquant face down to the delicate slippers peeking out from beneath her far-too-thin sprigged muslin gown. Good manners, however, prevailed. The introduction produced a decided gleam in her cousin's eye as he pounced on the young lady's name.

"The Cit has a sister, imagine that!" Mr. Trevor declared with something akin to glee. "How very fortunate—for me," he added with a graceful bow in Miss Lanning's direction, "that I decided to call and see how my dear cousin was going on."

"Mr. Trevor," said Miss Augustina Aldershot with little subtlety, "we are surprised to see you. I understood that you had business elsewhere."

The Terrible Twyford gave a negligent wave of his hand. "A party here, a party there, don't you know? *On-dits* flying in every direction. When I heard my dear cuz might be all alone, and she so newly married, I thought company might be welcome."

The sly insouciance of Mr. Trevor's smile was enough to make Relia long to throw something at him. "Mr. Lanning has a great many interests in London which he cannot abandon at such short notice—" Oh no, she could not have made such a foolish error!

Mr. Trevor's brows shot up. "I was under the impression your betrothal was of long-standing, dear cuz. Surely, even a Cit such as Mr. Lanning could have arranged his affairs so he could spend a proper amount of time with his bride."

"My brother has a great many affairs!" Olivia Lanning interjected, sitting very straight in her chair and glaring at Mr. Trevor as if she had not spent the last ten minutes casting simpering glances in his direction.

"I have no doubt," The Terrible Twyford replied, with a distinct smirk. Gussie made a strangling sound, while Relia turned pale.

"I trust you are now on your way home for the holidays," Miss Aldershot stated when she had recovered her countenance.

"Indeed," Mr. Trevor concurred, once again turning the full force of his personality on Miss Lanning.

It was, Relia thought, rather like a bull assessing a newborn lamb. How could Thomas Lanning have had the arrogance to think his dragonslaying permanent? Her cousin Twyford was turning out to be more like the multi-headed Hydra. Destroy one head, and two, even more dangerous, took its place.

"But now," Mr. Trevor said, continuing to use false charm like a bludgeon, "I believe I will accept the invitation to Gravenham after the holidays."

"Gravenham?" Relia echoed, surprised to hear the earl was entertaining as word had come of Captain Alan Fortescue being wounded on the Peninsula.

"Yes." Her cousin preened at being the bearer of significant news. "It seems the captain's wounds were not so terrible that a few months at home will not have him right as a trivet. So Lady Gravenham is planning a party of Fortescue's old friends after the holiday. The captain is, I believe, expected home in time for Christmas."

The remainder of the conversation flew by unheeded as Relia clasped her hands tightly in her lap and willed herself to stay upright on the sofa. Alan Fortescue was coming home! If only she had waited, she might have—

She was the wife of Mr. Thomas Lanning and must make the best of it.

Of Mr. Thomas Lanning, the Cit, who had not even been able to rid her of The Terrible Twyford!

"Ma'am? Ma'am?"

"Aurelia!" Gussie prodded.

Mrs. Lanning broke out of her disconcerting thoughts to see Biddeford standing a few feet away, looking more portentous than usual. "Yes?"

"There is a traveling coach coming up the drive, ma'am. I thought you would wish to know. 'Tis possible it is Mr. Lanning, ma'am."

Olivia, heedless of propriety, jumped to her feet and ran to the window at the far end of the drawing room. "Yes, yes," she cried. "I'm nearly certain 'tis Papa's old coach. Thomas never uses it, but . . . yes, I see him. It is he! Oh, no!" Miss Lanning added on something between a shriek and a groan. "He cannot have brought the Beast. He always goes to the Wilsons' for holidays. Aunt Browning would not have him in the house."

Beast. What beast? Relia wondered. Had Mr. Lanning brought a dog? One thing was certain, she would not lower herself to ask.

As Gussie ordered Miss Lanning back to her seat to await her brother as a proper lady should, Relia noted that Mr. Twyford Trevor had disappeared. Simply vanished without so much as a farewell. Perhaps she had maligned Mr. Lanning's dragonslaying skills a bit too soon. At this very moment The Terrible Twyford was likely slipping down the back stairs.

And then her husband was standing in the doorway, framed in ornate plasterwork, and looking larger and even more intimidating than she recalled. A big man, though lean and graceful like some giant jungle animal, to whom all other creatures granted a respectful amount of space. He was more attractive, also, than she had allowed herself to remember, although it had been quite impossible to forget his strength as he had kept her from tumbling down those lethal-looking flagstone steps in Tunbridge Wells.

"Aurelia, Miss Aldershot, Livvy." He nodded to each in turn, then stepped further into the room. Reaching one hand behind him, he dragged forward a youth of some eleven or twelve years. Already handsome, if yet an unlicked cub, the boy gave every evidence of becoming the image of the man beside him when he grew up.

Relia, who had been about to rise to greet her husband, realized her legs had turned to water. Olivia might have turned out to be Thomas's sister, but this—the Beast—must surely be his son.

"Nicholas, make your bow to your new sister," Mr. Lanning ordered.

Sister. *Sister.* Somehow Relia, still seated, managed a welcoming smile. In his stiffly new high-topped trousers and short jacket, his cravat tied in a flourishing bow and his hair freshly combed, young Nicholas Lanning looked anything but a beast. The expression on his face, however— holding, as it did, traces of hostility, belligerence, bravado, and something close to panic—promised a challenging holiday season, to say the least. *Years* of challenge, more like, Relia amended, unless she could somehow make friends with the boy. But Nicholas Lanning gave every evidence of being as willful as the other members of his family. If not more so.

"Our mother was Papa's second wife," Olivia contributed when Thomas remained silent, seemingly absorbed in studying his wife's reaction.

"Then the resemblance is even more remarkable," Miss Aldershot noted. "I take it you both look like the late Mr. Lanning?" she said to Thomas.

"Peas in a pod, that's what Papa always said," Olivia confirmed. "But Papa was never a beast," she emphasized with a vicious glare at her younger brother. "Nor Thomas—well, not very often."

"Am not!" Nicholas hissed.

"Are too!"

"Silence!" Thomas snapped. "Nicholas, you will go with Biddeford, who will find you a suitable room."

"If you do not mind, I shall accompany him," Miss

Aldershot declared, leaping at this further challenge like a firehorse racing to the smell of smoke.

Mr. Lanning gave her a small bow. "I should be pleased, Miss Aldershot. Thank you. Though you should know," he added in a tone that came as close to chagrin as anyone had ever heard from Mr. Thomas Lanning, "he has been requested not to return to school until spring term. I fear he will be here for a while."

"Olivia, you will join us," said Miss Aldershot in a voice that allowed no room for argument. As the three left the drawing room, Gussie carefully shut the door behind her.

"I am sorry," Thomas declared stiffly to the pale stranger, his wife. "Although I confess I had thoughts of your introducing Livvy to the *ton* at some time in the future, I did not expect to bring either one of them down upon your head so soon. When Nicholas is not in school, he spends his time with the families of his friends, who have been exceedingly kind to him since his mother's—ah—departure. I anticipated neither Livvy's rejection of her Aunt Browning nor Nicholas being sent down from school. When it happened, only the day before I received your letter about Livvy, I realized I had no choice. Although I have a house in London, it is not . . . a home. It is not equipped to deal with youngsters."

Nor was she, Relia thought. "All the time we were in Tunbridge Wells and I told you of my life here at Pevensey Park, not once did you mention their existence."

"I thought . . . it seemed we had enough problems confronting us. It was foolish to add more, if it were not necessary."

"But now it is."

"Yes."

Relia raised her chin. "Please sit down . . . Thomas." Mr. Lanning, flipping up his tails, though never taking his eyes off his wife's face, sat in a chair directly across from her. "I have made your sister welcome here," she informed him, "and I am happy to do the same for your brother. You are quite correct. This should be their home. I have loved Pevensey Park all my life, and it is my duty to share it with them. I had no brothers or sisters, so I fear I am ignorant on the subject of children, but Gussie is a marvel and will undoubtedly make up for my mistakes."

"You are most gracious," Thomas responded with as much formality as if he were speaking to a duchess. "Yet I fear they will be a considerable disruption to the quiet life you cherish here."

Relia bent her head, hiding her expression. Her husband certainly had the right of it, but she was not such an ogre that she could not feel sympathy for orphaned children, no matter how difficult they might be. Nor did a Trevor ever shirk her duty. This was her hired dragonslayer, and even if he had not yet done as thorough a job as she might have liked, she was honor-bound to fulfill her part of their peculiar bargain.

"Aurelia . . . is the renovation of our bedchambers complete?"

Abruptly, Mrs. Lanning returned from righteous self-satisfaction to the realities of the moment. "Nearly," she responded, plucking an invisible spot of lint from her gray woolen gown. "I did not expect you back so soon."

"Nearly? And pray tell just what remains to be done?"

"The sitting room and your bedchamber are complete. You will find them most comfortable, I am sure. Mr. Arnold was a most clever man."

"But *your* room is not ready, I take it?"

"Ah . . . no. Mr. Arnold is in London searching out the precise fabric I require."

"I see." Such innocence in those gray-blue eyes, Thomas thought. Almost, he believed her. "I see no evidence of holiday decoration," he commented casually, as if dismissing the incomplete refurbishment as of little importance. "Perhaps you may make use of Nicholas's services in that regard. He is one who needs . . . ah—a good many tasks, preferably interesting ones, to occupy his time."

"Of course," his wife responded smoothly. "An excellent suggestion. And now . . . perhaps you would care to see what has been done to your rooms?"

An hour later, Thomas Lanning sent for his wife's maid. Tilly, as he recalled, had seemed to approve of him after his rescue of her mistress from almost certain injury. The tale he pried out of her, however reluctantly, turned him even more stony-faced than usual. Dismissing the maid, he rang for Biddeford.

"You will restore the bedhangings and draperies Mr. Arnold provided for my wife's room," he told the butler. "Immediately."

"I fear there may be some delay, Mr. Lanning," Biddeford replied, stoically loyal to his mistress, though he could not quite hide his apprehension. "They have been boxed and sent to the attics. The draperies match the bedhangings, you see, sir, and Mrs. Lanning's room has a good many windows. There are a staggering number of boxes," the butler concluded, trailing into silence.

Though still scowling, Thomas, a reasonable man, nodded, for it was late in the day, nearly time to dress for dinner. "Very well, you and—what is the housekeeper's name? Ah, yes, you and Mrs. Marshcombe will see to the matter in the morning. And then you may supervise the removal of Mrs. Lanning's belongings to her new room." Thomas paused, skewering the butler with his sharp gray eyes. "I trust I make myself clear, Biddeford?"

The elderly butler drew himself up into a stance as stiff as a soldier under inspection by a general. "Yes, sir. Indeed, sir. I assure you, Mr. Lanning, all will be as you wish it."

As he reached the hall, Biddeford's shoulders slumped. Poor Miss Aurelia. She had married a sharp one. Wasn't taken in by her tricks one little bit. And with two more Lannings come to Pevensey Park—and neither of them with cobwebs between the ears—it was going to be a lively holiday. Most lively.

For a moment Biddeford allowed his lips to curve into a smile. It was possible . . . yes, indeed it was, that they had all become too set in their ways at Pevensey Park. The new broom had swept clean; a new era had begun. For a short while it looked very much as if the young miss had sacrificed herself, but now it appeared as if Mr. Lanning had no intention of abandoning his wife to her own devices in the country. No, indeed. Almost . . . yes, almost Biddeford could hear a creaking of timbers, the soft swish of silken hangings as the old house stirred to life. Perhaps even the patter of little feet on the stairs, childish shouts of glee, Miss Aldershot's stern admonitions rising over all . . .

With his shoulders returned to their customary stately grace and his face to its impassive butlerish mask, Biddeford pushed open the door and headed toward the kitchen.

Chapter Twelve

*R*elia's steps increased in pace as she moved down the hallway until, by the time she reached her room, she was close to a jog. Bursting through the door, she slammed it behind her, stalking to the center of the bedchamber, where she stood, breathing hard, eyes squeezed tight and fists clenched. The serenity of her household had disappeared up the chimney like so much unwanted smoke. At dinner, Gussie had concentrated her attention on the two younger Lannings, who seemed to require constant supervision to keep them from quarreling like toddlers on leading strings. Which left her husband as her sole conversational partner. And he—abominable man!—except for assuring her he would search out a tutor for young Nicholas so the boy did not always have to eat with the adults, quickly reverted to the dull, innocuous phrases that had marked their brief sojourn in Tunbridge Wells. To everyone in the household he turned a face full of animation, even fire. To his wife, however, he presented nothing more interesting than a whitewashed wall.

It was maddening.

And now a tutor was to be added to the mélange. As if her household were not already turned topsy-turvy. All Pevensey Park needed was yet another bedchamber filled by a perfect stranger.

With the automatic response of long practice, Relia shrugged out of the gown that Tilly had just unbuttoned, allowing it to pool about her feet. Nimbly, she stepped out of it, then raised her arms to allow her maid to pull her chemise over her head. Her mind still fixed on the unexpected disturbances brought to Pevensey Park by her marriage to Thomas Lanning, Relia paid little attention to the bedgown Tilly was offering, merely accepting it with gratitude, for, in spite of a glowing fire, the room was chill. She would welcome the warmth.

And yet . . . she was still cold. A fact uncomfortable enough to distract Mrs. Thomas Lanning from her dire thoughts. She looked down, saw an expanse of transparent lawn, bare arms. In *December*! "Tilly!"

"Yes, ma'am?" The maid's eyes, as full of romance as they had been in Tunbridge Wells, gleamed expectantly.

Relia could not possibly say what she wanted to say. She could not admit she had no need of bridal finery. "The velvet dressing gown, if you please." She snuggled into the soft dark blue fabric, then settled at her dressing table so Tilly could braid her hair. Brushing and braiding were so soothing. . . . Almost, she could dismiss her sulks.

When Tilly left, leaving the faint drift of a romantical sigh behind her, Relia, wincing, headed for the warmth of the fireplace, where she curled up in a comfortable upholstered chair and forced herself to face a healthy dose of reality. She *had* been sulking. And all because her world was changing. Changing in the manner she herself had precipitated.

She had a husband. An enigma, at best, but a far better choice than any of the others.

If only Alan Fortescue . . . *Foolish twit!* That was a road down which she could never go.

And as silly as the barely seventeen-year-old Olivia seemed at times, she, too, had livened up their lives. Indeed, Gussie was more animated than Relia had seen her in years. And Nicholas? Relia suspected the loss of both parents at such a young age had affected him more than it had his sister. And Thomas seemed to have sent him to school and to the homes of friends, seldom allowing the boy into his life. Until now.

And what had happened to Olivia and Nicholas's mother,

who must have been still a young woman when she died? Childbirth? In spite of the fire, Relia shivered.

A cursory scratching, and her door swung open, the sudden gust of air from the hallway causing the candles to flicker wildly and the flames in the grate to whoosh up the chimney. Aurelia bounded to her feet. "What," she demanded, "are *you* doing here?"

Thomas raised dark brows only a few shades lighter than his black satin dressing gown. "Visiting my wife? Is that not what everyone expects—a grand reunion after my long stay in town?"

"You cannot come in *here*," Relia sputtered.

"I am in," her husband told her calmly. "And, I assure you, the entire household would be gabbling in the morning if I had not come. In fact, I suspect that was Nicholas I saw just now, peeking round the corner. You would not wish me to offend his boyish sensibilities."

"*His* sensibilities?" Relia gasped. "And what is that?" she added in ominous tones, as Thomas hauled a flat wooden box out from beneath his robe.

"Chess. Do you play?"

"You come to my room at this hour of the night and you wish to play *chess*?"

"In all truth," Thomas returned after due consideration, "I would prefer an alternate method of passing our time. I am aware, however, that you would likely prefer to play chess." Mr. Lanning set the box down on top of a small round table, then carried the table across the room and set it between the two chairs by the fire. Waving his speechless wife back into her seat and taking the opposite chair himself, he began to set up the chessboard and its pieces.

"Of course," Thomas said as he sat back and surveyed the kings, queens, rooks, knights, and pawns, all exquisitely carved of ivory and ebony, "it would seem this game may be superfluous, for I believe we are already engaged in a surprisingly intricate game of chess."

"In which you seem to be playing with more pieces than I!"

"Touché, my dear. The point is yours." Thomas leaned forward, making his opening gambit with a black pawn.

Not fifteen minutes later he swept his wife's queen from the board. "I do not believe you are paying attention, Aurelia. I understood that you frequently played with your father. I expected a better game."

"I have never played chess with anyone *but* my father."

"Ah . . . then he let you win—"

"He did not!"

"Then can it be you are distracted because playing chess reminds you of your father, as sleeping in your parents' chambers offended your tender sensibilities?" said her husband with a sangfroid that was almost cruel.

Dangerous ground. Relia knew a trap when she heard it. "The renovations are nearly complete, sir. The next time you are here—"

"Thomas!" her husband snapped. "And Mr. Arnold's draperies and other gewgaws will be back in place tomorrow. As will my wife. I have given Biddeford orders to move your things as soon as the hangings are once again in place."

"You *dare*," Relia raged, "you dare to order me about when you cannot even get rid of The Terrible Twyford. You fill my house with—"

"Stop!" Thomas roared, sitting up so fast he nearly toppled the chessboard. "Trevor was *here*?"

"In the drawing room as you arrived," Relia informed him with great satisfaction. "Though when I turned around, the coward had slipped out. Down the back stairs, no doubt."

"And well he might," Thomas ground out. "Good God," he muttered, his fury suddenly distracted by a thought more horrifying than Trevor's mere presence. "Did he meet Livvy?"

"Yes."

"Hell and the devil confound it!"

"Mr. Lanning!"

"Thomas!"

For all of ten seconds the belligerents glared at each other. Relia found her tongue first. Chin high, she announced, "Twyford said my abandonment was an *on-dit* at a houseparty he attended, and so he had come to see how I went on."

Thomas closed his eyes and leaned back in his chair, wishing he had brought a bottle of brandy. It wasn't that he had not thought of it, but he had feared the sight of him with a bottle in hand might cause his wife to flee in terror. Frightening her would not further his plans.

Nor did he wish her ill, even though there were times he longed to pick her up and shake some sense into her stubborn, and deplorably narrow-minded, head.

Methodically, he packed up the chess pieces and the board, locking them into the thin wooden box. "I do believe I have stayed long enough to present the proper picture of a husband rushing to embrace his leg shackle," he informed his wife of six weeks. Thomas stood, tucked the box back beneath his dressing gown. His voice took on a more uncompromising tone. "Do not forget—tomorrow night you will join me in the master suite. As a good wife should."

Relia sat by the fire, shivering, her heart a block of ice. Thomas Lanning was a . . . a *gargoyle,* straight off the ancient Gothic church in Lower Peven. His Cit soul had been perverted by *commerce.* She should have married Harry. She should have waited for Alan. Even a nonentity like Lord Hanley would have been better than . . . *this*!

It was full half an hour before Aurelia dragged herself up from in front of the fire and sought her bed. The warm brick Tilly had left there had gone cold. Relia pulled the covers high, seeking a spot of warmth. Cold hands, cold toes, cold heart. She heaved a great sigh, knowing quite well what Gussie would say—what she had already repeated countless times over: *You've made your bed, child, now lie in it!*

For a few magical moments on her wedding night, she might have been able to do so. And then her husband had run off as if the Hounds of Hell were after him. Just as he had abandoned her for London. And Eleanor Ebersley. And Aurelia had discovered that, instead of a properly humble Cit grateful for his advancement, she had married an arrogant, high-handed monster who did not so much as deign to touch her. . . .

*In all truth, I would prefer an alternate method of pass-
ing our time.* Recollection of her husband's words, the
barely repressed acquisitive gleam in his eye as he said
them, had Relia burrowing further into the covers, wrapping
them around the back of her head until only her eyes and
nose peeked out. She needed her night cap, but *nothing*
could convince her body to move from under the covers to
fetch it.

She shut her eyes very tight. *Dear God in heaven!* To
think she had assumed that marriage would solve all her
problems!

"A fine day for gathering greens, is it not?" Thomas declared at the breakfast table, in a manner Relia found nause-
atingly hearty so early in the morning—as she also found
the mound of food piled high upon his plate. "You *do* plan
to decorate, do you not, my dear?" her husband added, an
odiously benign expression on his face.

"Oh, please," Livvy cried unexpectedly, "may we?"

Relia ceased layering blackberry jam on her toast. Laying down her knife, she cast a swift glance around the table.
Gussie's lips were twitching—the traitor! Thomas was
blandly expectant; his sister, eyes shining, was breathless
with anticipation. Mr. Nicholas Lanning, seemingly indifferent, kept his head down, steadily eating his way through
a haphazard pile of food that rivaled his brother's.

In spite of almost no experience with children, Relia was
not fooled. Nicholas, as would almost any young man his
age, longed to go on an expedition to gather greens. Yet . . .

"I fear the footmen are occupied today," she responded
with grim satisfaction. "A matter of bringing boxes down
from the attic, but they should be available tomorrow."

"Could not the gardeners or the grooms show us—" At a
sharp look from his brother, Nicholas broke off his telltale
interjection.

"Tomorrow will be acceptable," Thomas said. *Another
point to you,* said the look he exchanged with his wife. "And
do you bring in a Yule log? I should like to be part of that

expedition also. It is not something we can do in town, and I find myself intrigued by the tradition."

"It is pagan, you know," Relia said before attempting to hide behind a quarter of toast.

"One of many ancient traditions adopted by the church," Thomas agreed smoothly. "And a fine one it is."

"It is best managed in a medieval hall," Relia countered.

"True," Thomas agreed, "but I trust that somewhere in this vast pile you have a fireplace of sufficient size."

Relia did not care for the spark in Gussie's eye. House of mourning or not, obviously her old governess did not care to disappoint the younger Lannings, let alone the eldest, for whom she seemed to have developed an unaccountable approval. "Very well," Mrs. Lanning declared. "I will have the grate removed from the fireplace in the entry hall. That is where we used to have a Yule log before Mama became ill."

"And today?" Livvy asked, looking hopeful.

"Today . . . today, if you wish, you may bring in greens from close to the house," Relia conceded. "Holly and ivy—although you must not take so much that the gardeners will be complaining to me tomorrow," she warned with a smile. "And perhaps Nicholas will wish to help you."

"If you can work together in harmony," Miss Aldershot cautioned.

"I will go with them," Thomas said. "They have both had experience of decorating for the holidays. I have not. As long as I am rusticating," he added with seeming indifference, "I may as well join in country customs."

Later, when the three Lannings had gone off, bundled up against the cold, and Relia and Gussie were tucked up, warm and cozy under lap robes in the morning room, Miss Aldershot declared, "That was well done of you, my dear. Your papa would have approved, I am certain. You have ensured a happy Christmas for the Lannings."

Relia looked up from the list she was making of tasks that must be accomplished if they were giving up mourning long enough to celebrate the holidays. "I confess I am surprised," she admitted. "I would not have expected Mr. Lanning to show any interest in holiday decorations."

"Do you not recall the thrill of gathering greens, my dear? As a child, you always went out with your papa. I believe Mr. Lanning, born and raised in the city, was not able to participate in such family traditions, but he has made sure Olivia and Nicholas spent their holidays with good country families. This has not perhaps"—Gussie hesitated—"not helped make them a family of close-knit bonds, but I believe Mr. Lanning is attempting to rectify that now that he is married."

"Oh." Chagrined by her lack of sensitivity, Aurelia contemplated her faults. Her husband and his brother and sister were making an effort to become a family, while she, his wife, sat before a fire and made *lists*. She should have put on her warmest gown, her stoutest boots, her oldest cloak and bonnet and joined them in their raid on her holly bushes.

They had not invited her.

She had shown not the slightest interest.

Once, she had loved life, Relia recalled; she had been eager and carefree. Now . . . she had become a great glump. It was her duty, as chatelaine of Pevensey Park and wife to Mr. Thomas Lanning, to make an effort to do better.

But today . . . today was the day she had to move into the bedchamber separated from her husband's only by the width of their shared sitting room. It was not a propitious moment to soften her attitude. Every instinct warned she should, instead, add another layer of armor before any chink could be discovered.

When the three foragers returned to the house, with sparkling eyes and red cheeks, Relia was watching from the gallery above. *Cits!* They were close to staggering under their armsful of greens, yet they had not called for help. Just the three of them, laughing and triumphant, as if the holiday could not happen without their contributions of prickly greenery. And, of course, they did not stop their Cit behavior there. After dropping their burdens onto the highly polished and pristine tiled floor, the Lannings set off a great flurry by descending into the kitchen, where they sat at the servants' dining table and enjoyed thin slices of roast beef on fresh-baked bread, augmented by mugs of hot spiced cider.

Thomas and Nicholas paused their chewing only long enough to bound to their feet with lively grace when Aurelia joined them, making a valiant effort to look as if she sat at the servants' dining table every day. *Once again the goat,* Thomas thought. In his wife's eyes he was guilty of causing so much disruption among the kitchen staff that life below stairs might never be the same again. Perhaps that was just as well. And tonight . . . ah, yes, tonight he would have his wife exactly where he wanted her.

But, in the end, he let the moment pass. For that evening he found himself basking in a strange warmth as he listened to his wife—*his wife*—play the piano with all the grace and skill he should have expected. After that, Livvy actually displayed a talent, which might have been short on technique, but was filled with considerable feeling for the simple tunes she was contributing. And then he turned to discover his little brother actually regarding his sister with something close to appreciation. *Remarkable.* The holiday spirit must be having more of an effect than he had thought. Perhaps the manner in which he had teased his wife last night was enough for a while. And no one would be the wiser about the distance between them when they were safe behind the closed doors of the newly redecorated rooms.

An odd little creature, this child-woman he had married. Wise and capable, and at times so infantile and childishly innocent that he was tempted to throw up his hands and walk away from it all.

But he could not, of course. There was too much riding on this marriage. And he could no more truly abandon her than he could have sent his sister back to her aunt or failed to bring his younger brother, whom he scarcely knew, to the home he had at long last acquired for them. She would come round, his wife. Aurelia Trevor Lanning, who was so grimly determined to do her duty, even though she felt tainted by her marriage to a Cit.

When, after the tea tray was brought in and duly sampled, his wife excused herself and followed Miss Aldershot up the stairs, Thomas did not follow. Waving Olivia and Nicholas to their rooms as well, he shut himself in the library and sampled the brandy he had not had the night before. Brandy, and perhaps a good wassail bowl, it would seem, were the only comforts he would have for the holidays.

His step on the stairs, very late, was a trifle studied. But he made it through the sitting room without knocking anything over. Opening his wife's door, he peeked into the room, glumly expecting to find the bedhangings still tied back against the posts and an untouched coverlet.

Thomas swayed, blinked, looked again. His wife's bed was solidly enclosed in some material light and shiny enough to reflect the flickering glow of his single candle. Was she actually inside that rectangular tent, or was it all a sham? That was it. . . . The minx had had her maid drape the bed, while she slept quite peacefully at the opposite end of house!

Only one thing to do. . . . Thomas crept forward, pausing with a hand raised toward the crack in the hanging at the foot of his wife's bed. A hardheaded man in more ways than one, he could actually feel sobriety chasing away the brandy fumes inside his thick skull. What in God's name was he doing here in his wife's bedroom, about to intrude on her privacy while she slept?

And who had a better right? asserted the other part of him that he tried so hard to ignore. Holding the candle high, Thomas parted the satin hangings with his other hand and peered in.

She was there—Mrs. Aurelia Trevor Lanning, his wife— sound asleep, her braids trailing from beneath a nightcap that was a rather amazing confection of ribbons and lace. Ah . . . so there *was* a bit of vanity beneath all those ugly mourning gowns. She stirred. Thomas dropped the bed-hanging back in place, turned his back to shield the candle-light. But not before he had the memory of what he had seen firmly fixed in his rapidly sobering mind.

He had married a beautiful woman, an intelligent woman. One capable of appealing to the more gentle senses he had long ignored.

And capable of making him take to the bottle.

What he had was a wife who was bravely upholding her share of the devil's bargain they had made, however repugnant she found it. And when she discovered the rest of it? Thomas shuddered. He had always thought himself a brave man, but . . .

After the holidays was soon enough. The joyousness of the season seemed to be spawning a few brief moments of rapport between himself and his wife. Yes . . . in spite of Charles's admonitions, the fall of the axe could wait.

Chapter Thirteen

$\mathcal{B}$y evening of the following day Pevensey Park's elegant entry hall was engulfed in greenery, from genuine laurel wreaths adorning the brows of the classical statues, peering down from their niches, to trailing vines wound round the banisters on staircase and gallery, while evergreen boughs, swagged with red velvet, were suspended in great splashes of color against the pale green walls. Although it had been many years since Pevensey had worn so much green, Relia could still hear her mother's cautions quite clearly. *What goes up must come down!* Frequently, in showers of unwanted tiny needles well before Twelfth Night. Therefore, following the principles laid down by Lady Ralph, decoration in the state rooms consisted solely of trailing vines and red bows over mantles and doorways, thus avoiding a daunting clean-up of Aubusson, Axminster, and Persian carpets.

The entry hall, however, with its tile floor and direct access to the outside, could be decorated with near reckless abandon. With a shake of her head, Relia finally gave up all attempts at supervision when it became apparent that the three Lannings, aided and abetted by a full complement of footmen and a bevy of housemaids, had plunged hip-deep into exercising their creative imaginations. Retreating once again to the gallery, Relia simply stood and watched. Truth to tell, the hall looked quite lovely. If it brought back bittersweet memories, then she alone should suffer them, for the Lannings had not known her parents. Nor was she so unreasonable as to think they, too, should mourn.

Mr. Lanning's voice rose above the excited buzz below, giving orders. Then he stood with his head cocked to one side, clearly pondering what to do next. A question from Nicholas, remarkably handsome with the sullen look gone from his face. A consultation between Thomas and Olivia. Quick smiles between brother and sister, then off Livvy went to drape a garland around the shoulders of one of the more forbidding Roman generals.

"It is all right, you know," Gussie said as she joined Relia on the gallery. "You will notice even the servants have taken the Lannings to their hearts. All this"—Gussie arced a hand around the bustling and colorful entry hall—"is so much better than finding they have acquired a new master who does naught but sit on his high horse and scowl."

The idea was so ludicrous when applied to the tall man handing up greenery to a footman, who was standing on a ladder laid against the gallery balustrade, that Relia could not suppress a giggle. It was true. As annoying as he could be at times, Thomas Lanning possessed a good nature. Although in *her* presence that nature was well hidden beneath a forbidding façade or a mask of faintly derogatory humor, her husband was . . . well, rather appealing, with his dark hair rumpled and his cheeks still pink from the cold. His gray eyes sparkling with something besides annoyance . . . or his latest effort to urge her in a direction she did not wish to go.

He should not be down there, of course, doing what he was doing. No matter what Gussie said, he should not be enjoying himself in such a plebian fashion. And stealing her servants' approbation. *Cit!* Had he no proper notion of how to go on?

Relia stepped away from the back wall of the gallery and, hiding herself behind a column wound with greenery, focused her gaze on her husband alone. He was . . . strong, dynamic, a true dragonslayer.

He was replacing her authority in her very own household. Filling it with strangers. With noise, laughter . . . perhaps even joy.

And she hated him for it.

No, she did not.

Shoulders slumping, Relia turned and headed blindly toward her bedchamber, her feet finding their way to the room of her childhood, now stripped of everything that had been hers. She sat, shivering, before the cold grate, her mind lost in a confusion of contrary emotions. Was this what was meant by that old saying about winning a battle only to lose the war? Was that what she had done? She had saved Pevensey Park . . . by losing it?

Or was it she herself who was lost?

Excitement hummed at breakfast the next day, for the great Yule log expedition was about to commence. Relia, nagged by her conscience, rose early to see them off. Fortunately, Olivia had conceded that two days of winter cold were quite enough and did not insist on joining what was generally an exhausting all-day male event. So the ladies enjoyed the comforts of home—Relia making a list of the amounts to be given to each servant on Boxing Day while Miss Aldershot and Olivia worked on the boxes to be given to the poor. Thomas, however, rode off on the bench of a farm wagon, with Nicholas tucked up behind among a collection of men that included Pevensey Park's gamekeeper, two gardeners, two stableboys, and three footmen, all wearing their oldest and warmest clothes. They were also accompanied by a long two-handed saw, plus an intimidating array of sharp axes. Behind them trudged a farmer, leading the team of heavy workhorses that would be needed to haul the great log home.

What was that old nursery rhyme? Thomas thought as they bounced along the road, wheels clattering and harnesses clanking in the cold crisp air. Something about, *Lawks-a-mercy me, can this be I?* Said by an old woman, as he recalled, but the words were all too apt. If his friends from the City could but see him now. And the friends from Mayfair? Thomas laughed aloud. His true friends, like Charles, would rejoice for him, even while shaking their heads. The others did not matter.

His wife, of course, thought him an ill-bred lout. Yet disconcerting her by demonstrating his Cit ways was remarkably enjoyable. And yesterday, Nicholas, in a moment of unrestrained excitement while teetering on a ladder, had actually addressed him as Thomas. A good lad beneath his sullens, Thomas surmised. Perhaps being sent down from school was not such a bad thing after all. It was high time he became better acquainted with the child not born until he was at university.

Thomas judged that with most of Pevensey's people, if not his wife, he had made considerable progress. Next . . . next must be Squire Stanton and his family, important acquaintances to steer him through the maze of county neighbors. Mourning or no mourning, Thomas determined, there must be some sort of social mingling this holiday. Perhaps Miss Aldershot could advise him.

A shout went up as a likely log was found, already felled by lightning and lying conveniently on the ground. Thomas gave the gamekeeper an inquiring look. But it seemed the log was too dry and would burn too quickly, unable to last the proper length of the twelve days of Christmas.

Oak, declared the head gardener. Ash, countered the gamekeeper—all knew the Yule log must be ash. The argument lasted off and on for half a day until the perfect tree was found and felled, its branches lopped off. Thomas, asserting his rights with a good-natured grin carefully calculated not to offend, confirmed the gamekeeper's measurements by pacing off the length for himself. The entry hall of Pevensey Park was not the ideal place to discover another two inches must be sawn off before the log would fit. He tended to offend his bride all too easily without being blamed for a mound of sawdust or—heaven forfend!—nicks in the tiles.

The early dark of the winter solstice was beginning to settle over Pevensey Park before the Yule log party was heard jingling up the drive. The ladies, throwing on their heaviest cloaks, stepped out onto the broad landing to watch as the horses were brought to a halt, leaving the great log they were dragging directly before the front steps. The men piled out of the wagon, and in a short time the heavy ropes hitching the log to the horses had been transformed into three loops for pulling the trimmed tree trunk up the twelve imposing steps.

In spite of the lowering light, Relia had no trouble finding Thomas, as he topped the tallest of the other men by at least three inches. And Nicholas . . . she smiled to see the boy rushing in, right at the forefront of the work and the men cheerfully making room for him. With three men who sported the most stalwart shoulders pulling, and the bravest pushing from below, the Yule log bounced slowly up the steps, Relia, Olivia, and Gussie retreating before it. Inside at last, with their goal in sight, the men dragged the log across the tiles with renewed vigor. As they were removing the ropes before the final shove into the fireplace, Relia looked up to discover a good portion of her household ringing the room, including her housekeeper.

"Mrs. Marshcombe," she asked, "is it possible you still have the remains of our last Yule log put by? It has been so long—" Relia added, hoping she had not put her housekeeper out of countenance by asking.

"Of course, ma'am," Mrs. Marshcombe declared, as if the proper storage of a five-year-old charred bit of wood was a foregone conclusion. "Wrapped in stout canvas and still where I placed it when Lady Ralph last celebrated Christmas."

"Thank you," Relia murmured just as a shout arose behind her.

"It fits!" Olivia cried. "With scarce an inch on each side. Oh, well done!"

Relia swept through the crowd about the fireplace. Indeed, the Yule log fit to perfection. And high time she shook off the sad echos of nostalgia and did her duty as lady of the manor. "The wassail bowl is ready," she declared, raising her voice to be heard over the happy noise of satisfaction and congratulations. "My thanks to you all!"

The men swiftly doffed their caps, offering her appreciative grins and salutes before sweeping off in a general rush for the table set against the far wall that held a huge silver punch bowl, steaming with hot spiced wine. The table also groaned under a layer of meat pies, tarts, and other pastries that could be easily devoured by men who had done a hard day's work. Swiftly, Relia grabbed Nicholas and Olivia, pointing them toward the pitcher of spiced cider. But where was Thomas?

Being offered the first mug of wassail, of course. He raised his drink high, in salute to all those who had helped, before lowering his dark head to take a swallow of the heady brew. Another triumphant shout echoed through the festive hall.

Miserable man! Only a few days in Kent and he had won the men's good will. *Dear God, his hands!* Relia charged straight through the men crowded around the trestle table. "What have you done to yourself?" she hissed at Thomas, tugging on a cape of his greatcoat to get his attention.

"My dear, there you are!" he exclaimed, admirably playing his role in their charade.

"You're covered in blood," Relia snapped. "Come with me!"

Thomas held up both hands, one still clutching his mug of spiced wine. "An exaggeration," he proclaimed, regarding his hands with interest. "Nothing but a few scratches."

"Men have lost hands, even arms, for little more," Relia returned, transferring her grip to the sleeve of his greatcoat. "You may keep your wassail, but those cuts must be cleansed at once."

Meekly, and to the accompaniment of urgings from all those around him, Thomas Lanning allowed himself to be led away. But, once out of earshot, he said to his wife, "I am surprised you did not cart me off by the ear, my dear."

"I cannot reach that high," she retorted as she plunged down the stairs to the basement, still holding fast to his coat.

"Are you taking me to the dungeons?" Thomas inquired amiably as they continued down the long corridor, marked by closed doors on each side, barely visible in the dim light of a few tallow candles.

"Palladian houses do not have dungeons."

"I am relieved."

As the smell of roasting meat grew stronger, indicating they were approaching the kitchen, Relia opened a door and swept inside, still dragging her husband behind her. "Sit," she told him, indicating a plain wooden chair set under a long deal table whose finish had long since disappeared under numerous vigorous scrubbings. "No, wait!" Relia amended. "I will help you off with your coat, else you will have blood all over it. If you have not already," she added, casting a swift glance over him.

But the room was lit only by what little light there was in the hall, and she could see nothing. When her husband was seated, she took a spill from a jar and, obtaining a light from the hall candle outside, she soon had a candelabrum and an oil lantern casting their glow over the table. Visible now, though lurking in shadows, were row upon row of wooden shelves, lining two walls of the stillroom and holding a massive collections of glass jars filled with jams, herbs, spices, and medicaments reflecting the wavering light from the candles. From ropes strung across an ell near the fireplace depended a variety of plants, brought in from outside drying racks as winter approached. On a short third wall were two ceiling-high cupboards, filled with miscellaneous supplies. Along the outside wall was a cast iron double sink with its own pump, a long drainboard, and a cooling rack.

Although Relia did not consider herself an expert, she was proud of Pevensey's stillroom. Here, she and her staff were capable of maintaining a long tradition of efficacious remedies without having to rely on the area's aging doctor for every minor ailment. In fact, now that the only younger doctor in the neighborhood had gone off to the Peninsula, Relia suspected Pevensey Park was better off following the old ways than allowing the doddering doctor to come through the door bearing his box of leeches or with his lancet at the ready.

Thomas watched with interest as his wife retrieved clean cloths and a towel from one of the tall cupboards. She pumped water into an earthenware basin, which she laid on the table . . . and then she disappeared out the door, leaving him wondering. Somehow he doubted she had gone to find help, for she seemed surprisingly at home in this strange room with its heady mixture of intriguing odors. *Stillroom.*

He had never seen one before, but the name popped into his head. A traditional part of country living. He should bring the children here. They had no idea—

Relia interrupted his thoughts, dashing back in, a steaming kettle held fast in huge pads that seemed much too large for her hands. Thomas winced as the kettle wavered, the spout all too close to his lap, then heaved an audible sigh of relief as the boiling water made it into the basin. Relia set the kettle onto the table, tested the temperature of the water in the basin, added a bit more hot.

"Well done," Thomas murmured. "I had no idea doctoring was among your skills."

"Lighting a lamp? Pouring water in a bowl?" his wife scoffed.

"Ah—but I suspect you will manage the rest of it just as competently."

"If you did not have such soft hands, this would not have happened," she scolded as she dipped a cloth into the warm water.

"I must appear very feeble to a young lady accustomed to hearty country gentlemen," Thomas offered humbly, as his wife picked up his hand and began to wipe off the blood.

"If you'd ever done a day's work—"

"As titled gentlemen do," Mr. Lanning supplied.

Relia dropped his hand a shade too swiftly and took her time rinsing out the cloth before reaching for his other hand. "Many go to Gentleman Jackson's," she countered primly. "They fence, shoot, hunt."

"Make asses of themselves."

"Mr. Lanning!" Relia flung the bloody cloth onto the table.

"My apologies, my dear," Thomas sighed. "I could not resist. Please continue, for without the blood I can now see some of the cuts are a trifle deeper than I had thought."

Somehow the devil to whom she was married managed to assume a look so humble and woebegone that Relia found it quite impossible to stay angry with him. Or at least impossible to walk away and leave him to his own devices. But she had to repress a wicked smile as she reached for a bar of yellow soap that was far from the lavender-scented variety made for the bedchambers upstairs. Dipping a fresh cloth in water, she applied the soap liberally. This was going to *hurt.*

Blasted female! Thomas grumbled to himself. This was going to hurt, and he probably wouldn't even notice, as he was so distracted by the feel of her hands on his, the nearness of her—the two of them bathed in a pool of light in the center of a dark room seemingly cut off from the rest of the household. How strange that he should be alone with his wife in such conditions of intimacy, and he had not even planned it.

He could not quite repress a flinch as she attacked his right hand with the cloth. Nor did he fail to notice his wife's grimace of satisfaction. But, still, he couldn't think of a single place he would rather be. It was possible marriage had advantages he had not yet considered.

Other than the obvious.

If his wife was nearly seven months into her year of mourning when they had married, and he had stayed in London for six weeks, then her period of mourning must be—

His other hand screamed in outrage, but Thomas was too busy counting to pay attention. Three more months, or close enough to make no difference, before . . .

He'd been a fool to make such a careless promise. Trying to out-noble a nobleman, was he? Or demonstrating he was not impressed by her grandfather, the marquess, or by her titled parents? Or had he truly been so focused on what he would gain from this marriage that he simply had not cared? Women had never been more than a casual convenience, colorful beings to add grace and beauty to his surroundings and occasional spice at nights.

But this one—his wife, *Mrs. Lanning;* there! he'd actually said it—added spice even without warming his bed. If he weren't careful, he might actually like the arrogant little she-devil. As well as desire her.

Thomas broke off his reverie to discover that one hand was already covered in strips of cloth, and the other, slick with some mysterious ointment, was fast disappearing under a similar cover. "I won't even be able to eat!" he protested.

"Yes, you will. I've left your fingers free. But the basilicum salve will not stay on without the cloth, so you will simply have to make do."

"Yes, ma'am," said Thomas Lanning, hunching his broad shoulders and looking as if he had never thought to give an order in his life. "I suppose I should have stayed home and tended to my knitting—"

For a moment he thought the bowl of bloody water was headed straight for his face. But, obviously, his wife did not care to douse her handiwork along with his head, for she dumped the contents into the cast iron sink instead. "I will send Higgins to help you dress," she told him. "If only you had a valet!"

Another black mark against the vulgar Cit. Of that accusation, at least, he could plead innocent. "I have a valet," he told her, "but I sent him home to his family for the holidays. Oddly enough, I had thought our relationship might benefit from a bit of privacy." Thomas stood up. "I will welcome Higgins, however. Obviously, I had not thought of doing something so foolish as to injure myself bringing in a Yule log." He bowed and left her there.

By the time Thomas made his appearance in the festively decorated entry hall, he was once again himself. Confident, smiling, slapping backs in spite of his bandaged hands. A man of the people, waving farewell to the last lingerers with a grin on his face and strength in his step. His plans were all in order, and tomorrow was another day—

Ah, no. Tomorrow was Christmas Eve and the lighting of the Yule log for the twelve days of Christmas. Although two footmen and a bevy of maids were already at work cleaning the hall under Biddeford's watchful eye, Thomas paused in the middle of the tile floor, feeling very much alone. He was the stranger here. He had taken a great gamble—nothing so unusual for Thomas Lanning, of course—but this was the biggest risk he had ever allowed himself. And only the good Lord—or was it the devil?—knew how it would turn out.

Chapter Fourteen

*R*elia knelt on the tiles before the cold hearth of a hall almost as freezing as the winter night outside. Behind her, and above on the gallery, stood every member of her household, solemnly observing the first lighting of a Yule log at Pevensey Park in five long years. Biddeford stepped forward, proud and erect, to hand her the hotly glowing brand that was the last remains of the Yule log her mother had lit the Christmas before her illness descended upon them all.

Relia's breath caught in her throat. Her grip tightened on the slim, glowing remnant of wood, even as her hand shook. *Pevensey. Hers now.* Her responsibility to maintain tradition, even while lighting a symbol of the beginning of a new era at Pevensey Park.

Everyone was here. Watching. For, somehow, from Biddeford to the youngest tweeny, they all seemed to care. Gussie, Thomas, Olivia, Nicholas—gathered close in front of the hearth, as if she were rekindling the heart of the house instead of a huge green log that might be expected to catch and burn with great reluctance.

Relia blinked, forced herself to concentrate on the task at hand. With great care she set the brand to the piles of shavings, twigs, and larger kindling that had been placed around the great log. It must burn, and burn well. Fire—that age-old symbol of warmth and light, prosperity and good fortune. A pagan ritual adapted to the bright new world of the nineteenth century. And still casting its spell, Relia thought, for it was plain all present were caught up in the ancient magic, as huffing and puffing could be heard from all around her, as nearly every last soul joined the two footmen who were wielding bellows, coaxing the great log into life. A peek at her husband revealed that Thomas Lanning looked as eager as the rest, watching the softly licking flames with an encouraging eye, as if by sheer authority he could help the kindling do its job instead of being consumed to ashes, leaving the giant log untouched.

A third footman rushed forward with an armload of leftover greenery. Suddenly, Relia found herself swept up and away from the fire as the greens the footman was laying on top of the log burst into leaping flames. The pungent odor of pine filled the room, but Mrs. Thomas Lanning was too disconcerted to notice, for she was held hard against her husband's chest, and he showed not the slightest sign of letting her go.

Indeed, he was worse than The Terrible Twyford. How dare he display such intimacy in front of her entire household?

"It's a-catching, ma'am!" Tilly cried.

"I do believe she is correct, madam," Biddeford declared, but not before casting a minatory glance at the outspoken maid.

"See, there!" Nicholas pointed. "The bark's glowing—that little patch on the left."

Olivia, completely forgetting the ladylike manners Miss Aldershot had been attempting to instill, squealed with delight. The circle of servants in the hall and those lining the gallery leaned forward, nearly in unison, attempting to confirm the good news.

"Twelve days for sure," proclaimed the footman who had contributed the pine boughs. In triumph, he glanced at his mistress, encountering Mr. Lanning's eye instead. "Sir?" he inquired, stepping close in response to the unspoken order from the new owner of Pevensey Park.

"Mills, is it?" Thomas asked in a tone intended to be heard by as few people as possible.

"Yes, sir."

"Mills, I hold you personally responsible for seeing that this fire burns for all of its twelve days. Do I make myself clear?"

The footman grinned. "Yes, Mr. Lanning, you surely do. Twelve days it is. Watch it like a hawk, I will."

"Good man." Thomas released his grip on his wife. "Come, my dear. If we are to live without frivolity this Christmas, let us at least remove ourselves so the servants may enjoy their fun and games. Olivia, Nicholas, come along!"

"May we not have a glass of wassail?" Livvy protested.

"And I want to play games!" declared Nicholas, reverting on the instant to the sullen, willful boy who had descended from the coach only a few days earlier.

"Pevensey is still a house of mourning," Thomas informed him in the tone that reduced his junior clerks to little more than grease puddles melting into the office floorboards. "Your new sister has graciously allowed the servants to enjoy the old customs for Christmas Eve, but *we* will join her and Miss Aldershot in a quiet evening in the drawing room. You may, if you wish, Nicholas, retire to your room."

The younger Mr. Lanning, mumbling words Relia was relieved she could not hear, bolted up the stairs, scattering servants in his wake.

"My apologies," Thomas pronounced stiffly to his wife and Miss Aldershot. "He has much to learn yet."

"He, too, has lost his parents," Relia responded, surprising even herself. How odd. Instead of censuring the boy, she had no difficulty understanding how lost he must feel. His parents, his home, even his school taken away, only to be thrust into a house of mourning when it was Christmas and he was only twelve years old. "I think you should go to him . . . Thomas," she said, placing a hand on his arm. "There are, perhaps, things you, as brothers, should know about each other. And tell him"—Relia paused, her gaze drifting briefly toward the Yule log—"tell him I will arrange a party for the young people in the neighborhood for Twelfth

Night. And he and Olivia may help me plan the games and pantomimes and the food."

"It's discipline he needs," Thomas declared grimly, "not cosseting!"

Relia peeped up at her husband with a look that took his breath away. Intimate. No . . . wheedling, that's what it was. The wench!

"But it is Christmas, Thomas. And he is only a boy."

Thomas threw up his hands in the classic gesture of defeat. Not only was his wife being kind to his brother and sister, she was calling him by his first name. Deliberately, of course, manipulating him as easily as a puppet. Controlling little chit that she was.

"A party!" Olivia threw her arms around Relia. "Oh, thank you, thank you!"

Disengaging herself from her sister-in-law's embrace, Relia smoothed her lavender satin gown while composing her features. She had touched, and been touched, more times in the past week than she could recall since she was a child. It was . . . not unpleasant. There was surprising warmth in the human touch, like the glow spreading from the great log in the fireplace, licking at the icy edges of the frozen world of Pevensey Park. Yes . . . lurking at the edges of her vision she could see the ice cave that had formed around her. Like Merlin, she had been trapped inside. Seemingly forever. Yet now, by her own doing, she had cracked a chink, let in a breath of fresh air. A slice of light that threatened to grow and spread until . . .

Relia scrambled to regain her composure, ruthlessly blocking out the insistent brilliance of that narrow ray of light. "To show your gratitude," she said to Olivia, "you may play some Christmas tunes for us, while your brother speaks with Nicholas."

Reminded of his duty, Thomas headed for the stairs, albeit a bit reluctantly. What did he know about children? It was nearly twenty years since he had been Nicholas's age. Perhaps football or cricket? Did the boy hate Greek as Thomas had? Did he miss his mother—of whom no one ever spoke? Should he tell the boy of his new half-sister, born to his mother and her lover in Italy?

Yes, he should. Nicholas was old enough for reality. Perhaps, together, they could decide what to tell Livvy. They were, after all, the only remaining males of the Lanning family. As he walked down the hall to his brother's room, Thomas's step was far lighter and faster than when he started up the stairs.

Christmas morn was marked by a journey into Lower Peven for church, with Nicholas grandly perched on the box with the coachman, rather than being thoroughly humiliated by being squeezed inside between his brother and his sister. His spirits rose still further when, during their sumptuous Christmas dinner, he pulled the coin from the plum pudding and was promptly rewarded by a golden guinea from his brother's pocket.

In contrast, Miss Aldershot turned an unbecoming shade of puce when her portion of pudding was found to contain the traditional ring. "Absurd!" she muttered, carefully setting the tiny ring aside. Then, with the cool calm she had attempted to instill in her pupils, she picked up her fork and took a bite of the steamed pudding.

"Oh, no!" Livvy wailed, as she withdrew a miniature thimble from among a dark nest of raisins, fruits, and nuts. "That is not at all fair. Why should Miss Aldershot get the ring and I the thimble?"

"It only means you will not wed this year," Relia interjected hastily. "And that cannot possibly offend, as you will not make your come-out until a year from this spring."

"And I," said Thomas, "seem to have the button, which, as Miss Aldershot has pointed out, demonstrates the absurdity of this particular tradition, as I am already married, so can scarce remain a bachelor this coming year."

The words were no sooner out of his mouth than Thomas heartily wished them unsaid, for his wife was staring at him, openmouthed, in one of her rare unguarded moments. *Devil it!* It was plain as a pikestaff what she was thinking. They did not have a true marriage. . . . And this sad state of affairs was to continue for another whole *year*!

Only if he were dead and buried, Thomas vowed.

Yet . . . he bent his head to his pudding, lips twitching. It was not altogether unpleasant to discover that his wife had been stricken by the thought of continued celibacy.

If, of course, he had interpreted her expression correctly. Possibly, she had merely been appalled by the thought of Thomas Lanning across the table tomorrow and tomorrow and tomorrow, and was wishing him a bachelor forever, as, indeed, finding the button in the plum pudding was said to indicate in some parts of the country.

Though none would ever admit it, of those at Pevensey Park's Christmas table, only Nicholas truly tasted the rich ingredients of plum pudding on which Cook had expended both labor and love.

Neither the four Lannings nor Miss Aldershot had time for reflection on Boxing Day, as each of the servants, both inside and out, received a purse, with a little something extra this year for those who had helped with the Yule log. And this year Relia was able to give all the servants a day off, as there were enough members of her new family to help distribute the boxes to the poor, as well as the gifts she gave each year to her tenants and, particularly, to their children. If the sound of hunting horns or the sight of red-coated riders in the distance disturbed any of the Lannings, not a word was said. But, truthfully, Relia had been angered by the looks on people's faces when her husband had refused the squire's invitation to the Boxing Day hunt, delivered after church services the previous morning.

"I fear I do not hunt," Thomas had told Squire Stanton, managing to look both properly regretful and suitably honored by the invitation. "And I believe my wife wishes me to accompany her on her Boxing Day visits. There are, I believe, a few of our tenants whom I have not yet met."

"You do not hunt?" the squire barked, looking as outraged as if Mr. Lanning had told him he did not eat meat.

"I am greatly honored to be invited, I assure you. But I am a man of the City, born and bred. I promise you, I should make a great fool of myself if I went out with the hunt." Mr. Lanning offered his best smile, which, as Relia well knew, was formidable. "And probably be brought home on a gate."

"Well . . . can't have that, of course," the squire had mumbled, obviously making a heroic effort to hide both scorn and irritation. "Good day to you, sir."

Which was all well and good, Relia thought, for she herself was not fond of hunting—but she had looked around to discover condemnation on the faces of many who were just leaving the church. Obviously, the incident was an all-too-clear reminder that Thomas Lanning was not one of them, but a Cit who had married far above himself.

The hunting horns died away in the distance, and Relia's wandering thoughts were soon back to the duty at hand, as she introduced Thomas to the manager of their hops farm and processing barn, and to his wife, and promising family of four boys and three girls.

That evening the family dined on a cold collation, which they dished up for themselves, while the servants enjoyed the remainder of a well-earned day of rest. The following day was devoted to creating a guest list and to considerable haggling over plans for the Twelfth Night festivities, most of which Relia rejected out of hand. Livvy coaxed, Nicholas sulked, Thomas persuaded. Somehow the group of older guests—"But you cannot fail to invite the parents, my dear"—grew out of all proportion to Relia's original plans. The squire and his wife and children, of course, could not be forgotten. And the parents of the Trent children, Gussie added. And didn't they have a sister at home, widowed at Talavera?

"Is there not an earl about somewhere?" Thomas inquired blandly later that evening, as Relia sat at the delicate rosewood *bureau de dame* in their sitting room, nibbling the feathers of her pen and muttering over the scribbled additions to her guest list. "Are you on visiting terms with him, and does he have children?"

"Gravenham," Relia returned shortly. "And yes, we visit, and yes, he has children of a suitable age. But his second son is just home from the Peninsula, recovering from severe wounds, I am told. I doubt they will wish to come."

"It will do no harm to invite them. Perhaps they will do us the honor. After all, I am anxious to meet my neighbors," Thomas added suavely. "Attempting to fulfill my obligations, do the pretty, don't you know." He sketched a flourish with his hand, a salute in the style of a courtier of an earlier era.

He was mocking her again! That curl of his lips, the enigmatic gleam in his eye. If only she might peek beneath the façade for only a moment . . . and discover if the man she had glimpsed in Tunbridge Wells for so short a time after her near accident was truly inside.

Why she bothered to wait in her sitting room each evening she could not imagine! It was a lovely room, of course. Relia was pleased with her first attempt at decoration. No longer a lady's boudoir done up in delicate silks and pale colors, the sitting room was vibrant in shades of cherry and rose, accented with dark blue and cream—colors selected to match the fine new Axminster carpet. There was a sofa in French blue velvet, brightened by loose pillows in the same striped cherry-and-rose satin as the two wingchairs. The wallpaper was cream, flocked in dark blue, the draperies and deep swags of cherry damask. It was a room designed not simply for the lady of the house, but for a man as well.

Though why she should consider pleasing her husband Relia could only ascribe to her determined efforts to uphold her part of their bargain, even if Thomas Lanning was quite, quite impossible. To her, he was blasé, indifferent. Amused, but not amusing. Yet somehow each night, after dismissing her maid, Relia found something to do in the sitting room they shared. Lists, letters, a book to read before the fire. All while charmingly *en déshabillé* in the fine dark blue velvet dressing gown she had worn in Tunbridge Wells, or in one of several other equally charming confections she had acquired in London.

And although she shied from admitting the truth, even to herself, Relia ended each day in her sitting room because her

husband must pass by on the way to his bedchamber. She
had found him not averse to a few moments' conversation
before retiring, even though she found herself wondering if
he ever felt as awkward as she, as they moved cautiously,
tentatively, in a game more complex than chess. Explor-
ing—

He was staring at her, one eyebrow raised, undoubtedly
wondering to what far realm her wits had wandered. And
why.

"Very well," she murmured, and reached for one of the
invitations Miss Aldershot and Olivia had so laboriously
penned that day.

As Relia wrote, she felt a hand come to rest on her shoulder. Her pen wobbled, ink splattered. The searing warmth of
her husband's fingers promptly disappeared. "My apologies," Thomas muttered and strode from the room.

It was some time before Relia reached for a fresh invitation to inscribe to the Earl and Countess of Gravenham and
their family.

To Relia's astonishment, the Fortescue family accepted.
All of them, including the earl and the countess and that veteran of the Peninsular War, Captain Alan. News of such il-
lustrious guests sent the household into even more of a
twitter than it already was. Mr. and Mrs. Lanning almost immediately discovered one more bone of contention.

"We may not hunt or have a Yule log in town," Thomas
informed his wife, as they continued an argument, begun at
dinner, in the privacy of their sitting room, "but celebrating
Twelfth Night is a tradition with which we are quite familiar."

"This is a party for young people," Relia asserted. "We
are not going to have a bottomless wassail bowl!"

"But not all of us are children," Thomas reminded her.
"Surely the chaperones are to have something stronger than
cider. Somehow," he mused, "I cannot picture Gravenham
and his son or Squire Stanton—"

"There will be wine with supper—"

"And something stronger in the card room," Thomas declared. "You may stand a footman at the door to make sure none of the youngsters wander in."

"Thomas!" Relia caught her wail, stifling it into a gulp. "You do not understand. If we have a party for the adults, we are *entertaining*."

"Well, of course, we're entertaining." Puzzled, Thomas frowned down at his wife, who was once again seated at her small desk, working on a list of tasks still to be accomplished before Twelfth Night.

Relia plunged her head into her hands, the feathers of the quill she had been using sticking out between her fallen tresses.

"Oh . . . deuced dense again, am I?" Thomas muttered. "Once again, I have trod on your sensibilities. Yet . . . I think we cannot call it off."

"No, of course not." Though muffled, Relia's response was clear. She raised her head, pushed back her wayward strands of honey brown hair. "Gussie has begun to remind me, almost daily, that I cling too much to my grief. It is only right that you should have an opportunity to meet so many of the families in the county. Quite everyone has accepted. Indeed, I am surprised. . . ." Relia broke off, hiding her face as she once again bent over her desk.

"You are surprised they all agreed to come," her husband supplied. "Surprised they would honor the home of a Cit. Curiosity, my dear, simple curiosity. A trait found in high and low alike. Nor do they wish to offend a long-standing friend, of course." His wife, eyes averted, failed to see his conciliatory smile.

"Thomas?"

"Yes, my dear?"

"Why is it you accommodate yourself to everyone but me?"

Thomas did not pretend to misunderstand her. Placing his hands behind his back, he thought before he spoke. For once, he displayed not a single hint of amusement at her question. Truthfully, his wife was beginning to drive him mad. Lying in wait for him, expecting him to carry on a perfectly normal conversation in the intimacy of their private rooms, with her wearing . . . well, practically nothing.

Deliberately, Thomas allowed his slowly simmering temper to blot out the images threatening to overcome his good sense. It was time his dear wife heard some home truths. "I am accustomed to having the upper hand, Aurelia. Making plans, making decisions, giving orders. So are you. I am a difficult man. Arrogant, accustomed to having my own way. Ask anyone in the City and they will tell you so. Again, traits not unfamiliar to you. But, yes, I have learned to accommodate myself to those who can be of use to me. It is good business. But to those of my own family . . . I am not so adept. You must have taken note of my feeble efforts with Livvy and Nicholas."

"Yet with me you make no effort at all!"

"Not so!" Thomas's sternly disciplined calm, which had been dissolving as slowly but surely as the burning Yule log, totally deserted him. "Who has brought life back to this household?" he roared. "Renewed old traditions? Do you think I did this for myself? Solely for Livvy and Nicholas? You are an ice maiden, Aurelia. Frozen in time. A child who never wants her world to change. Grow up, girl. I am a man, not a puppet. And I want a wife, not a puling infant."

Appalled by his loss of control, Thomas plunged his head into his hands as his wife swept from the room, slamming the door of her bedchamber behind her. Hell and damnation, how could he have been such a fool?

In the few remaining days before Twelfth Night the strained relations between the master and mistress of Pevensey Park, never noticeably cordial, went unremarked in a household frantically preparing for its first party in more than five years. Only husband and wife were aware that when Thomas Lanning entered their private sitting room at night, he no longer found his wife bent over her desk or toasting her toes before the fire. Lit by a single wall sconce and the embers of a dying fire, that quiet haven, which had seemed on the verge of creating an aura of intimacy between them, was empty and chill. A silent reminder that the gap they were attempting to bridge was, perhaps, too wide. An insurmountable barrier erected by centuries of tradition, and all the more invincible for its invisibility.

Each night Thomas extinguished the candles in the sconce, poked at the embers in the grate, then stood for a moment, eyeing his wife's bedchamber door. Each night, he turned away, walking through the door to his own bedchamber, his grim face illumined by the single candle in his hand.

Chapter Fifteen

"*T*hat young scamp—beg pardon, madam!" Mrs. Marshcombe, the housekeeper, took a heaving breath that sent a ripple through the black bombazine covering her more than ample bosom. "Master Nicholas," she amended, "wishes to add Snapdragon to the games. I know 'tis none of my business, madam, but that boy's got poor Miss Aldershot wrapped round his thumb, he has. The games they have planned!" The housekeeper threw up her hands. "Needing something new every minute they are. And Snapdragon! 'Tis the devil's own brew, miss—madam! Raisins and brandy it is, and lit all on fire. And many a singed finger we'll have, and belonging to little Lord This and Lady That, I promise you. Weeping and wailing and gnashing of teeth is what we'll have, and all the governesses and nursery maids down upon us and the parents soon after—"

"Mrs. Marshcombe!" Relia cried, effectively stopping the spate of words and leaving her irate housekeeper with her jaw hanging open. "Surely I recall playing Snapdragon on many occasions in the past. Snatching the raisins from the flaming brandy was rather . . . well, rather exciting."

"And, as *I* recall," the housekeeper responded firmly, "year after year Master Twyford and his friends seized the raisins while the young ladies watched, offering noisy and inelegant encouragement to their favorites."

It was true, of course. Relia did not bother to repress her smile of nostalgia. For all Twyford was a spoiled bully, there had been some good times at the Christmas holidays. "I imagine it will be much the same this time, Mrs. Marsh-combe," she said. "Nicholas may have his Snapdragon. The boys will be daring, and the girls will cheer them on. Just be sure there is a footman standing by with a bucket of water."

"But, madam, they will *eat* the raisins!"

"Have you turned Methodist, Mrs. Marshcombe?"

"Indeed not, madam!" Another broad ripple of black bombazine. "But the brandy—"

"The brandy burns, Mrs. Marshcombe. It is consumed by fire, not by young stomachs."

The housekeeper sniffed. "Very well, madam." After a pause long enough to express her continuing disapproval, Mrs. Marshcombe curtsied and headed for the staircase to the kitchens below.

Relia sighed. They had been standing in the entry hall before the remains of the Yule log, now reduced to no more than three broken lengths of charcoaled wood. But the great log had made it through the twelve days of Christmas, whether on its own or by whatever encouragement—or possibly discouragement—Mills the footman had managed when no one was looking. Her husband had a way of making events occur as he wished—was that not why she had married him? Which was all the more reason his harsh words had hurt so ferociously. Thomas Lanning was a man who made things happen. If he wished to return to the rapport she had thought was developing between them, then surely he would have found a way to—

A scream. A shout. A drawn-out wail.

Relia picked up her skirts and dashed toward the commotion, flying past a bevy of maids poised with dust clothes in their hands as she hurried through two great salons before finding the source of the problem. A maid, wailing loudly, was sitting on the carpet, her apron thrown up over her face. Beside her two footmen scrambled about on all fours, apparently searching for something. Suspended only a few feet off the floor was the Venetian Murano glass chandelier, which evidently the maid had been cleaning in preparation for this evening's party. Even without its candles lit, the crystals, both clear and colored, sparkled in the sunshine from a southern wall of floor-to-ceiling windows.

One footman caught sight of his mistress, poked the other. The maid peeked out from under her apron, then renewed her wailing on a higher pitch. "What has happened?" Relia demanded. Both footmen spoke at once, to the accompaniment of the girl's sobs. "Mills, you first," she snapped.

"I was holding the rope so's Maggie here could clean the crystals, ma'am. And . . . and one of them fell," Mills choked out. "Jemmy and me was just trying to find it, but—"

"Mills, Jeremiah, you will lift Maggie up, please, and all of you step to the side. There . . . that is better," Relia declared, staring intently at the intricately patterned, high-pile Isfahan carpet onto which the clear crystal had disappeared as if by magic. Eyes left, eyes right. Slowly, Relia and the two footmen circled the area, willing the crystal to catch the light.

"There, ma'am!" Mills called, pointing. "You was right. Maggie was a-sitting on it."

Dropping to her knees, Relia picked up the two-inch crystal that had dangled from the lowest tier of the chandelier. She held it up to the sunlight, slowly turning it around as the three servants and those hovering in the doorways held their breaths. "It is perfectly fine," she declared, followed by whooshes of relief from all sides.

"My dear Mrs. Lanning, are you hurt?" cried a voice from the doorway. "Allow me to help you!" Charles Saunders rushed forward, arms outstretched. It was, Relia noted, the first time she had ever seen the solicitor lose his equanimity.

"Mr. Saunders! What an unexpected pleasure," Relia beamed, allowing Mr. Saunders to help her to her feet. "I am perfectly fine, I assure you. I fear you have caught us in the midst of a small domestic crisis, which is now resolved. Maggie, you will cease your caterwauling this instant. It was an accident. The crystal is unbroken." Relia handed the errant object to Mills with the adjuration to see it reattached to the chandelier immediately. "And now, Mr. Saunders, allow me to tell you I am delighted you have arrived just in time for Twelfth Night."

"And allow me to apologize for charging in, as curious as everyone else, to discover what the fuss was all about," said Mr. Saunders, white teeth gleaming beneath his patrician nose and clear blue eyes. "There seems to be a dash of knight errant in every man, I confess, although I am pleased to discover you have the situation well in hand." He favored Relia with the boyish smile that never failed to charm, even though she knew quite well that it covered an intelligence and a will almost as formidable as that of her husband.

"And is it not just like Thomas," Mr. Saunders added, "not to apprise you of my coming, particularly when I made such an effort to break away from my dear mama so I could be here before the others arrived. And, speaking of my mama, she would be quite horrified to have such an unexpected intrusion into a party of hers. If I have overset your table arrangements, I will dine in my room."

Relia, slightly overwhelmed by this torrent of words, assured Mr. Saunders his arrival was a delight, not an intrusion. "In fact," she told him, "you will balance the table, for Lady Gravenham has just sent a note requesting permission to bring an unexpected guest. My cousin Twyford."

"Good gad, I thought we had vanquished him!" Mr. Saunders exclaimed.

"Twyford tends to be irrepressible," Relia noted wryly. "He keeps popping up, like the proverbial bad penny. He quite delights in twitting me; he always did. Though how he has pulled the wool over Lady Gravenham's eyes I cannot imagine, for she has known him since he was in short coats. Ah, Biddeford," Relia added as she caught sight of the butler, who had been dealing with the hysterical maid Maggie and supervising the repair of the chandelier, "Mr. Saunders's room has been kept ready for him, has it not? And please inform Mr. Lanning of his arrival."

With a look that quite rivaled her husband's for bland suavity, Relia turned back to her guest. "Now tell me, Mr. Saunders, precisely what you meant when you said you wished to arrive before the others."

"I—I . . ." The London solicitor fingered his watch fob, twisted his neck as if his cravat were strangling him.

"We are expecting some colleagues down from London, are we not, Saunders?" said Thomas Lanning from the doorway. "If I am to spend time in the country, then the City must come to me. I did not speak of it, my dear, because they are not expected for several days yet. Time enough to prepare after we are done with tonight's party. Come, Charles, into the bookroom where we can talk without cluttering up Mrs. Lanning's preparations."

As the two men escaped—there was no other word for it—Relia watched with narrowed eyes. If the men coming down from London were candidates for the position of steward, she would be glad enough of it, for she was more than ready to turn over that particular burden. But somehow she suspected this was not the case. She sensed a mystery, a subtle undercurrent that prickled the air around her. If she were speaking to her husband in anything other than necessary monosyllables, she might have pursued the matter, but their current relations were strained, to say the least.

And tonight was the party. Yes, devil fly away with the man! Tonight they were entertaining everyone who was anyone in a goodly portion of Kent. For it seemed those without children must also be included lest they consider themselves excluded from the Pevensey Park visiting list. Therefore, Mrs. Thomas Lanning now found herself entertaining in a manner far beyond anything she had envisioned when she had made her rash offer of a Twelfth Night party for the children.

Papa, forgive me. I've tried so hard, but I've made a rare mull of it.

The look on Thomas Lanning's face when he gazed down the length of the dining table that evening and saw Mr. Twyford Trevor happily conversing with Miss Olivia Lanning, while sneaking glances down her thankfully modest décolletage, Relia considered well worth the annoyance of enduring her cousin's presence. She supposed that placing the two together was unworthy of the gracious hostess she hoped to be, but the temptation for revenge had been too great. Relia looked up to find her husband's lethal gaze fixed on her. With a gracious smile, seemingly perfectly oblivious to the lightning bolts cast in her direction, she turned her attention to Baron Trent on her left.

Later, said her husband's steely eyes. *Just wait till later!*

When Relia gave the signal for the ladies to leave the gentlemen to their port, Olivia and Chloe Stanton hastened off to join Miss Aldershot and the younger Twelfth Night celebrants, both girls having been easily convinced that their help with the children would be much appreciated. Truth to tell, they were not beyond the enjoyment of games, and airy promises from both Harry Stanton and Twyford Trevor to look in on the children's festivities gave added incentive to their excitement. The girls' departure, alas, left Relia to entertain a bevy of older ladies, with the Trents' widowed daughter, Jane Edmundson, the only person close to her own age. And Mrs. Edmundson, Relia thought, would be of little use, for she seemed a quiet slip of a girl who wouldn't say boo to a goose. And help was surely needed when, after forty minutes of music dutifully performed by Mrs. Lanning and several of the guests, Lady Gravenham turned to her hostess and declared, "Well, girl, what made you do it? Come, come, I am certain we all wish to know."

"My lady?" Relia lifted her head high and stared with limpid eyes at Captain Alan Fortescue's mother.

Lady Gravenham, a handsome woman just barely on the shady side of fifty, looked down her considerable length of nose and sniffed her disdain. "Do not dissemble with me, child. You could have had your pick of the *ton*, including your cousin or even the squire's eldest, yet you chose a Cit. Tell us without roundaboutation, I pray you, what made you do such a daft thing. Your poor parents would never have countenanced such a maladroit misalliance." All around the drawing room heads were nodding.

So this is why they came, Relia sighed. Just when she thought the shock of her marriage had dissipated—that the ripples on the smooth pond of life in Kent were going to be allowed to slide away unremarked. This must be where she was supposed to drag out the story she had hoped never to use except with Lord Hubert and his family. Somehow, here and now, it was much harder to tell, perhaps because the gap between herself and her husband had become a chasm.

They were all looking at her. Expectantly. Accusingly.

"Really, my dear," said Margaret Stanton, "I believe you owe us some explanation. All of us must live with Mr. Lanning in our midst."

"And do not tell us it was a love match," said Lady Trent, a gray-haired matron whose strident voice belied her wispy figure, "for we shall not believe you. The only glances exchanged between you and Mr. Lanning at table appeared to carry nothing but the gravest animosity."

Caught. As neatly as a gamekeeper's trap.

"You cannot know that, mother," said Jane Edmundson, quite unexpectedly. "You know couples are not expected to live in each other's pockets. And you also know there is a good deal of strain in entertaining. Just because Mr. and Mrs. Lanning have had a falling out is no reason to assert theirs is not a love match."

Oh, thank you, my dear Mrs. Edmundson.

Solemnly, as if from the witness box, Relia repeated the story of an old attachment between herself and Thomas Lanning that had been given to the Hubert Trevors. Then, in all fairness, since she was speaking to her closest neighbors, she added a bit of the truth. "Pevensey Park is a business. It seemed best to find a man of business to take charge."

"Your father managed quite well," Lady Gravenham pointed out. "As do all our husbands. What does a man of the City know about a country estate?"

"He is learning." And why on earth was she defending him? It was absurd. If only Captain Alan had come home sooner . . .

"Madam." Biddeford's voice interrupted the uncomfortable scene. "Master William Stanton has just poked Master Nicholas in the cheek with a billiard cue. The matter is not serious, but I felt you should know."

God bless all butlers!

Relia and Margaret Stanton dashed off to determine the

extent of the emergency, leaving the remaining ladies to continue to dissect their host's antecedents and their hostess's good judgment. By the time Mrs. Lanning and Mrs. Stanton returned to the drawing room, the gentlemen had just come bursting into the room on a wave of alcohol fumes and raised voices, the Earl of Gravenham preceding his host through the door. "Ah, ladies," he boomed, "we have had a splendid idea. What think you, Lady Gravenham, of having an MP for a son? There's a By-Election coming up for old Yelverton's seat. The squire thinks our Alan should run."

"How wonderful!" Relia cried. "You are quite correct. A splendid idea indeed."

"No, no," Captain Fortescue protested. "I cannot at all picture myself in Parliament."

The ladies, their attention totally diverted, protested loudly. The captain would be an ideal candidate for MP. They could not imagine why no one had thought of it sooner.

"Surely there would be no opposition," Lady Trent declared. "Who would dare run against the son of an earl, a wounded veteran of the Peninsular War?"

"I believe that would be I," Thomas Lanning said as the laughing murmurs of agreement began to die away. "I am the Whig candidate for Marcus Yelverton's seat."

Chapter Sixteen

*W*ith grim deliberation Thomas Lanning walked down the long corridor toward the suite of rooms he shared with his wife. His feet made no sound on the hall runner; his candle cast wavering shadows against the walls. Except for the silence, this, he thought, must be how prisoners must have felt on their last few steps to Tyburn hill. Pevensey Park's last astonished guest had departed long since; even the servants had sought their beds. But Thomas had lingered in the library, swirling brandy round and round in its glass, holding it up to the flickering firelight, then staring off into the dark corners of the room. He never touched a drop. He had had enough wassail for one night. Enough to make him careless. Enough to bring out the bravado he usually kept well hidden.

In front of the most powerful man in the district—the man whose son was likely to be his Tory opponent—he had announced his own candidacy for Parliament. He had taken a social affair that was intended to enhance his status with his neighbors—his voting neighbors—and managed to alienate them all when it became so glaringly apparent that his wife was as surprised as everyone else. And yet . . . what else could he have done? He *was* running for Parliament. And concealing the fact under such circumstances would have been worse, making him appear sly and devious—not at all the portrait of the sophisticated, knowledgeable man of the world he wished to present as MP for this particular portion of Kent.

She'd been splendid, of course, his wife. Aurelia Trevor Lanning—a lady to the core, revealing yet again her strong sense of honor. She had recovered swiftly, putting a fine face on it all. Calming Gravenham, who looked as if he were about to have an apoplexy. Bravely exclaiming about what an *interesting* By-Election this would be. And then there had been that moment in the general confusion following his announcement when Captain Fortescue had told his host, most discreetly, that he would visit him on the morrow. Now that was definitely interesting, for Thomas rather thought Fortescue meant it when he said he did not care to be an MP. And if so . . . there was no one else who could present a sufficient challenge—

He had arrived at the end of the corridor, where the narrow top of the T-shaped hallway led left and right to nearly invisible doors into their respective dressing rooms. The door to the sitting room, however, loomed straight in front of him. If he were a coward, he would sneak into his bedchamber through his dressing room . . .

But, of course, Thomas Lanning was not a coward. Not in business, not with people . . . but a wife was something else altogether. Aurelia had been avoiding him since his outburst a few days ago. Although he had sent her a written apology the following morning, the sitting room had remained empty each night, the door into her bedchamber firmly in place. For a few precious moments after her near disaster in Tunbridge Wells, they had hovered on the brink of openness with one another. Then he, who was never open with anyone, had retreated, shutting her out, even before he had fled back to London.

It wasn't that he did not want more from his marriage. She was a lovely creature. Soft skin, shining hair, eyes alight with intelligence . . . and barely concealed scorn. Pride had demanded he grant her a reprieve from her wifely duties. His body, however, had little use for such nonsense. Each day he kept his promise he was forced to draw further back. Each day the breach between them grew wider, more difficult to close.

But tonight . . . tonight she would be waiting. He could

have lingered below until Hell froze over, but still she would be waiting. The guilt was all on his side. And a most uncomfortable place it was—not at all where Thomas Lanning was accustomed to be.

Had Charles not warned him of the risk? Thomas took a deep breath and opened the door.

He was right. She was there, her midnight blue dressing gown a dark swath against the lighter blue of the sofa, her face a pale oval where it rested on a cherry red cushion, her nightbraids catching a glint of firelight. For a wild moment, unworthy of him, Thomas wondered if he could tiptoe on by, save this confrontation for morning. He was never to know what he might have done, for his wife's eyes flew open, and in an instant she was erect, sitting primly on the edge of the sofa, hands folded in her lap. Gray-blue eyes regarded him with considerable solemnity. She opened her mouth.

"Before you say a word," said Thomas, holding up his hand, "kindly allow me to explain."

"Explain?" declared Mrs. Lanning, her voice as steady as it was cold. "I assure you no explanation is necessary. You have used me quite brilliantly for your own ends. 'Tis perfectly plain now why you married me. In my naïveté I thought Pevensey Park was the attraction, but it was Pevensey's power and prestige you wanted, was it not? In fact, if Marcus Yelverton had not died, you would not have married me—"

"If Marcus Yelverton had not died," Thomas retorted, stung out of his bemused contemplation of his wife, "you would not have needed me. He was a good man, a strong one. It is one of the reasons I wish to take his place in Parliament."

She stared up at him, half her face illumined by his candle and the dying fire, half lost in shadows. "Then we are even, I think—you and I," she murmured. "Though how we will manage to go on I do not know. This is a far greater blow than I had expected."

"Aurelia—" Her eyes flashed at him out of the darkness. Thomas threw himself into the cherry-striped chair, which was angled toward the sofa. He leaned forward, straining to see her face. "Relia, you have a man's sense of honor. I admire that—immensely—but sometimes I wish you would scream at me. Rant and rave about what a thoughtless brute I am. Tell me that I have turned your peaceful world upside down. Instead, you absorb each blow that comes your way, straighten your shoulders, square that lovely little chin of yours, and determine to uphold your part of the bargain. This, you tell yourself, is the price you must pay for searching out a mate to save Pevensey Park. Well, let me tell you, my girl, even though I am a man who does not like to be gainsaid, your accommodation is positively frightening."

Daringly, Thomas laid a hand over hers. "Relia, look at me! It is all right to quarrel with me. I am just as much of an arrogant, unfeeling wretch as you think I am."

Her lashes fluttered. A quick peep, then her gaze returned to the large fingers clasped over her own. "I fear I do not know how to shout," she told him.

Thomas heaved a sigh. "Very well. . . . But I still need to explain why I did not tell you I was running for MP." Slowly, she nodded, but she winkled her hands out from under his, hiding them behind her back. Thomas leaned back in the wingchair, choosing his words with care. "Listen to me, Relia. I have never spoken to you about my life. I should have, but ours was a business arrangement—we both knew that—and our personal lives did not seem to enter into it. You deigned to trade yourself to a Cit in return for the enticement of a vast country estate. That was our bargain. It seemed unnecessary that you should know that I had no need of Pevensey's income. Or that I did indeed welcome the power and prestige that went with the estate. An arrogant assumption, I grant you," Thomas added quickly, "but I have long been accustomed to keeping my own counsel in business arrangements." He managed a rueful half-smile. "But I had no experience at all in being married."

His wife's nod of understanding, however slight, broke the dam of Thomas's long-held reticence. "I had not had any family life since my mother died when I was nine," he told her. "Again, a similarity in our situations which you can appreciate. And when my father married again, my life and his became almost totally estranged. I did not care for my step-mother, and when she ran off with Nicholas's tutor, I felt only grim satisfaction." Ignoring his wife's gasp, Thomas continued his confession. "I should have shown sympathy—for my father, for the poor abandoned children. Instead, I did nothing more than duty demanded, not even after my father passed on, leaving me guardian to a girl and boy I scarcely knew."

"You sent them away to school. And to Aunt Browning." It was an accusation, not a commendation.

"Yes. And Nicholas to strangers for his holidays, as his aunt would not have him in the house. Neither of the children was real to me. They were not part of my life. Which was all the more despicable, as I am not the vulgar self-made Cit you expected, Relia. My family has been in banking for three generations. I came into this world with more substance than most young nobles, and I was given the education and training to make the most of it. Which I have done. But I wanted no part of my father's other family."

"And then you received an offer of marriage."

Thomas allowed his gaze to wander over the delectable vision, so close, yet so far away. "And then I received an offer of marriage," he agreed. "And I began to think of the advantages for Olivia and Nicholas, as well as for myself. Livvy was growing up, soon to be ready for a come-out. And Miss Aurelia Trevor of Pevensey Park could ensure vouchers for Almack's and all that went with it. And Nicholas was beginning to cause enough trouble that I knew it was well past time I personally shouldered the responsibility. But I couldn't bring myself to mention them to you any more than I could mention my political ambitions. . . ." Thomas paused. *Devil it, but this was difficult!* "Truthfully, when Charles first brought the matter to my attention, I thought him mad. Marriage to some female I had never heard of . . ." One who was such an antidote she had had to employ a so-licitor to find her a mate.

"Then I began to listen, really listen. And I realized the match had possibilities. That we could be of use to each other. You needed a dragonslayer. I needed a family. You needed a replacement for Marcus Yelverton, and I was more than willing to be exactly that. Except"—Thomas shook his head—"by the time I met you and thoroughly embraced the idea, I was unwilling to take the risk of frightening you off. Bad news, I thought, could wait until after the wedding."

"But you said nothing, even then," his wife reminded him, unbending in her hurt and anger.

"Our acquaintance was so new, so fragile," Thomas murmured. "My courage failed me. There was time, I thought, plenty of time."

"I suppose one could consider it amusing," Relia noted, "almost as if Fate took a hand in your downfall. For it was then that Olivia ran away from her Aunt Browning and Nicholas got himself sent down."

"And my wife took them in and gave them a home. In spite of the fact that she was a very private person, who had, until then, led a perfectly quiet life." Silence held them both as, for a moment, they teetered on the brink of a better understanding. "But we were in the midst of the holidays," Thomas said, "and I was at last making some feeble progress in becoming acquainted with my sister and brother. And you and I were also becoming . . . better acquainted. It seemed an awkward time to talk to you about elections. I told myself that after the holidays would be soon enough."

Thomas's voice trailed away. There, he had said it at last. Perhaps now they would be able to find some point of reconciliation.

"Is this you, Thomas?" his wife asked, examining his face with care. "Is this the real person behind the façade? Or is this yet another face you are putting on to cajole your wife into helping with your campaign?"

Thomas blinked, drew in a sharp breath. "I suppose I deserved that," he conceded. "But, truly, Relia, you have heard it all. I have no more secrets." What an odd child she was. An indomitable spirit inside a porcelain doll. Grimly determined to do what was right. Yet so private, so sensitive. He was not the only one who masked his feelings. Would he ever discover what lay behind the Lady of the Manor?

And she thought *him* a mystery!

Hell and damnation, she was sitting there still as a stone, contemplating the blasted cushion as if it were the Oracle at Delphi. He had bared his soul, as he had never done with anyone before in his life, including Charles. What more could she possibly want?

One slim hand drifted out, clutched at the striped cushion, traced a seam. "I thought," his wife said softly, "that after the holidays you would return to London . . . and to your mistress."

"Beg pardon?"

"To Mrs. Ebersley. Olivia has told us all about her." Relia's fingers dug into the cushion as if she wished to do the same to his throat.

Livvy knew about Eleanor? How? Sister or no sister, he'd murder the chit with his bare hands!

And then it struck him. His wife *cared*. Or was she merely suffering from pride of possession? Was that not how she thought of him? An acquisition, bought and paid for? An upper servant somewhere between steward and governess?

Although Thomas had a bitter recollection of the last time he had lost his temper, his wife tended to precipitate emotions he could not control. Bounding to his feet, he paced the dimly lit room like a panther on the prowl, while his wife followed his progress with wide-eyed wonder, astounded, even fearful, because the mention of Eleanor Ebersley had provoked such an outburst. Truly, she had thought gentlemen tended to be sophisticated about their *chère amies*. He must love Mrs. Ebersley very much.

And suddenly he was there, hip to hip beside her on the sofa, his hands on her shoulders, turning her to face him. His fury—or whatever emotion had driven him—was gone, replaced by a look so serious it was clearly visible, even though the candles had burned down to stubs.

"Listen carefully," he told her, "for this is as sincere and truthful as you will ever hear me."

His hands tightened. Though there would be bruises in the morning, Relia felt no pain. He was so very close. He was *touching* her. Not as close as in Tunbridge Wells, but he was actually touching—

"It should be perfectly apparent to you by now," Thomas declared, his face hovering inches from hers, "that I am not in the petticoat line. If I were, I would be much more adept at handling the intricacies of marriage. My life is filled with business matters from morn till night. If a female has crossed my horizon on occasion, it is only because I am, in the end, made of flesh and blood. But from the moment I agreed to this marriage, there has been no one else. Indeed, Charles tells me . . . well, never mind that, but let me assure you I have no mistress except my work."

"A more formidable opponent, I think." Though where those words came from Relia did not know. It must be some strange wisdom brought on by the ambiance of intimate conversation in the wee hours of the morning, shut away from the world in their own private apartment.

"You have the right of it," Thomas admitted, his hands loosing their grip, falling to his sides. "The weeks ahead, the chaos of a political campaign will not be easy. I am aware the loss of peace and quiet will be offensive to you. I did not understand that when we were married. . . . I never thought—"

"And if you had, you would have married me anyway."

"Yes."

"Good night, Thomas," Relia pronounced, rising to her feet, carefully replacing the cushion against the dark velvet of the sofa, hiding her face as she did so. "This has been a most enlightening conversation. I assure you I will do my best to support you in your campaign."

"Good God, girl, you can't go off like that!" Thomas cried, jumping to his feet.

Relia picked up a candelabrum, whose flickering light played over her look of faint surprise. "And what else is there?" she inquired. "It is you who have set down the rules of our relationship."

She left him there, gaping after her, the great Thomas Lanning, Prince of the Exchange, outgunned by a chit of one and twenty. His wife.

Was she governed solely by the Trevor pride? he wondered as her door shut softly behind her, leaving the sitting
room in almost complete darkness. Or had there been an undercurrent of something more? Did she, perhaps, feel a stirring of tenderness beneath her anger?

Did he?

Damnably foolish question. He had found her appealing
from the first moment he saw her, else *nothing* would have
induced him to marry her. He would have found another
way to gain a seat in Parliament.

Thomas's bed was cold. And lonely. For a few fleeting
moments the very air had vibrated between them. The world
stopped, and his hopes soared. The burning inside him was
not anger. And then the clock ticked, and the Beauty beneath
his fingers was once again the Ice Maiden; he, the lowly
Frog.

A few steps. That's all it would take to go back, cross the
sitting room, enter his wife's bedchamber . . . end this stu-
pidity once and for all.

And what would she do? Scream the house down, or submit as a good wife should?

Submit. A shiver rocked him, but it was not from the cold.
Shakespeare had it right. *Oh, what a tangled web we weave.*
How would he ever find his way through the maze of pride
and arrogance, through the morass of nasty surprises and
hurt feelings?

The gray light of predawn was tinging the cold January
morning before sheer exhaustion overcame the turmoil be-
setting Mr. and Mrs. Thomas Lanning. Later, each would
look back on that evening's strained conversation as the last
quiet moment in the chaotic weeks to come.

Chapter Seventeen

"*C*olors," Livvy declared. "Bright colors to catch every eye. Indeed, you must have a whole new wardrobe, Relia, for Nicholas says Thomas cannot possibly win against Captain Fortescue unless you are there at his side, showing your support. You simply cannot go around looking like a raven strayed from the tower—"

"Livvy," her sister-in-law responded sharply, "you know quite well I have put off my blacks—"

"For grays and lavenders that quite fade into the woodwork. Truly, Relia—"

"Pray do not tease her, Olivia," Gussie Aldershot interjected. "A lady must always stop and think before she speaks."

Miss Lanning, who had been standing, arms akimbo, examining her brother's wife—who, quite out of character, was simply sitting in an armchair, gazing out at the frosted park—flounced across the morning room to drape herself artistically across the length of the rose damask sofa. She picked up a book, opened it with a flip that rustled the pages. The corners of her mouth drooped into a pout.

"Olivia." Relia bit her lip, tried again. "Livvy," she said, "I know you wish to help, but picture, if you will, what all our neighbors would say if I suddenly donned bright colors three months before the anniversary of my father's death. I would be condemned out of hand, even if there were many among them who did not themselves observe a full year's mourning for their departed. That is simply the way of the world. And I understand that the world of politics is far harsher than most. One single mistake could cost your brother the election."

Miss Lanning slammed the book shut, tossed it at the table, where it missed, falling to the carpet with a dull thud. "You are such a saint, Relia!" Livvy declared, tears springing to her eyes. "I swear I cannot bear it. You are even kind to the Beast, though how you manage it I do not know. I look at you, and sometimes I swear I see a halo shining over your head. You are too, too perfect. I can never live up to your expectations!"

"Oh, my dear," Relia cried, jumping up and dashing across the room, only to come to an abrupt halt a few feet from the sofa, long years of being alone keeping her from embracing her sister-in-law as she knew she should. "I am so far from perfection that I sometimes think I am doing absolutely everything wrong. Just ask your brother. I am certain he will tell you so."

"My brother!" Olivia cried. "Thomas quite worships the ground you walk on. Did you not know that?"

Which just went to show how mistaken they could all be, Relia thought. Perhaps it was best to let the girl keep her illusions.

"Ah, good, here you all are," said Charles Saunders from the doorway. "Mrs. Lanning, Miss Lanning, Miss Aldershot, please allow me to introduce Mr. Hugh Blacklock, who is to be Nicholas's tutor."

Even as she examined Mr. Blacklock, Relia was aware of a stirring on the sofa as Livvy came to attention, undoubtedly arraying herself just as she had been taught—back straight, feet together, hands artfully arranged in her lap. She should have done so for any guest, of course, but Mr. Hugh Blacklock was a striking young man in his early twenties, with enough countenance to send flutters through ladies far older and more experienced then Miss Lanning. Of medium height, he boasted locks as dark as his name, melting brown eyes, and facial features just enough off perfection to give character to his face. His eyes were alight with a natural curiosity about his new surroundings, and his lips curved into a friendly smile as he shook the hand Relia held out to him. It was, in short, impossible not to like Mr. Hugh Blacklock.

As soon as everyone was seated, Mr. Blacklock declared, "Please allow me to tell you, Mrs. Lanning, how honored I am to become part of this household."

"We are all gratified by your sentiments, Mr. Blacklock," Relia responded with an indulgent smile, "but I would have thought there are many households of greater consequence than our own."

Practically quivering with enthusiasm, Mr. Blacklock declared, "I assure you the opportunity to work for Mr. Thomas Lanning is much sought after, ma'am. As I am sure you know, he is financial adviser to the cream of the *ton*. The Prince of Wales calls him friend. Indeed, it is he who termed Mr. Lanning 'Prince of the Exchange.'"

"It is true," Livvy affirmed. "Thomas is invited everywhere. Perhaps you did not know that, Relia, living so shut away here in the country," she said, snatching at her moment of smug superiority. Which she promptly followed with an even more unexpected pronouncement. "And I expect you did not know our great-grandfather was Duke of Twineham, for Thomas never speaks of it. Your grandfather, Relia, was only a marquess, was he not?"

"Olivia, I believe this is not the moment for a discussion of respective antecedents," Mr. Saunders interjected sternly, as both Mrs. Lanning and Miss Aldershot appeared to have lost the power of speech. "Come, Mr. Blacklock, we will leave the ladies to their morning tasks. There will be plenty of opportunity for conversation at a later time." The two gentlemen bowed themselves out.

"Oh, was he not quite splendid!" Livvy cried, clapping her hands.

"Olivia," said Gussie Aldershot, as Relia was still sitting, looking down at her hands, seemingly oblivious to all around her, "why did you never tell us you were a member of *that* Lanning family?"

"But I thought you knew. Until I saw the look on Relia's face when Mr. Blacklock mentioned the prince."

"Perhaps you might tell us how this all came about."

"It is quite simple really," Miss Lanning said, confining herself to only one sly look at her sister-in-law. "My grand-father was a younger son who did not wish to enter the mil-itary or clergy. 'Tis said he was a brilliant student, gifted in mathematics, so he searched for a bride in the world of banking and found an only child who was heiress to an en-tire banking empire. My father did well enough following in his footsteps, but everyone says 'tis Thomas who is like our grandfather—truly gifted in commerce. He has enhanced the fortunes of all who have listened to his advice. And his personal fortune is immense. It is just that . . . well, he has never had time for anything else. I was astounded when he wrote to say he was married, for I could not understand where he had found time to court a wife—"

"Captain Alan Fortescue," Biddeford intoned, exercising his butler's discretion to interrupt Miss Lanning's waterfall of words.

Ruthlessly, Relia gathered her wandering thoughts and invited the captain to be seated. In spite of a pronounced limp, Captain Fortescue was a fine figure of a man. Tall, but still too thin from his long days of illness, with hair the honey brown of her own, and fine blue eyes with the pierc-ing yet vulnerable look of a man who has seen more of the world than he might have wished.

"I have come to see Mr. Lanning," the captain said, "but I asked Biddeford to show me here first, as I wished to ex-press my thanks for the delightful party last evening. My first in many months, Mrs. Lanning, and I truly enjoyed my-self."

"You are very kind, Captain, considering . . ." Relia paused, suddenly at a loss for words.

Captain Fortescue proffered a gentle smile. "I daresay the evening did not end as either of us anticipated, Mrs. Lan-ning. My father quite seized the bit and ran with it. But I am here to set matters straight. You need not fear that I mean to run in the election. After three years on the Peninsula, I wish only to retire to my own small manor and lead a quiet life. London is not for me. And the thought of standing up in Par-liament and making a speech quite sets my knees to quaking. Better to face a whole regiment of Boney's men, don't you know?"

"Nonsense. You would make a fine MP," Relia protested, even as she was swept by a wave of relief. How very odd. She was actually glad the captain was not going to oppose her husband. Which could only mean she wanted Thomas to win.

Which would be perfectly dreadful. Not at all the life she wished to lead!

Should she not, then, be wishing to share the captain's quiet life—thinking, yet again, what a shame it was that she had not waited for him to come home? But here she sat, rejoicing that the captain was bowing out, leaving the way clear for Thomas—who wanted political power so much he had been willing to marry a stranger.

My husband, the MP. How utterly mortifying to recognize that sinful pride was tempting her astray!

You are an insidious worm, Thomas Lanning. Burrowing your way into my privacy, forcing me to change . . . grow . . . move, most painfully, into a world I never wished to know.

By some miracle wrought by strict training in good manners, Relia upheld her portion of the conversation with Captain Fortescue. She smiled, wished him well in his continuing recovery. And sighed with relief when he took his leave and was led off toward the bookroom.

There, Thomas Lanning awaited him with considerable curiosity. And there, the two men drank Madeira and came to a surprising meeting of the minds. Long after the captain took his departure, Mr. Lanning sat at his desk, lips curled into the thin, calculating look his colleagues had come to recognize as the sign of intense action to come. There were difficult weeks ahead, but the biggest challenge had just taken himself out of the race. For who else could the Tories find to run?

Who else, indeed?

Relia tripped lightly down the stairs, then followed the various twists and turns of the flagstoned corridor that led to the estate room. Although she carried several sheets of paper in her hand, her mind was far from the gloomy underground hallway. Here, in the late afternoon, were the first precious moments she had had alone since her remarkable interview with her husband the night before. Even though she had no love for entering figures in the household accounts, she welcomed this opportunity to shut herself away from the bustle above stairs and contemplate what had happened in the wee hours of the morning.

She was, of course, furious with him. He had hurt her beyond redemption. And yet . . . her feet slowed, her heartbeat quickened as she recalled the feel of Thomas's fingers on her shoulders. Truly, she who had never fainted had almost done so. Only the Trevor pride had kept her from swooning at his Cit feet. Who would have thought that being alone with a man could be so . . . overwhelming?

That was certainly not the way she felt when Twyford had held her. And this morning it was as if she had seen Alan Fortescue through a glass darkly. He was everything she had ever wanted in a husband, the epitome of her girlhood dreams. As recently as over the holidays, she had castigated herself for not waiting for him to return. But this morning she had felt only the pleasure of renewing an old acquaintance. She had even been . . . disappointed. Yes, it was true. The great hero of the Peninsula had feet of clay. He wished to run away from life, whereas Thomas was ready to stand and fight—

Unkind. Each man must fight in his own way. Alan Fortescue on the field of battle, Thomas Lanning in the House of Commons.

And while she was being perfectly honest—she, Aurelia Trevor Lanning, was a fool. She had searched frantically for a port in her personal storm, yet when safe harbor was found, she had changed tack, turning her back. If anyone had sent her life spinning topsy-turvy, it was she herself. There was no one else to blame.

Relia opened the estate room door and charged inside on a wave of self-disgust. Skidding to an abrupt halt, she demanded, "What are *you* doing here?"

Thomas raised his dark head from the ledgers spread out in front of him. "Checking the accounts?" he ventured.

"Should you not be making plans for your campaign?" Relia bristled.

Thomas leaned back in *her* chair and answered with a slow smile. "I have a veritable army to do that for me. And it is the end of the year. I felt it my responsibility to be certain that all was right and tight." One dark brow arced in query. "Can it be I am encroaching again?"

Relia could feel her pale complexion turning some horrid shade of puce. "I—I—" She glanced down at the sheaf of papers in her hand. "I have not yet entered the servants' Boxing Day gifts," she murmured. "The party . . . the confusion. I am so sorry. . . . I fear the household accounts are not—"

"Good God, child!" Thomas crossed the room in a few strides, swept his wife into the leather armchair he had just vacated, then stood looking down at her, frowning mightily. "I have no interest in the household accounts, Aurelia. Before the new steward arrives, I wished to make sure that all was in order in Pevensey's agricultural accounts. I am well aware it has not been easy for you—"

"You did it on purpose! All these weeks without a steward. You wished to punish me for daring to want to manage Pevensey Park myself."

Thomas drew a deep breath, shoved aside a large leather-bound ledger, and eased himself onto the mahogany desk top. "Good stewards are not easy to find, Aurelia. Particularly one responsible enough to oversee all the enterprises at Pevensey Park."

"You are the great Thomas Lanning, are you not? Livvy, Mr. Saunders, Mr. Blacklock—all believe you walk on water. You could have had someone here long since, but you wished to demonstrate I was nothing but a foolish female incapable—"

"Nonsense!" Thomas roared, smashing his palm hard against the mahogany. Relia gasped. "Beg pardon," her husband muttered. "But how you can so willfully misunderstand—" He broke off, closed his eyes for a moment, sternly reminding himself that he was on the verge of losing what little gain might have been made last night. "Firstly," he pronounced with exaggerated clarity, "good stewards—of the quality you wish for Pevensey Park—must be found, then enticed away from their present employer. After that, at least a month's notice to said employer is required. That is only common courtesy. It is, therefore, nothing short of a miracle that we have found a man we believe will do. He is expected here within the next few days."

His wife's glare was lethal. "You have hired someone without my meeting him. Without my approval?"

"Devil it, Relia! If you do not like the man, you have only to send him away. Turn him off without a character. Let his wife and children starve, after he gave up a most satisfactory position in Yorkshire so he might come to Pevensey Park."

"You are impossible," Relia fumed. "No matter what I say or do, I am wrong!" She went very still as fingers brushed her cheek.

"How very odd, my dear. I feel exactly the same. We make a sad pair, do we not? Do you suppose all marriages have these struggles?"

"Probably not," Relia conceded. After a pause, she added grudgingly, "I suspect most wives are not quite so determined to have their own way."

A burning log sputtered in the grate. Wind whistled along the windows high above. "Strange," Thomas said at last, "but I find I cannot now imagine being married to a woman who defers to my every wish. I should, in fact, probably wish to strangle her from sheer boredom." He tilted up his wife's chin, studying her with a long, thoughtful look. "Do you think we might declare a truce, Aurelia, at least for the duration of the By-Election? I need your help, my dear. Your support."

"But if Captain Fortescue is not running, surely it will be an easy victory." Limpid blue-gray eyes stared directly into his own. But Mr. Lanning was becoming better acquainted with his wife's tricks, else he might have been diverted.

"Relia!" Thomas's fingers tightened on her chin. "Do you never stop arguing?" She ducked her head, leaving his hand dangling in the air. "Well? I want an answer, wife. We will not leave the matter thus."

Aurelia Trevor Lanning raised her head, stiffened her shoulders. "It will be as my dragonslayer wishes," she declared. "For the duration of the By-Election."

Thomas held out one large hand. To Relia, it seemed the size of her face. With ill grace, she grasped it. Suddenly, her imprisoned fingers were moving toward his mouth, lips touched her knuckles, lingered . . . and then her hand was back on the desk, and Thomas Lanning was striding toward the door, leaving her in a welter of account books. The Cit, who could read them as easily as Livvy read a novel, was abandoning her to the role she had insisted on assuming.

With a new steward bearing down on Pevensey Park . . . and her personal life at sixes and sevens . . .

Thomas had kissed her hand.

And declared the gorgeous, sophisticated Eleanor Ebersley a thing of the past.

He had declared a truce. And, truth to tell, it seemed about time.

I have a veritable army to do that. Thomas's words seemed to echo through the basement room. A noisy, conniving political army was descending on Pevensey Park. Along with a new steward and a tutor who caused Miss Olivia Lanning to lose, on the instant, all interest in Harry Stanton and Twyford Trevor.

A truce. If she bottled up her emotions over these various invasions of her privacy, Relia very much feared she would explode, rather like an inexpertly bottled jug of wine.

But they had shaken hands on it. And . . . well, other things—silent, private things—had passed between them at that moment. Like her marriage, they had just made a bargain.

Chapter Eighteen

"*T*homas! Thomas!" Charles Saunders cried, charging past the astonished Biddeford to burst into the book-room. "You will not credit it. I have just come from the village. Gravenham was so incensed over the captain's refusal, he has chosen the first alternate in sight." Mr. Saunders paused, waiting expectantly for his friend's perspicacious mind to leap to the correct conclusion.

"He would not be such a fool," Thomas enunciated slowly. "Never!"

"Ah, but he is," Charles told him. "Gravenham roared so loudly his entire household could hear him, and the village is talking of nothing else. In the midst of railing at his son, the earl clamped his mouth shut, turned to Trevor and barked, 'You! You'll do. My son may run off and hide, but I *will* control the borough! My name, combined with yours, boy, is all you need to win the seat.'"

Mr. Saunders sank into a soft leather chair, while his employer swore imaginatively and colorfully. "Trevor is from Sussex, is he not?" Thomas said at last.

"As you are from London."

"Our election laws are in sad need of reform, Charles," declared Mr. Lanning, with considerable irony.

Mr. Saunders made a noise that could only be described as a snort. "Our election laws are a frightening hodge-podge needing sweeping reform from the Highlands to Land's End. That is, as I recall, one of the reasons you wished to run for office."

After a few moments of glum silence, Thomas asked, in uncharacteristically plaintive accents, "Did we not banish The Terrible Twyford, Charles? I am unaccustomed to being such an inept dragonslayer."

"I am beginning to fear there is only one way to banish him, and that, my friend, is a path we cannot walk."

Thomas tapped a thumb against his lips, his gray eyes reflecting the depths of an arrogant, stubborn determination second to none. "Then we must do it at the polls," he said.

"This borough is even more peculiar than most," Mr. Saunders replied, with a shake of his head. "The earls of Gravenham controlled the vote for years, but they grew complacent, forgot their obligations, and Yelverton beat out the Tories by a goodly margin. Gravenham's determined to get the seat back."

"And yet some of his tenants must have voted independently," Thomas mused. "We must make certain they do so again."

"As they will, if you are generous in your largesse, munificent in your promises, and lay on ample amounts of charm, as well as pounds sterling."

"Delightful." Thomas lowered his head into his hands. "I wanted this, did I not, Charles?" he added softly. "I have turned my life upside down so I could run for Parliament. I have acquired vast country holdings I did not want. I have married—"

"And gained a great deal even if you never become an MP."

"Thank you, Charles. What would I do without you to provide my conscience?" The sarcasm was tossed like a knife from Mr. Lanning to his long-suffering solicitor.

"Our agents and workers will be arriving over the next few days. We will canvass door to door, stand drinks every night at The Hound and Bear. Perhaps an assembly or two. A picnic party in the park would have been splendid, but the timing is wrong," Charles sighed. "But perhaps a parade, handbills . . . and you must think of some good works. You will recall we spoke of this in London. Something grand—

enlarge the village school, add to the bells in the steeple, a new organ, an almshouse—"

"I am a wealthy man, Charles," Thomas groaned, "but you would bankrupt me."

"You could buy and sell Gravenham three times over," Charles declared. "Believe me, I investigated the costs when you first spoke of running for MP. Funds are not a problem."

Thomas nodded, but did not raise his dark head from his hands. "You are aware," he said, "that my wife is going to hate every moment of this campaign. And likely every moment of being a political wife thereafter."

"Mrs. Lanning is a lady who always does her duty."

"Yes, of course," Thomas murmured, his fingers clutching at his hair. Aurelia and her blasted sense of honor. Aurelia, the Ice Maiden. Lady of the Manor in inch-thick armor. His wife.

His penance.

He couldn't look at her now without being consumed by guilt. No matter. Once he won the election, he would go back to London, leaving her at Pevensey Park, as she so clearly desired. They would lead separate lives, as so many married couples did. An occasional visit, of course, to ensure continuation of the line. . . .

"You're smiling," Mr. Saunders said. "What miracle has brought that about?"

"Just a thought that crossed my mind, Charles. Just a thought."

On the fifth day after Twelfth Night, Relia looked down the length of her greatly expanded dining table, rejected an almost overpowering urge to grimace, then firmly replaced her inclinations with a gracious smile, albeit a trifle wan. To her right was Mr. Carleton Westover, her husband's Election Agent—a tall, distinguished man of indeterminate years, whose streaks of gray hair merely added authority to a dynamic and commanding presence. Gussie Aldershot had taken one look at Mr. Westover when he arrived and tottered off to her room, later sending word that she would not come down to dinner. Relia, respecting her companion's privacy, had not pressed the matter. Tomorrow, however . . .

With a table predominantly male, there had been no hope of balance, so Thomas had allowed Nicholas to join them, remarking that the boy might as well learn about politics. Olivia and Relia, therefore, were the only ladies in a veritable sea of males. On Thomas's right was Thaddeus Singleton, a writer. Speeches, squibs, handbills, poems, newspaper articles, he told her grandly—everything a candidate needed in the way of words. A man in his mid-forties, Mr. Singleton was short of stature, almost as broad as he was tall, and in imminent danger of becoming completely bald. But he brimmed over with confidence and loquacity, his stream of conversation providing a steady drone over which all others must attempt to converse.

Nicholas, seated next to Mr. Singleton and almost opposite his sister, was, Relia noted with considerable interest, as animated as the day he had helped bring home the Yule log. Evidently, like his brother, he found politics fascinating. Never . . . absolutely never would she be able to understand why! The other newcomer at the table this evening was Mr. Patrick Fallon, an Englishman of Irish ancestry. His job description, when offered to Aurelia at teatime, was so vague that she had not been able to make sense of it. But, interpreting the sly smiles, the winks and nods exchanged by the other newcomers during Charles Saunders's glib introduction, she could only suspect that Mr. Fallon was the man who handled the aspects of the election campaign that were not discussed in the drawing room. This suspicion might, of course, have been augmented by the very large, very brawny behemoth who hovered at Mr. Fallon's side, a man who topped even her husband by several inches and at least three stone in weight. He had a face that looked as if he had spent his life in the prize ring. His name, Mr. Saunders told her, was "Big Mike Bolt." The man-mountain had promptly tugged his forelock, obviously fearing to take her delicate hand in his. His relief, when swept below stairs by Biddeford, was patently obvious.

Thaddeus Singleton's voice rose above the others. "We

need an artist, Lanning. And a musician," he boomed. "I can write, but I cannot draw worth a brass farthing. We must have cartoons, caricatures of this Trevor. I understand there's enough material to draw on! And songs. Poems alone won't do, no, indeed. We need music, catchy tunes for people to sing. We'll parade 'em down the street with your colors flying—"

"A fine picture, Singleton," said Mr. Westover, "but we must move one step at a time. First, we must form a committee, with strong locals we can trust. And we must listen to what they have to say. Nothing riles up the local electors more than someone dashing in from the outside and telling them what to do."

"He is right, you know," Thomas said to Mr. Singleton. "The earls of Gravenham have greatly influenced the vote for more years than any of us have been alive. In order to win, we have to cultivate every last freeman in the borough."

"You are wrong," Relia said to Mr. Westover in a voice that carried the length of the table. "Nothing riles the local freemen more than being ignored by their supposed aristocratic patron, Lord Gravenham. He has expended little money and less energy in cultivating the vote in this borough. That is why his candidate lost to Marcus Yelverton in the last election. I heard Mr. Yelverton and my father speak of it many times."

Thomas leaned back in his chair and regarded his wife with the amused expression she found intolerable. "My dear, I had no idea you knew anything about politics."

"I don't, nor do I want to," she snapped, much stung by his despised patronizing look.

"But my dear Mrs. Lanning," cried Mr. Singleton, "you will be an immense asset to your husband in this campaign. A lady's touch is just what is needed, I assure you." Smoothly, he turned a beaming smile on Olivia. "And Miss Lanning's also. Lovely ladies standing by the candidate's side are precisely the image we want. They are a glowing example of womanhood, an inspiration to all those of lesser stature. Beauty, elegance, noble bearing. The men will be dazzled, the women charmed." Thaddeus Singleton waved a hand above the table, nearly oversetting his wine glass. "And if you do not think women have an influence over how their men vote—"

Thomas grabbed the swaying wine glass, as Mr. Westover interrupted the spate of words. "I am certain Mrs. Lanning will be happy to do all she can, Singleton, but you will leave her role in this election to me. And to Thomas. We will not discuss it again at table." The momentary silence following this pronouncement left no one in doubt about who was in charge of Thomas Lanning's campaign.

"I draw," ventured Hugh Blacklock. "And I've a sketchbook full of caricatures. It seemed a talent I would never use, but I should be happy—"

"Excellent," Carleton Westover beamed. "You may show them to me directly after dinner. A resident artist would be most convenient."

"Now all you need is a musician," said Patrick Fallon.

"And some locals willing to serve on our committee," declared Charles Saunders, who was seated to Relia's left.

"Do you not have to choose colors?" Livvy asked, speaking up for the first time since the table conversation became general.

"Blue," Nick declared. "Everybody likes blue."

"What do the Tories use?" Fallon asked.

"Burgundy and gold," Relia supplied.

"Blue and white, blue and tan, blue and yellow?" Thaddeus Singleton threw out.

"Blue and red?" Nick said. "Like the flag?"

A general chorus of *aahs*. Eyes gleamed. "By Jove, perhaps the lad's right," said Mr. Fallon.

"A bit bright, but I like it," Thomas agreed. "Nicholas, we thank you. Choosing the right colors is not only important, but it lets us move forward with the banners. Which, I am assured by my faithful town crier"—Mr. Lanning tossed a conciliatory grin at the chastened Thaddeus Singleton—"is of utmost importance."

"Ribbons and cockades," Fallon added. "And we'll find people to paint our colors on the handbills with your picture." He broke off, turning to Hugh Blacklock. "Do you do portraits, as well as caricatures? We need a noble view of our candidate."

"I shall most surely try," said Mr. Blacklock earnestly. Turning to his employer, he inquired, "Can you manage a sitting in the morning, sir?"

"I can see by the anticipatory grin on young Nick's face that I must agree," Thomas declared. "No doubt this education in politics will do him more good than the lessons he will be missing."

"The time of year is unfortunate," Mr. Singleton sighed, looking doleful. "Saunders was saying your park fairly begs for a lawn party, Mrs. Lanning. Such an event would have garnered a great many votes."

"Could we not have a skating party?" Livvy asked.

Thomas offered his sister an indulgent smile. "I fear that many people would shatter the ice of our small pond. We would drown our electors rather than secure their vote."

"But it snowed again last night," Nick said. "We could have sleigh rides and sledding. There's a fine hill out beyond the ha-ha."

"Do you skate, Thomas?" Relia inquired sweetly into the silence following Nick's suggestion.

"I'd fall flat on my—" Thomas bit back his words, adding ruefully, "in front of all the constituents."

"Do you have a sleigh, Mrs. Lanning?" Carleton West-over inquired.

"Yes. At least I think so. It has not been used in many years. And there are sleds somewhere, I believe—"

"And we could borrow from the Stantons," Livvy cried. "On Twelfth Night Harry mentioned organizing a sleigh ride sometime soon," she added on a blush.

"We certainly need the squire's support," Thomas mused.

"The Stantons dislike my cousin Twyford," Relia said. "It is doubtful they would support him. And the Trents are staunch Whigs," she added thoughtfully. "It is possible they, too, would contribute."

"If necessary, I'll buy new," Thomas declared. "I like this idea. Livvy, Nick, I thank you." Then, tempering his enthusiasm, Mr. Lanning studied his wife. "Is this feasible, my dear? Can we manage hot food and drink for such a crowd? Fires and shelter for the faint-hearted? I know how much work a simple Twelfth Night party caused. . . ."

Mrs. Lanning's serene expression never changed. "Of course," she told him. *Monster!* He knew quite well she could not resist such a challenge to her management skills. Nor could she resist his open, if manipulative, attempt to placate her by consulting her opinion. *Impossible man!*

Her husband would make a superb Member of Parliament. Born to guile.

"And what if it warms up and rains away the snow?" Mr. Singleton inquired, patently enjoying his role as the Voice of Doom.

"You are paid to look on the bright side," Thomas told him a tad sharply. "You write glowing words about me, while making dire accusations about my opponent. Which, believe me, is an easy task. Do not trouble yourself about the weather. I shall ask the vicar to pray for us. I understand that, his cloth not withstanding, he is a devoted Whig. Most odd for an Anglican clergyman, but in this case, quite true."

For perhaps the hundredth time Relia wished she could tell when her husband was joking.

Thomas looked up, caught the gaze of his Election Agent. "Ah, Westover, are you about to tell us you do not care for our scheme?"

"Not at all," said Carleton Westover. "There is little so effective as an expensive treat for the electors and their families. You will have to do more, however. Some lasting project, I think. Something the constituents can see and admire every day . . . something to improve their lives."

Thomas's nod was echoed by the other men at the table, even young Nick demonstrating his understanding of this aspect of courting the vote. Livvy was frowning. Relia looked thoughtful. A long-term benefit to the borough? If politics could accomplish that, perhaps it was not as much of an anathema as she had thought. And . . . she knew the very thing!

"What's burgage?" Nicholas's demanding voice, plainly

lacking in proper dinner-table manners, interrupted Relia's thoughts. But before she could chide him for interrupting the men's conversation, Carleton Westover spoke up.

"In some boroughs, young man, votes are tied to a specific piece of property. Whoever owns that property—even if the building where a voter once lived is now used only as a barn, or is perhaps nothing more than a tumble-down chimney or a pile of rocks—has the right to vote. Those are said to be Burgage Boroughs."

"And then," said Thomas, eyes twinkling, "there are Scot and Lot Boroughs and Potwalloper Boroughs."

Nicholas blinked, grinned, then demonstrated that behind his frequent sullens was a wit that would one day rival his brother. "Does that mean that anyone who can wallop a pot may vote?"

"Exactly, my boy!" Patrick Fallon chortled. "A man must only attest that he is head of a household and has a pot to cook in. A far more fair and equitable means of choosing electors, to my way of thinking, than ancient burgage rights."

Nicholas frowned. "What was the other one you mentioned, Thomas?"

"Scot and Lot, boy. In those boroughs a man may vote if he has enough substance to pay the poor rate."

"In other words," Relia declared, "our methods of selecting voters are a maze of inconsistency. Yet not a one of them includes females."

Every male face, including young Nicholas's, went blank. Livvy's mouth fell open. "I fear, my dear," said Thomas, at his most bland, "that even if I should win this election—and even if I should succeed in accomplishing much-needed reforms—the vote for females is quite out of the question. Not in our lifetimes at least."

"Good God, I should hope not!" cried Patrick Fallon.

"Women are very important, however," said Charles Saunders, ever the peacemaker. "Any assistance you are able to offer in this campaign, Mrs. Lanning, would be invaluable. Yours is an old, established family, with a vast number of tenants and employees. Although this is a Free-

man Borough, Gravenham controls most of the ancient burgage rights. He did not exercise them in the last election, but
since his candidate lost, who knows what he will do this
time? I fear Singleton was right. Your style and elegance, the
woman's gentle touch, would work wonders with the voters." Charles executed a half-bow, proffered his open and
patently genuine smile. "I assure you, the electors cannot
fail to be charmed."

"Charles!" Thomas barked from the far end of the table.

Carleton Westover, an interested observer of Mr. Saunders's remarks and of Mrs. Lanning's expression, looked
thoughtful. His employer's instructions regarding his wife's
role in the campaign had been vehement. Yet . . .

"I believe, Thomas," said Mr. Westover, "that you may
wish to rethink the matter of your wife's participation. I am
quite certain Mrs. Lanning is a lady of great pride. A lady
who has no desire to be the wife of the losing candidate for
Parliament."

Chapter Nineteen

$\mathcal{A}$s if a general political conversation at the dinner table were not sufficient breach of proper conduct, later that evening Relia and Livvy suffered the ignominy of having their most skilled efforts on the pianoforte go unheard and unnoticed. The men, huddled in deep discussion over the intricacies of something called the canvass, did not even lift their heads when the two women exchanged exasperated looks, then exited the drawing room. Relia's visit to Gussie Aldershot was equally frustrating. A sudden indisposition, her friend and companion murmured. It was nothing. She would be her old self in the morning. Relia was still frowning over this patent untruth while she allowed Tilly to prepare her for bed.

"The new dressing gown arrived today, ma'am," Tilly announced with some glee. "The quilted rose satin with the Chinese embroidery. Right gorgeous it is, too." With a grand flourish the maid swirled the dressing gown off the bed and held it up, turning it around so her mistress could admire the full length of the intricate design on the back. "Mr. Lanning'll figure it money well spent, I promise you."

As Relia allowed Tilly to slip the new dressing gown over her nightwear, she noted in her full-length cheval glass that her cheeks were the same rose red as the satin. Drat the man! Even with a truce in effect their lives were awkward. As if they were attempting to walk along the top of a wooden fence, teetering one way, then the other, constantly searching for balance. Always on the edge, gazing longingly, hopefully, at the safety of firm ground below.

At least tonight she would not have to manufacture an excuse to linger in the sitting room. Relia dismissed Tilly, then settled at her *bureau de dame*. She lit a brace of candles and began to record the endless lists necessary to organize a Winter Festival to which every freeman and his family would be invited. Copious quantities of food and drink, activities for every age group, sports and games that could be played in the snow. Or on ice. Bonfires—yes, definitely bonfires—and where they might safely be lit. A list of those from whom they might borrow sleighs and sleds. Surely her old one-seat sleigh was still in the stables somewhere. How she had loved gliding along, a groom trotting beside her pony—almost as if . . . ah, yes—as if she had acquired fairy wings and was flying above a sea of ice crystals.

Relia smiled and made another note. No doubt the mothers would queue up for the opportunity of allowing their little ones to ride in her elegant miniature sleigh. And return home with warm memories of Pevensey Park. And not be averse to whispering kind words in their husbands' ears about Thomas Lanning's candidacy. Perhaps in the dark of night, in the warmth of the marital bed . . .

Relia was swept by an even stronger wave of heat than the rosy blush that had matched her new nightrail. *Impossible man!* As if she truly cared if he won or lost. She forced herself back to the list at hand.

Her pen was still scratching away when Thomas entered the room. Wearily, he pulled up a chair, turned it around, and dropped into it, folding his arms across the back. A barricade? Relia wondered. If he needed one, that was perhaps all to the good. Or was it simply the lateness of the hour and her brain turning fuzzy?

His gaze moved appreciatively from her face, past her shoulders, down to the point where the hem of her rose satin dressing gown lay in graceful folds against the carpet. "My head may be whirling with the idiotic intricacies of politics," her husband said, "but I am still capable of noticing your new finery. Most attractive, my dear. An excellent choice."

"I am indeed surprised you noticed," Relia responded coolly.

"A-ah!" Thomas nodded sagely. "We were shockingly rude, I daresay. Rattling on about committees, canvasses, and charity projects with not a thought to the ladies amongst us."

"Indeed you were."

"So you took yourself off without so much as a 'Good night, sweet prince.'" Mournfully, Thomas shook his head.

"I will take myself off to my grandmama in Bath," Relia snapped back.

Thomas chuckled. "No, you will not, for you would be certain we were tearing Pevensey Park to bits in your absence. And"—he cocked his head to one side, examining her face with some interest—"I do believe Westover is right. You would not wish to miss the excitement of helping your husband become an MP. Nor the triumph when I win," he added softly.

"Speaking of winning," Relia said, ignoring her husband's annoyingly sharp assessment of the situation, for which she was unable to summon a suitable retort, "I know what charity work you should pursue. Mr. Yelverton first proposed it, and Papa was going to pay half the cost. An almshouse," she declared. "The expense of building and upkeep are great, I know, but it is much needed—"

"An almshouse?" Thomas straightened in his chair, frowning thoughtfully.

"I am sorry," Relia apologized. "It is probably more than you can afford, but you could use funds from Pevensey, just as Papa was going to aid Mr. Yelverton, and—"

"Mrs. Lanning," Thomas pronounced, "have I told you you are a remarkable woman?"

"I am arrogant, independent, sharp-tongued, and stubborn. I can assure you no one, including yourself, has ever termed me 'remarkable.'"

"Then consider it said." Thomas proffered a lopsided smile. "We will be assembling an election committee in the next few days. If they give their approval, an almshouse it is. And, Relia . . . I do not need funds from Pevensey Park to build it. I never needed funds from Pevensey," he added, "though I assure you I fully appreciate its value." *Ah, good.*

His wife was looking thoughtful, assimilating the wonder of a husband who did not need her money.

"There is another matter," Thomas said. "Have you spoken with Miss Aldershot this evening?"

Thomas could clearly see the play of emotions as his wife's thoughts changed direction from his wealth, to puzzlement, to dawning understanding. Suddenly, her eyes snapped fire. "Do not tell me you have learned what I could not!"

Thomas shrugged. "We were all tired, we'd drunk a bit more than we should have. Westover was last to take himself off to bed . . . and eventually a bit of the story came out."

Fascinated, Relia leaned forward—a mistake, as she found herself only inches from her husband's lips. Swiftly, she straightened her back to ramrod, clenched her hands in her lap. Thomas, she noted, was wearing his amused look again. "Well?" she demanded.

"It seems Westover and your Gussie were childhood sweethearts, but he was full of dreams and ambition, and must be off to London. She was tied down with an ailing mother and could not leave home. And, as happens, he was dazzled by the city, letters were severely restricted by her father, Other Interests came along."

"For *him*," Relia interjected bitterly.

"Naturally," Thomas murmured. "It is always the fault of the man, is it not?"

"Do you think . . . is it possible there is still some interest there?" Relia asked, making a valiant effort to recall that she and Thomas had declared a truce.

"I have never before seen Westover even close to maudlin. He was tonight. I believe he was quite as shaken as Miss Aldershot."

"And Livvy has fallen under the spell of Mr. Blacklock," Relia sighed.

"Good God!"

"'Tis far better than her making sheep's eyes at The Terrible Twyford, I do assure you."

Thomas groaned and dropped his chin onto his folded

arms. "Ah, Relia, what have I done to you? If I were the devil creating a hell designed exactly for you, with all the things you hate most, I could not have done a better job."

Mrs. Thomas Lanning stared at her husband for some moments. In spite of the lateness of the hour and the amount of drink consumed, his eyes were wide open, studying her as intently as she was studying him. "You know, Thomas," she said at last, "you are the perfect candidate for Parliament."

"Somehow I know that statement is not a compliment."

"I find I am no longer certain of anything," his wife responded, "except that you have the gift of telling people exactly what they wish to hear."

"If I am improving in what I say to you, then I have exceeded my wildest fancies. No? I am not improving, or you do not wish to admit it? Come, my dear, there is no one else here. Can you not concede that I am becoming more experienced in the business of being a husband?"

"Perhaps."

Thomas noted, however, that his wife was regarding him as if he were one of the lions in the Tower. An animal ready to spring and gobble her up at a moment's notice. "Relia . . . Westover is not the only one who feels the need to bare his conscience tonight. It's more than time I fully explained why I went off to London directly after our return from Tunbridge Wells."

"To see Mrs. Ebersley?"

Thomas's head shot up, his hands tearing at his dark locks. "Damnation, woman, no, *not* to see Mrs. Ebersley! I mean, yes, I did see her, but only to reaffirm what I had told her earlier. That I had given her her congé."

His wife's nod was slight. She still looked as if she were confronting a ravenous beast.

"Just as I told you, I went to London to take care of business matters left unresolved by the haste of our marriage. . . . But I stayed there, in spite of the short journey down to Pevensey, because . . ." Thomas gripped the side rungs of the chairback, leaned away from his wife and admitted, "I have always been a very controlled person. I give great thought to every action. In Tunbridge Wells I discovered I was not the iron man I had supposed, but a male as vulnerable as any other. A creature whose mind could be sent reeling by the sight of his wife about to break her pretty little neck. By sharing a sitting room with a woman *en déshabillé*. By knowing this woman was my wife. *My wife!* And yet I was no more ready for marriage than you were. So I ran back to the safety of the City, to the only home I knew." Thomas paused, regarding his wife with a silent plea.

Her response was . . . applause. "Oh, bravo, Thomas. You are indeed learning the art of being a husband," she informed him with dignity and no little sarcasm. "But perhaps you would care to tell me what other matters kept you in London for six long weeks after only three days of supposed connubial bliss?"

Thomas had the grace to chuckle. Truly, her quickness of mind delighted him, even if he might wish her less stubborn. "Very well. If you must have the wood with no bark on it, in addition to being terrified of failing to keep the ridiculous promise I made to you, I was deliberately shirking my responsibility to you and Pevensey Park, as I had to Livvy and Nicholas. I wanted the life I had had for so long, free of all obligations except those of the empire I had built. Oh, I wanted the By-Election, but I was daunted by all that went with it."

"Such as a wife, a sister, and a brother."

"An agricultural empire I knew nothing about. County people, county ways. A world more foreign to me than Paris, Rome, or Athens."

"People who thought of you as a Cit."

"That, too."

"A wife who thought of you as a Cit."

"Yes," Thomas breathed. The air between them seethed with unspoken thoughts and chaotic emotions.

"Then it is fortunate we have a truce, is it not?" Relia declared. And fled the room.

As Thomas found his way to bed, he marveled, not for the first time, at the forethought of his wife's ancestors. In most households his bedroom would have been joined to his wife's by the width of his dressing room plus the width of hers. Their rooms would have had separate entrances. Husband and wife would converse only if one, usually the husband, sought the other out. Since this process tended to involve actions with little need for conversation, husband and wife could go for months, perhaps years, without private conversation. Without that blessed sitting room, he would not be any better acquainted with his wife than he had been after three days in Tunbridge Wells.

Nor would he feel as tormented—both physically and mentally. If not for the blasted election . . .

Get thee behind me, Satan! The words of his Dissenter grandmother echoed down through the years.

No, he dare not chance it. He needed his wife's support. And yet . . . Thomas pictured Relia's sharp eyes turned sultry, her lips as inviting as the rose red satin of the new dressing gown. A garment never intended to keep a husband at bay. The woman was driving him mad!

After the election, Lanning. After the election!

Malcolm Reaves, the new steward, arrived with his wife and three children on the day the hustings went up in the market square. Although his north-country accent brought the inevitable speculations about his ancestors earning their name by reaving other people's cattle, it was generally agreed that Mr. Reaves was a good choice. Mrs. Thomas Lanning handed over Pevensey Park's daily problems and its accounting ledgers with a right good will. On the following day, accompanied by Miss Olivia Lanning, Relia sat, proud and erect, behind her husband on the banner-draped raised platform while he declared his candidacy, speaking to the crowd with a power that confirmed her belief that he was born for politics. And shamed her cynical conviction that such a gift was not a virtue.

And yet . . . she was sitting here, was she not, as a candidate's wife should? She and Livvy, shockingly garbed in bright blue velvet pelisses with small matching hats that did not hide their faces—hats topped, quite outrageously, by two scarlet ostrich plumes. What did it matter that she was wearing a proper half-mourning gown beneath? All anyone could see was blue and scarlet. It was humiliating. They looked like lightskirts!

Relia raised her eyes from her toes, which were beginning to go numb with cold, and caught the broad smirk of a rider hovering at the back of the crowd. Twyford! And she could not blame him for laughing. Who would have thought when Nicholas proposed blue and red for Thomas's colors that matters would go to such an extreme as scarlet feathers on a blue hat!

Her cousin Twyford was wearing a cockade on his top hat, Relia noted, almost grinding her teeth, for it was a tasteful arrangement of burgundy and gold pinned to one side of his black beaver. His jacket was burgundy, his waistcoast striped in burgundy and gold. Beau Brummel himself could not have faulted The Terrible Twyford's appearance. Relia sighed.

The crowd burst into applause, then into full-throated roars of approval, as Thomas ended his maiden speech in ringing tones. Carleton Westover rose and, taking the arms of both women, drew them forward to stand on either side of Thomas, where they smiled and waved . . . and did exactly as they had been instructed.

Relia greeted those nearest the hustings by name. She kept smiling, waving . . . and wondered, deep down, if she truly wished her husband to win. If he did, her life was never, ever, going to be what she wanted it to be.

What she had thought she wanted it to be.

Thomas was bending down, shaking hands. At the back of the platform, Patrick Fallon and Big Mike Bolt, with the aid of several committeemen, were attempting to match those in the enthusiastic crowd with the poll lists in Fallon's hand. The crowd surged forward, sweeping around the platform into The Hound and Bear for a round—several rounds—of ale, laid on by the Blue and Red Election Committee.

With a wave of his riding crop Twyford Trevor saluted his cousin and trotted off. The campaign had begun.

Chapter Twenty

"*M*y dear," declared Margaret Stanton, her generous bosom overhanging her lap in a manner reminiscent of a pouter pigeon, "you are aware, I trust, that you will be entertaining every butcher, baker, and candlestick maker in this part of Kent."

"Mama!" Chloe Stanton protested.

"It is the nature of politics, my dear Margaret," declared Lady Trent, looking down her nose at the squire's wife.

"In Freeman Boroughs, at least," Livvy qualified.

"Innkeepers, brewers, mercers, grocers, shoemakers, glovers, cabinetmakers, tailors," Chloe intoned.

"Soldiers, sailors, bankers, wool buyers, booksellers, solicitors," Jane Edmundson added.

"Apothecaries, surgeons, blacksmiths, leather workers, jewelers," said Gussie.

"Enough!" Relia laughed, holding up her hand. "Indeed, Mrs. Stanton, I am well aware of the numbers and occupations of the electors in this borough. I have heard little else this past sennight. Which is why I have asked you ladies to join me for tea. The men have their Election Committee; now we ladies must have ours. I am not so arrogant as to think I can manage the entertainment of the entire borough without assistance." Mrs. Thomas Lanning smiled benignly at her circle of Whig neighbors. "Ladies, may I have your support? My husband and I will be eternally in your debt."

Visions of advancement for younger sons danced enticingly through the elegant drawing room at Pevensey Park.

Of houseparties filled with distinguished and influential gentlemen down from London for the weekend—eligible suitors for the hands of Kentish daughters. While Lady Trent, Margaret Stanton, and others of their generation examined the advantages of actively supporting Thomas Lanning, Jane Edmundson studied the toes of her half-boots with a small, secret smile. "What if . . ." she ventured, "what if Captain Fortescue were to support Mr. Lanning?"

"Do not speak nonsense!" Lady Trent told her daughter. "Go against Gravenham? Absurd!"

"But Alan—Captain Fortescue—refused to run," Jane persisted.

"That was personal inclination, I believe," Relia said. "But go against his father's wishes? I doubt it. And Twyford is his friend. . . . although how the captain could be so indiscriminate in his taste I have never understood."

"Nonetheless—"

Relia eyed Jane Edmundson with sharpened interest. "Do you, then, have some idea of the captain's feelings in this matter?"

The widow ducked her head, hiding a blush. "The captain has been gracious enough to call at Trent Manor once or twice since Christmas."

"Or four or five or six," intoned her mother, with a self-satisfied curl of her lip.

Relia leaned forward. "Is it possible, then? Will he come out for Mr. Lanning?"

"He likes him. Very much," Jane confided softly. "I will ask."

"Is it possible?" Later that night, in the privacy of their rooms, Thomas Lanning echoed his wife's question. "The endorsement of Gravenham's son, a wounded veteran of the Peninsula? Lord!" Thomas paced the carpet in the sitting room, running his hands through his dark hair until it is was nothing more than a disheveled heap.

"I am almost sorry I mentioned it," Relia said, "for family loyalty is always strong. The captain may wish to endorse your candidacy, but whether or not he will actually do it . . ."

"After what happened today, he may very well do so."

"Tell me."

"Gravenham is so fearful of losing again that he's invoking the old burgage rights. Today he served eviction notices on thirteen widows living in burgage properties."

"Whatever for?" Relia cried, instantly outraged, though not quite understanding the significance.

"Because the right to vote is tied to their cottages, and they cannot vote."

"Merciful heavens," Relia breathed. "That is despicable."

"Indeed. Westover is arranging to bring in voters from London to counteract Gravenham's maneuvering—"

"London? But how is that possible?"

"Ah, such political naïveté," Thomas teased, coming to a halt and managing a wry smile. "And, no, you need not tell me you would know more about politics if women had the vote. My understanding is capable of anticipating that remark." His wife sniffed, but kept silent. "Any man who has ever had the vote in this borough may return for the election. We, too, will bring in voters from beyond the borough— from as far away as the Midlands and the West Country, but the majority will be from London."

"A transportation nightmare, surely?"

"Which is why I have employed so many experts. Voting is to be spread over six days. We will manage."

"Thomas?"

"Yes?"

"Every morning you hold breakfasts at the inn, with, I'm told, as much ale as food. All day you canvass door to door, showering the constituents with smiles and handshakes, wringing from them the promise of their vote. Then every evening it is back to The Hound and Bear for more food and vast quantities of drink. How is it you return home so remarkably well preserved and steady on your feet?"

"Good God, my dear, was that a compliment?"

"It was a serious question. I am curious." For once,

Thomas noted, his wife's smile was close to winsome. It became her.

"Then it deserves a serious answer." Thomas sank into one of the comfortable chairs facing the fireplace. "I suppose . . . yes, I endure because I must. Because campaigning is only a few short weeks, and needs must when the devil drives. I find I draw energy from the people. Each person is different—a challenge. Someone I am promising to serve in return for his vote. Each day I learn more about what is needed, and, like you, I make lists of what needs to be done for this borough after I win. As for the ale?" Thomas proffered an almost boyish grin. "It is the floorboards of The Hound and Bear that should be reeling with drink. I have grown adept at letting gravity empty my mug."

Relia shook her head. "Political smoke and mirrors. I should have known."

"Would you rather I had to be carried home each night?"

"As if that would gain you votes!"

Thomas thought it was a propitious time to change the subject. "Has Miss Aldershot shown any signs of softening?" he inquired.

"Gussie will not do more than bid Mr. Westover good morning," Relia replied. "Yet she works for your campaign as if she herself were running for office. But with all of you out of the house from seven to midnight, there is little opportunity for any form of reconciliation."

Thomas stretched and yawned, the comfort of the sitting room, the pleasure of his wife's presence, making him careless of his words. "I have promised myself we will go away somewhere after the election, perhaps back to Tunbridge Wells, where I plan to spend at least a week in bed."

Silence. Thomas's eyes snapped open, encountering the stunned look on his wife's face. "Devil it!" he growled. "Do you think I'm made of iron? That I'm not aware I am married to a woman of wit and beauty? A siren who waits in her lair to taunt me night after night, even though she's a Lady and I'm a lowly Cit? Do you actually think I do not care? Well, woman, say something!"

"I think," said his wife, rising to her feet, "that you have endured too many days of seven to midnight and that it will only get worse. Therefore the *siren* will avoid this sitting room for the duration of the campaign. As for a week in Tunbridge Wells, you may find your bed exceedingly lonely."

Mrs. Thomas Lanning crossed to her bedchamber, head high, chin in the air. She threw open the door . . . then paused upon the threshold. "On second thought," she amended, turning toward her husband, "I imagine the newest Member of Parliament would have no difficulty finding dozens of women to warm his bed. Therefore— purely to be my usual difficult self, you understand—I shall accompany you, after all."

This time, it was Thomas who applauded.

Mr. Blacklock's sketch of the Whig candidate for MP was so successful, portraying Thomas Lanning in a noble pose yet with his eyes somehow promising he would never forget he was a man of the people, that Carleton Westover ordered it printed on enough handbills and posters to wall-paper the entire borough. This, of course, also did much to ensure the vote of every printer and papermaker, not to mention those put to work painting bright blue and red cockades in each corner. And then there were the drapers who pro-vided endless ells of blue and red fabric for banners, stream-ers, and the ribbon bouquets the candidate's supporters wore pinned to their lapels. *Buy local, buy local,* intoned Mr. Westover each day. And so they did. Even if it meant driv-ing loads of country-made goods up to London, where Mr. Lanning donated them to the poor.

Mr. Hugh Blacklock's caricature of the opposing candi-date was equally successful. Enough so that heated words, exacerbated by the eviction of widows, escalated into row-dyism, with Mr. Trevor's followers ripping down their can-didate's unflattering caricatures and, shortly thereafter, spilling over into ridding the walls of Mr. Lanning's portrait as well. Since both aspiring members of Parliament had set up headquarters in rival inns a scant half mile apart, the con-troversy rapidly turned physical.

If anyone had asked her, Relia thought when regaled with this news one morning at breakfast, she would have had to admit she had every confidence in Big Mike Bolt. One look at the bruiser, and, after the initial shock, she had not doubted his ability to handle any sort of violence. She should be appalled, but, truth to tell, she felt only satisfaction at the routing of Twyford's bully boys. Not that she would ever tell Thomas so.

As if she would have the opportunity! For she never saw him now. He was gone off to The Hound and Bear before she rose, and came home long after exhaustion had forced her to seek her bed. Relia suspected he was using the dressing room entrance to his bedchamber, for not a sound could she hear from the sitting room, though many nights she lay awake, listening for the slightest sound of an opening door. Of footsteps tiptoeing over the carpet. Yet had she not told him she would not be waiting? Why should Thomas do anything but straightaway seek his bed?

She missed him, Relia admitted later that morning, as her fingers paused over the prize ribbons for the Winter Festival she, Gussie, and Livvy were assembling in the morning room. She missed their moments of late-night privacy, even the times when their words were few. And she was proud of him. For all her cynicism, her latent scorn, Thomas Lanning was going to be a splendid MP. One who would serve his people. One who was likely to rise, like rich cream, above the other four hundred and two Members of Parliament.

"You have visitors, madam." There was something ominous in Biddeford's tone that snapped Relia out of her reverie in a trice. Gussie and Livvy, also alerted, ceased their low-voiced conversation. "It is Lord and Lady Hubert, madam. And Mr. Trevor."

Livvy gasped. Miss Aldershot clutched her heart. Relia's body went cold.

Thomas! Dragonslayer! Where are you when I need you?

"Biddeford, you old fool," Lord Hubert shouted, pushing the butler out of the way. "How dare you keep us cooling our heels in the hall? Aurelia, Miss Aldershot, good day.

And who the devil are you?" he demanded, catching sight of Miss Lanning.

"Ungrateful child!" spat Lady Hubert, hard on her husband's heels. "You have ruined us all. Disgraced the family name. We have come to give you a last chance to redeem yourself, to allow your poor mama and papa—God rest their souls!—to lie easy in their graves. Tell her, Twyford," she declaimed, with a dramatic thrust of her hand toward her only son. "Tell her she must immediately abandon this monstrous behavior."

"Morning, cuz," drawled The Terrible Twyford. "Ah . . . the exquisite Miss Lanning." He bowed.

To Relia's disgust, Livvy colored up and simpered. *Good God, had the chit no discrimination?*

To Mr. Trevor's credit, he displayed more sense than his esteemed parents, calmly ushering them to the morning room's lyre-back chairs before taking a seat directly across from his cousin. "All alone, Relia?" he inquired softly. "Your houseful of hucksters have deserted you?"

"You know quite well they are out canvassing. As you should be. Or is Gravenham doing all your work—buying outsiders willing to vote as he tells them?"

"Naughty, naughty, dear cuz. Association with your cur of a husband has obviously tainted your reasoning."

Livvy leaped to her feet, Mr. Trevor's open admiration of her person forgotten. "You are despicable!" she cried.

"Olivia!" Gussie Aldershot put an arm around Miss Lanning and murmured in her ear. Both women subsided onto the gold-and-cream-striped settee.

At least Livvy was no longer dazzled by The Terrible Twyford, Relia thought as she gathered her courage. "If you have come to insult me," she said, "you may leave now. I have no wish to hear anything you might say."

"Come, come, dear girl." Twyford offered the smile that had once presaged his tearing the wings off butterflies. "We are here as your family. Because we are concerned for you. We wish to rescue you from the monster you chose so misguidedly. Come with us now, we beg you. Fly back to the safety of Middlethorpe Manor and escape all this nonsense.

We know you cannot like it. Such a quiet country mouse—always so grave and bookish. You stand beside Lanning, pale and suffering. 'Tis plain to see you hate every moment—"

"That's not true!" Relia cried. "I have smiled until my face cracks, shaken hands until I cannot move my fingers. I have admired every last baby and half-grown child in the borough, poured so many cups of tea I sometimes imagine doing it in my sleep. I am a good campaigner. Never say I am not!"

"Methinks the lady doth protest too much."

"Go away, Twyford. You are not wanted here."

"We will not go away!" Lord Hubert roared. "This is my brother's home."

"This is *my* home. My husband's home. As long as you speak ill of him, you are not welcome here." And she meant every word of it. Even if she had liked the Hubert Trevors and their abominable son, she would have repudiated them today. Because they had insulted Thomas. Her husband. The Cit.

The Whig candidate for the House of Commons.

Who was somehow standing in the doorway, large and vital, looking ready to harness thunderbolts and cast the intruders from the room. For a moment Relia felt dizzy. He had heard her. Every word.

And God bless Biddeford, who must have sent for him. Or perhaps someone had seen the Trevor carriage rolling through the village.

"I heard you needed a dragonslayer, my dear," he said, but his unwavering gaze was fixed on his opponent. "Lady Hubert, Lord Hubert, Trevor, when this election is over, we will honor the family connection—at christenings and weddings, perhaps. But at the moment we find your visit most inappropriate. Just imagine what our respective supporters may say about such a private meeting. I fear both our candidacies could suffer. Do you not agree, Trevor? Biddeford, I believe Lord Hubert and his family are leaving. Would you be kind enough to show them out?"

Christenings and weddings? Relia did not even notice

the Trevors's departure. Thomas spoke of christenings. Whose christenings?

Foolish female, she knew quite well what he meant. The christening of little Lannings, who would tumble over the park, race across the bridge to the rotunda, which would become—as it once had for her—a castle, a pirate ship, Sherwood forest, a high mountain, a beleaguered desert fort.

Her children. Thomas's children. Not so startling after all. They were married, were they not? And among his campaign promises, had her husband not included a return to Tunbridge Wells?

Miss Aldershot took Livvy firmly by the arm and led her out of the room, leaving Mr. and Mrs. Thomas Lanning alone in the morning room. The look on both faces, usually well hidden behind their public façades, was suddenly naked. Vulnerable. Dear God, Gussie thought, how she envied them. For she had been even more of a fool than Relia. What good was pride in the long, lonely hours of the night? *Forgiveness is divine.*

But the men came home so late. When, during this interminable campaign, would she ever have the opportunity . . . ?

She was mistaken. Carleton Westover, Thaddeus Singleton, Patrick Fallon, Hugh Blacklock, Nicholas, and Big Mike Bolt were all gathered in the entry hall, a solid phalanx overseeing the departure of the opposing candidate and his family. Gussie felt a surge of warmth. She and Relia had found a most excellent dragonslayer. One with a great many assistants.

"Mr. Westover," declared Gussie Aldershot, "I wonder if I might have a word with you."

Chapter Twenty-one

To the ladies' astonishment, the candidate and his Election Agent forsook the nightly revels at The Hound and Bear and joined the family at dinner. Even Nick's excited revelation that it was he, while acting as messenger for the Election Committee, who had noticed the Trevor carriage and galloped *ventre à terre* for help, could not keep the three Lannings from noticing the startling change in the hostile atmosphere that customarily radiated between Gussie Aldershot and Carleton Westover.

"Smelling of April and May," Livvy giggled in Relia's ear later that evening as she turned pages for her sister-in-law's offerings on the pianoforte.

"More like September and October," Relia shot back, then missed a note or two as she realized how far her good manners had fallen. It was the Election, of course. Her association with so many vulgar people.

No, it was not. It was having another young woman in the house. Someone to talk to . . . almost like a sister. Indeed, Livvy was a sister, was she not? And in another year they would brave London society together. She, the wife of a Member of Parliament, and Miss Olivia Lanning, his sister.

Once again, Relia's fingers faltered. Somehow London no longer seemed so formidable, a *ton* jungle to be carefully avoided by remaining in the tranquility of Kent. Astonishing. When had she begun to look up and see a world beyond Pevensey Park?

The day she sat at the table in Sir Gilbert Bromley's office and saw Thomas Lanning walk through the door.

She must have finished her étude, for the men were applauding. Relia managed a grimace of a smile in response, then hastened to one of the tall windows, hiding her face as she pulled aside the drapery and peered out into the night. *Love at first sight. Impossible. Quite impossible.*

It had indeed been love at first sight, though she had been fighting most gallantly against it ever since. *Thomas Lanning, the Cit. Thomas Lanning, Prince of the Exchange. Thomas Lanning, Member of Parliament.*

Dear God, she loved him! How dared he do this to her? For in Thomas Lanning's life she came in a distant fourth at best. After politics. After Livvy and Nick.

Yet . . . all those nights they had met in the sitting room, he might have retired to his bedchamber via the dressing room door. But he had not. He had *wanted* to talk to her, she was certain of it. And had he not dropped everything today to dash to her rescue?

That was his obligation. The very heart of his promise to her. And Thomas Lanning was an honorable man.

Tunbridge Wells. He planned to spend a week in bed in Tunbridge Wells. Not alone.

Relia gulped, took another look out the window. Reality was needed, not flights of fancy. "I fear it will rain," she pronounced. "Two days till the Festival, and what if the snow is all gone?"

Thomas's hand came down on her shoulder. Dear God, he was standing directly behind her! "There's an old saying, my dear—*Do not borrow trouble.* And you will recall the vicar is on our side. It is indeed clouding up tonight, but the temperature is dropping. A fine covering of new snow is what we'll have. Conditions will be perfect."

Temperature. Dropping. Then why was she burning up?

Thomas leaned forward, his lips touched her ear. A wave of dizziness shook her from head to toe. "Ten days, my dear, and it will all be over. Win or lose, I promise we will go back to the Wells."

Ruthlessly, Relia settled her prideful armor back in place.

She turned and took her husband's arm. "I will go to the Wells accompanied by the newest Member of Parliament," she told him stoutly. Mr. and Mrs. Lanning then proceeded, arm in arm, toward the tea table, where Biddeford had just laid out their late-evening repast.

The next day Captain Fortescue left the shelter of his father's house and took up residence at The Hound and Bear, graciously refusing a bed at Pevensey Park. That, he told the Whig candidate with a grin, might indeed be the feather that broke the horse's back. He could endure the inn for the short time remaining in the campaign. After that . . . well, after that he hoped to retire to the estate left him by a doting uncle. With a bride, no doubt, declared Mr. Lanning, a knowing gleam in his eye. The captain responded with a wink and a hearty handshake.

Captain Fortescue's presence at Thomas Lanning's side was enough to sway a goodly number of his father's own tenants, as well as numerous freeman who considered themselves loyal to the Fortescue family, though not necessarily to the present earl. After all, the lad was a Fortescue, was he not?

The Earl of Gravenham was incensed. Eyeing his handpicked candidate with grave disfavor, he announced that stronger measures would have to be taken. "Snatch papers," he growled, considerably confusing his candidate, for Mr. Trevor had never heard of this esoteric approach to voting rights. "That's what we need, m'boy," the earl declared. "Snatch papers. I'll see to it at once."

As Thomas—the man of the City who should not have known about such things—had predicted, a fine new coat of snow blanketed the area. A soft, wet snow that turned the world into a fairyland of white-capped branches and amorphous shapes. On the morning of the Winter Festival the sun came out, sending rainbow sparks from a myriad ice crystals, casting dazzling brilliance over the landscape, almost as if Mother Nature herself were a Whig.

A crew was set to sweep the new snow off the pond. Tres-

tle tables dotted the terraces, which had also been swept
clean of snow. Beside each was a brazier designed to keep
hot food ready from morn till night. Tall stacks of wood
marked bonfires, ready to be lit. Six sleighs lined the drive
before the house, and on the distant hillside beyond the ha-
ha, ten sleds stood ready and waiting. Wooden benches had
been placed around the pond to ease the strapping on and
taking off of sharp skate runners.

As for games, three narrow strips had been trampled
down for ring toss. And in an empty sheep field, well away
from other activities, archery butts rose above the snow. Of
course, as Relia had noted during planning sessions, missing
arrows might not be found till spring, but archery they
would have, as long as the arrows held out. There was also
to be a snow castle contest, one for adults and one for children, and a tug of war, with the losers taking a snow bath
rather than a simple tumble onto soft grass. Relia herself intended to keep a close eye on her childhood sleigh, as it
brought back so many happy memories. For the convenience of the mothers, who would be able to watch their children ride from the comfort of the rotunda, she had set the
course near the foot of the cascade, where water churned,
deep and dark, before running downstream beneath the
frozen pond.

And now came that moment of inevitable silence when
Relia stood beside Thomas on the upper terrace and wondered if anyone would come. The sound and fury of the
campaign had vanished as if it had never been. The campaigners, the servants, were poised and ready, like ice statues dotting the landscape. The snow sparkled, the wind was
hushed. Nothing moved.

*Overnight the electors had all turned Tory. Twyford had
barricaded the roads.*

An hour later, three hours—five—Relia was so immersed
in tenants, townspeople, and children that she could no
longer recall when or where she had last caught sight of
Thomas. Or Livvy or Nick, or half the rest of her household.
She greeted and smiled, smiled and greeted, all the while attempting to keep an eye on everything that was happening.

A hundred times over she thanked God for Biddeford and Mrs. Marshcombe. And Malcolm Reaves was meeting and greeting as if he had been steward at Pevensey Park for twenty years. He was everywhere, as if he, too, were running for election. Charles Saunders, too, was everywhere, tirelessly helping where help was needed. The still-recovering Captain Fortescue, with Jane Edmundson on his arm, was not so active. He did not need to be. The constituents flocked to greet the wounded veteran of the Peninsular War. Now and again, Relia caught a glimpse of Mr. Westover, usually with Gussie glued to his side. And to think how appalled Gussie had been when she found the ring in the plum pudding!

Big Mike Bolt and some of his cronies hovered at the back of the crowd, ever vigilant. There were men patrolling the outer reaches of the Festival as well. Not for the first time Relia appreciated the forethought of Thomas and his cohorts, for security was not something that had ever entered the heads of the ladies' planning committee. She supposed . . . yes, she had to admit that men had their uses.

Right there, standing in the classic rotunda, surrounded by young mothers, Relia blushed scarlet.

She had been right about the child-size sleigh. There was such a demand for the youngest festivalgoers to ride in the tiny vehicle with its ornate wrought iron design and single seat, upholstered in red velvet, that Relia had been forced to assign each mother a number. Which, necessarily, she must supervise. Each small child was allowed to ride three times around a wide circle on the bank below the cascade, with a groom carefully leading the pony that pulled the sleigh. Eventually, Relia was able to turn over her duty to Jane Edmundson, who, thereafter, alternated with Livvy and Chloe Stanton. It was only late in the afternoon, as dusk approached, that she abandoned her role as hostess and returned to the rotunda, where she sat, with a great sigh of relief, on one of the rotunda's marble benches.

"I am done, Livvy," Relia announced. "All is a great success, but I swear I cannot stand on my feet another moment!"

"Well, I am glad enough to get up. I swear I am frozen to this bench! I cannot believe how many mothers are determined to see their little ones ride your infant sleigh. We have gone through two grooms and three ponies, and 'tis a wonder the mothers have not come to fisticuffs."

"O-oh!" All the women gasped.

"Fireworks!" Livvy cried. "Did you know we were to have fireworks, Relia?"

Fireworks. Not a word, not a single word. Not even from Nick, who ordinarily would have been bubbling over about such a treat. A Thomas surprise, then. And a very fine one, at that. For darkness came early, even in February, and the bright, sparkling colors showed clearly above the space just below the ha-ha, where the pyrotechnic experts must be hiding.

Everyone paused—the festivalgoers, the cooks, the servers, the security guards, the campaign workers. It was a beautiful sight, the perfect end to a perfect day.

The last child in line was set aboard the sleigh. The groom, stifling a weary groan, set off on his final three circles of the day. There was a nasty whine, a trail of fire low overhead. Shouts, cries of warning. An explosion rocked the area around the cascade, tearing a large branch off a willow, sending a shower of rocks plunging into the deep water below. The terrified pony tore free of the groom, running for his life, the sleigh rocking dangerously as he bolted for the safety of the stables. The child, a girl of not more than three years of age, was thrown free. People rushed forward, but they were too late. The child tumbled down the steep bank and disappeared beneath the black water.

Someone shot out of the crowd, scattering great coat and jacket as he ran. Two almost superhuman tugs, and his boots were off. He dove straight into the icy water. A full minute later, he bobbed up, empty handed. He gulped for air, plunged back under. This time Relia got a good look. Thomas. It was Thomas.

Dear God, of course it was Thomas. Who but Thomas Lanning was responsible for all this?

Big Mike Bolt stationed himself at the edge of the black

water, peering into its impenetrable depths. The mother was shrieking. Relia did not even hear her.

And then the little girl was in Big Mike's arms. He passed her to eagerly waiting hands, then turned and helped his employer escape the frigid water. A flurry of women swept the sobbing mother and unconscious child into the house, with the doctor trotting after. Behind them, a bevy of well-wishers surrounded the hero of the hour, escorting him in triumph into the warmth of the house, while cheers rang from a thousand throats.

It was more than an hour later, when the little girl had been pronounced well enough to go home, and she and her parents had been sent off in Pevensey's finest carriage, that Relia was able to think of Thomas. Biddeford had assured her he was fine, but she must, of course, see for herself. Even if it meant . . . indeed, yes, even if it meant entering that holy of holies, her husband's bedchamber.

"—demmed military rocket!" Relia heard as she sneaked open Thomas's door, her soft scratching having gone unheard.

"What!" Her husband's roar did much to reassure her that he was far from death's door.

"Trevor," declared Charles Saunders grimly. "I doubt Gravenham would stoop so low."

"You mean it was deliberate?" Thaddeus Singleton choked out. "Someone might have been killed!"

"Someone almost bloody was," Thomas ground out.

"I'll take care of 'im, guv'nor," Big Mike declared. Relia, with her ear to the crack in the door, almost gave herself away by applauding.

"As much as I appreciate the offer," said the candidate, "we'll settle for besting Trevor at the polls."

"Not a doubt about the vote after today," proclaimed Carleton Westover. "You're the hero of the hour, Thomas."

"Trevor likely thinks you staged the whole," crowed Patrick Fallon. "I couldn't have thought of anything better if I'd spent the entire campaign plotting it out."

"A plot that puts our candidate in grave danger of inflammation of the lungs," Mr. Singleton sniffed. "I think not."

Thomas, who was growing exceedingly tired of all the fuss and bother, as well as the adulation for what he looked upon as nothing more than an act of absolute necessity, glanced restlessly around the room. He noted the opening in the door to the sitting room with considerable interest. It might be his imagination. Wishful thinking, but . . .

"Out!" he barked. "Enough politics for one day. All of you, out, out, out! Use the dressing room door. Peace and quiet is what I need."

Liar.

As the door closed on the last of the Election Committee, Thomas closed his eyes, wondering if he had misinterpreted the crack in the door. If so, he was going to be gravely disappointed. "You may come out now," he called softly.

His wife peeked her head around the door, proffered a tentative smile. She appeared more than a little apprehensive, Thomas noted. To the best of his knowledge, she had not set foot in this room since she had approved Mr. Arnold's redecoration. "Come, come, Relia. I assure you I am not about to expire. I have been plunged into a hot bath, dried with warm towels, and been put to bed with hot bricks at my feet. I have had so many attendants I now know what royalty must suffer. But we *are* married, so you may safely enter without shocking the residents of Pevensey Park or the electorate."

Slowly, Relia advanced across the carpet, looking suspiciously like Eve directly after taking a bite of the apple. "You are all right? You are sure?" she breathed.

"Quite—" Thomas bit off his remark. "We-l-ll," he hedged, "I am still a bit chilled, but I daresay I shall recover." He allowed his voice to fade away on a sigh.

"Shall I bring you a hot toddy?" she inquired anxiously.

"I've already had two," Thomas admitted. "Relia?"

"Yes?" Eyes wide with concern, his wife awaited his next words.

"There is something you might do. . . ."

"Anything," she declared earnestly.

"'Tis said there's nothing as effective as body heat in warming up someone who is well nigh frozen."

His wife blinked. Her gaze plummeted to her toes. "Thomas," she whispered, "I am not quite certain what you mean."

"You know exactly what I mean." Instead of blushing, she turned pale. As if his bed were occupied by a ghost. A venal one, at that. "Be a good girl and lock the doors, Relia. The candidate would like a few moments alone with his wife. God knows I've earned them," he added softly, but not so softly she did not hear him.

Relia considered swatting him with a pillow, but decided, in all fairness, that he was probably right. Nor was she anxious to return to the days of their constant sparring. There were moments, like this one, when the wise woman kept her silence. Even if it meant . . .

She marched with deliberate step, crisscrossing the bedchamber to lock both the dressing room and sitting room doors. But her step slowed, the brave set of her shoulders slumped as she turned back toward her husband's imposing bed. He looked her up and down, shook his head. "Skin to skin, that's the only remedy," he told her. "Turn around, so I can do your buttons."

To his surprise, she approached the bed, meekly turned and presented her back. Thomas nearly stopped breathing. In his eagerness he fumbled the task, yet somehow her gown slipped off her shoulders, fell away. "Leave it," he ordered. "No hands," he added as she crisscrossed them over her thin chemise, eyeing him askance. If that was the only undergarment she had worn at the Festival, she needed warming as much as he! Incredible. She wasn't even wearing stays.

Thomas lifted the thick pile of bedcoverings, silently inviting his wife to join him. Truthfully, he was so hot he needed a dose of cool flesh to slow him down, keep him from frightening the dear girl to death.

Heart pounding, but spirit willing, Relia snuggled down beside him. *A-ah!* Poor darling, he must indeed be freezing, for there was a part of him that seemed as stiff as a board.

Men were built very oddly, it seemed. Her lips curved in a soft, secret smile. It was high time she discovered the why of male anatomy.

Mr. Lanning was all too willing to demonstrate.

Chapter Twenty-two

$\mathcal{M}$rs. Thomas Lanning and Miss Olivia Lanning stood shoulder-to-shoulder at the foot of the wooden steps that led up to the hustings. Both ladies were clad in the bright blue velvet pelisses and off-the-face hats with scarlet ostrich plumes that had been worn so frequently over the past weeks that they were now familiar friends instead of garments to be despised. Beside them was Master Nicholas Lanning, who had blossomed into such a quick-witted and competent young man during the campaign that few doubted he would one day follow in his brother's footsteps. All three kept their eyes fixed on the Whig candidate as he ascended the steps, stated his name, proclaimed his occupation as investment counselor, avowed he was a freeman, resident of the parish of Peven, and qualified to vote in said election. He then moved on to the table manned by a solemn-faced polling clerk and, in a voice that boomed out over the hushed crowd, stated that he voted for Thomas Lanning, the Blue and Red candidate for Member of Parliament.

A great cheer went up. A signal from Patrick Fallon, and the first parade of voters came marching up the street toward the market square, banners flying, feet synchronized to the tune of a lively band of musicians. It was the delegation of hops workers from Pevensey Park. Similar arrivals had been carefully scheduled to enliven the voting over the next six days, in addition to catching the attention of those laggard electors who had not yet made up their minds.

After Candidate Lanning descended from the platform,

beaming and catching outstretched hands proffered from all directions, he and his family were whisked off into the relative quiet of a private dining room at The Hound and Bear, where they sank gratefully into chairs around a table piled high with food and drink. No one could ever say Mr. Carleton Westover did not know how to manage every aspect of a campaign.

"Almost over," Thomas said to his wife, with a wink that promised so much more.

Although the candidate and his wife had reached an accommodation in the bedroom, Aurelia Trevor Lanning had not given up her spirit. "All this," she sighed into the quiet that ensued as the others turned their attention to the high-mounded plates of food, "for a job that pays not a single ha'penny." Hands froze in midair. Everyone stared. Thomas burst into laughter. From Carleton Westover down to Nicholas Lanning, the Whig campaigners, reassured that Mrs. Lanning was merely funning, joined in the general amusement.

"How fortunate that I married you," Thomas drawled, "for I have no doubt Westover has gone through my entire fortune."

"Thomas!" that gentleman protested, "we have spent a mere pittance compared to some campaigns I've managed."

"And more to come, I fear," said Patrick Fallon. "We haven't heard the last of Trevor's bully boys, and I'd swear Gravenham has a trick or two left up his sleeve."

"But the voting has begun," Nick said.

"Six days, lad. Six days," said Mr. Westover. "We're allowed up to fifteen, but this borough has a tradition of managing the matter in six. And campaigning continues as long as there's a voter who has not climbed the hustings. Anything may yet happen."

And, of course, it did.

"Thomas! Thomas! It's Charles. Wake up!" Although Mr. Saunders was well pleased by the reconciliation of his friend and his wife, on this, the eve of the fifth day of voting, their recent practice of locking all three doors into the hallway was a confounded nuisance.

Thomas dragged himself to awareness, fumbled to light a candle, then gazed down at his wife, who was also awake, eyes wide with anxiety. "I doubt the house is about to burn down about our ears," he assured her, "and all else we can manage." He brushed a kiss across her lips, threw on his dressing gown and padded barefoot through her dressing room, where he opened the door and peeked down the hall. "Wrong portal, Charles," he called with a wry grin to his friend, who was pounding on his own dressing room door.

"This is not the time for humor," Mr. Saunders grumbled, after jogging down the hall to meet his employer. "Gravenham has brought in men who are pitching tents on all the abandoned properties he owns. He's given them snatch papers to attest their right to vote. Big Mike just sent a messenger, wanting to know what he should do."

"Clever devil," Thomas murmured, rubbing his stubbled chin. "Tents, you say?"

"Yes. 'Tis enough to show the land is occupied. Devious, but legal. Each and every one of them has papers from Gravenham stating they have the right to vote that burgage property. Temporary, of course. That's why they're called snatch papers."

"Do we not have a hundred and more votes coming down from London in the morning?"

"We do, but I cannot like the earl's maneuvering. 'Tis not fair to invoke old rights that have fallen into disuse for good reason. Empty land should not have a vote."

"Ah, Charles, you would back me into a corner." Thomas frowned and shook his head. "I must think of Captain Fortescue and his family and the years to come when we must all live together in this borough, Whigs, Tories, and Independents alike."

"And I say Gravenham has gone too far," declared Relia from over his shoulder. "You will win, Thomas, and you must begin as you mean to go on. In this borough the electors should be freemen and freemen only. Marcus Yelverton broke Gravenham's stranglehold on the voters. You must make sure it stays that way. Is that not what the reform you want is all about?"

"Bloodthirsty wench," Thomas murmured, reaching behind him to draw his wife close. "Very well, Charles. Tell Big Mike that I find tents a disturbance to the fine Kentish landscape. And I also believe we should do these snatch visitors the courtesy of preventing them from freezing their—from freezing," Mr. Lanning hastily amended, dropping his voice. "Tents, snatch papers, and men are to be gone before the polls open in the morning . . . but with as few cracked heads as possible, if you please."

"It's done!" After a decisive nod, Charles Saunders made an abrupt turn and strode off down the main hallway at a rapid clip.

Thomas closed and locked the door, then swept his wife back through her dressing room to the warmth of her large bed, where they promptly encased themselves inside the screen of peach velvet bedhangings, newly fixed in place. The bedhangings that had once been such a bone of contention. The candidate rolled onto his side, propped himself up on one elbow and leaned over the vague pale shadow that was his wife's face. "Now that we're awake . . ." he said, his warm breath fanning across her cheek.

"Thomas?"

"Yes, my dear?" He nuzzled her ear, trailed butterfly kisses over her cheek, pulled aside the stiff white cotton of her winter nightwear to press lips of fire to her neck, her shoulder—

"Thomas!" The palms of two small hands delivered a surprisingly firm shove to his chest. "There is something I must say to you," Relia gasped. "I attempted to do so earlier, but you . . . we were . . . um . . ."

"Distracted?" Thomas suggested. "Like this, I believe." And kissed her full on the lips.

His wife pounded him on the back. "Stop it! There is something I must tell you before the votes are counted, and there is not much time left."

"Oh, very well, if you must." With a great sigh, the Whig candidate subsided onto his pillow.

"Well . . ." his wife whispered into the darkness. "I want you to know—" She clasped her hands tightly on her chest, took a shuddering breath. "Ah . . . this is so much more difficult than I had thought! No wonder you have never told me—" She drew a deep breath, began again. "It is quite simple, really. I sought long and hard for a dragonslayer. When I finally found him, I tolerated that he was a man of City because I had need of him. At least that is what I told myself. The truth is . . . the simple truth is, I took one look at you and knew that, for all the odd looks you cast my way, you would do. More than do."

Relia reached out, ran soft fingers down her husband's arm. "But it was only recently," she admitted in a rush, having gained courage from the feel of him, "that I realized I loved you. That I will love you, win or lose. That I wish to bear your children, grow old with you—"

With a groan Thomas took his wife in his arms, his mouth devouring hers in a kiss so intense they both forgot to breathe. When, after at last gasping for air, Thomas found his voice, out tumbled all the words he had hoarded up over the long months when he had been certain his wife scorned all but his abilities as a knight errant. Among them was the admission that he, too, had fallen in love at first sight. And was almost equally blind in recognizing that tender emotion for what it was. "Do you suppose," he said in one of those maddeningly analytical moments to which political candidates tend to be addicted, "that Westover and Miss Aldershot ever feel like this?"

"Thomas!"

"Your captain and Mrs. Edmundson?"

"He's not my captain!"

"Good. Then he can live," declared Mr. Lanning, expansively.

"I pray you, Mr. Candidate, do not let the election go to your head."

"Unlikely, for I shall always have you to remind me of my shortcomings, Mrs. Job-with-No-Pay."

Relia chuckled, then instantly sobered. "Do you truly

love me, Thomas, or was that just another campaign promise?"

"You have forgotten something, my love. Women don't have the vote."

"Oh. Then kiss me again, my princely Cit. We'll work on the rights of women another day."

In the By-Election for the seat held by Mr. Marcus Yelverton, the Whig MP, Thomas Lanning, won by a decisive margin. He endured the "chairing" with right good will, carried through the streets of Lower Peven in a chair festooned with blue and red streamers behind an honor guard of equally gaudily attired horses and riders. Fortunately, the occasional brick and roof slate, thrown by die-hard adherents of Mr. Twyford Trevor, missed.

Epilogue

Aurelia Trevor Lanning sat on the marble bench in the rotunda and gazed out over Pevensey Park in near perfect contentment. It was mid-July, and the countryside was so breathtakingly lovely that it might have been the product of some beatific dream. But, in spite of the verdant landscape, the soft warmth of the breeze whiffling around her face, and memories of countless political picnics over the last twelve years, one long-ago Winter Festival captured her thoughts. Those horrifying moments when she had thought Thomas lost beneath the icy black water. The look on his face—hopeful but wary—when he had lifted his bedcovers, inviting her in. The moment, a few nights later, when they had each shed the last barriers between them and admitted—

"Mama, Mama, Mama!" cried Miss Rosalind Lanning, dashing across the width of the rotunda and skidding to a halt before her mother. Arms crossed over her boyishly flat ten-year-old chest, she declared, "Trevor says I cannot be the pirate captain because I'm a girl. That's not fair. It's my turn. He says I must be a wench," she added on a sniff of great disdain.

Relia turned solemn eyes on her eldest. "A *wench*? Is this true, Trevor?"

"I'll be a wench," Julia Lanning piped up from the floor of the rotunda where she had been building a village of sticks and stones, framed by a carefully placed border of wilting wildflowers.

"You don't know what a wench is," declared Master

Geoffrey Lanning, nearly nine, whose first year at Eton had, unfortunately, convinced him that he now knew everything there was to know.

"Do, too," his little sister retorted.

"Trevor and Rosalind will both be pirate captains," their mother pronounced, neatly sidestepping the issue of wenches. "And Geoffrey and Julia may be your lieutenants. You may then see who is first to find the treasure."

"What treasure?" Julia demanded.

"A pretend treasure, silly," said Geoffrey.

"Oh, very well," Trevor sighed. "Come on, then." The three older children set off across the old wooden bridge toward the pond, with Julia doing a run-run-hop-hitch in a valiant effort to keep up.

Relia followed their progress, her emotion best described as awe. These four absolutely astonishing children were hers. Hers and Thomas's. They were real—every one a miracle. There had been no squabbles in her childhood. Except for occasional visits from The Terrible Twyford, she had been able to imagine herself as anyone she wanted to be, for there was no one to gainsay her.

She had not learned to share. To compromise. To think of someone other than herself.

Until she met Thomas Lanning. Who, truth be told, was nearly as spoiled as herself. A hard lesson had suddenly loomed before them—learning that the sun did not rise and set for their exclusive benefit. And yet . . . if she had not been so headstrong, so determined to save Pevensey Park, she would have settled for so much less. She would never have met Thomas. Never learned to love a Cit. Be proud of a Cit. Treasure a Cit.

And there he was at last! Bounding across the park at a far greater speed than a man well past his fortieth birthday should ever—

Relia came to her feet, her breath catching in her throat as she watched the precipitate arrival of that anomaly, a Whig cabinet minister in a Tory government run by His Grace, the Duke of Wellington. Though they had been separated only for a fortnight—since Relia had left their townhouse on Berkeley Square in order to be at Pevensey Park when the boys returned from school—she was, as always, breathless at the sight of him.

Thomas striding over the wooden bridge, up the marble steps to the rotunda . . . sweeping her into his arms. His lips meeting hers.

"Thomas," Relia sputtered when he finally let her go, "the children!"

Mr. Lanning lifted his head, eyed his distant, still-squabbling children with a considering gaze. "Are you quite sure we've managed the business correctly?" he asked his wife with a perfectly straight face. "Perhaps we should try for Number Five?"

After twelve years of marriage, Mrs. Lanning demonstrated that she could still blush. But her contentment was complete. Her Cit was home, and all was right with the world.

Author's Note

After researching the British electoral system prior to the reforms of 1832, I decided that the methods used to choose electors were so extraordinary and so varied that I might be forgiven for creating a fictitious borough where voters were selected both as freemen and by ancient burgage rights. Any political errors are mine, and not the fault of the learned gentlemen whose texts were invaluable in writing this book: *Voters, Patrons and Parties: the Unreformed Electoral System of Hanoverian England, 1734–1832* by Frank O'Gorman; *Electoral Behavior in Unreformed England: Plumpers, Splitters, and Straights* by John A. Phillips; *The Unreformed House of Commons: Parliamentary Representation Before 1832* by Edward Porritt. (Regretfully, I was unable to use the terms "plumpers," "splitters," or "straights," as these refer to standard elections, not to by-elections with a single candidate.)

My thanks also to Melanie Odom, Reference Librarian, and to Pamela Purch and Marianne Zaun of Interlibrary Loan, Sarasota County Library System, Sarasota, Florida. Their efforts to obtain books for me, and in a timely fashion, have made it possible for me to add far more depth to my stories than would otherwise have been possible.

—Blair Bancroft

About the Author

With ancestors from England, Wales, Scotland, Ireland, and France, **Blair Bancroft** feels right at home in nineteenth-century Britain. But it was only after a variety of other careers that she turned to writing about the Regency era. Blair has been a music teacher, professional singer, nonfiction editor, costume designer, and real estate agent, and she has still managed to travel extensively. The mother of three grown children, Blair lives in Florida. Her Web site is www.blairbancroft.com. She can be contacted at blairbancroft@aol.com.

Signet
Regency
Romance

Blair Bancroft

The Harem Bride

Once, Jason Lisbourne had played the knight
in shining armor—and now, no matter how
many women he seduces, he can't dislodge
the hold the beguiling Penelope Blayne has
on his very soul. Now he has a second
chance to save her, unless pride—and
a secret—rip them apart forever.

0-451-21006-9

Available wherever books are sold or at
www.penguin.com